POISON CONTROL

Eric Swan Thriller #2

DOM TESTA

Profound Impact Group

Poison Control: Eric Swan Thriller #2

By Dom Testa

This is a work of fiction, and a strange one at that. All organizations, events, and characters portrayed in this work are products of the author's imagination. Any similarity or resemblance to any person, living or dead — or reinvested — is not only purely coincidental, but incredibly bizarre.

Published by Profound Impact Group

PO Box 506

Alpharetta, GA 30009

Reach us at EricSwan.com

Library of Congress Control Number: 2019917955

ISBN: 978-1-942151-10-4

Cover art by Damonza

CONTENTS

CHAPTER ONE

When a bullet whistles past your head it's not always whistling. Sometimes it's more of a *pfft*, sometimes a solid *crack* as it breaks the sound barrier, and sometimes you don't hear the projectile at all because it's been overridden by the sound of the weapon's discharge. It all has to do with the particular firearm in question and your distance from the asshole shooting at you.

Science aside, there's also the unmistakable sound of the targeted person screaming *holy shit* or the disgusting noise as they soil their pants. The first time I was shot at I did both. Laugh all you want, then go put yourself in the line of a 9mm round, tough guy, and let's see how you do.

I'd just had two shots slam into the stucco above my head and wasn't in the mood to hear any more. The problem, however, was the triangulation. That's a fancy way of saying I was pinned down because two shooters were set up about 100 feet apart. They each covered one of my only two ways off the railed patio. I crouched below the decorative half-wall that may not have been very tall, but at least was thick enough to stop slugs.

Getting into this predicament could easily be blamed on Agent Ford, the DEA agent who'd bumbled through the patio doors even as I yelled at him to wait. He was sure he could make it to safety and then, with some luck, nab the bastards.

I'd feel like a creep blaming him now while he was lying in a puddle of blood in the center of the patio. In other words, he definitely didn't make it to safety. And since I'd temporarily teamed up with him — something that, as a Q2 agent, I rarely did — I'd rushed out to try to help him in case he was merely wounded. No. He was dead and now I was trapped.

Both of the armed jokers seemed competent in their marksmanship, but at the moment they were just wasting rounds. My fear was that eventually one of them would figure out an angle that worked. Which was the first of two reasons I couldn't just sit and wait for the cops to finally show up.

I glanced over the top of the stubby wall long enough to locate the guy on the left. Four or five more shots forced me back into my crouch. But that was enough time to see that he'd taken cover behind some poor soul's car. Looked like a newer Lexus SUV. Nice ride.

You might be thinking, *Just shoot the gas tank and make it explode*. You've confused Hollywood with real life. Bullets simply put holes in gas tanks, they don't cause eruptions. Looks good in movies, though, so directors will keep doing it.

Ah, but there was one other detail I'd picked up. Behind the Lexus and Shooter One was a large metal sculpture. I didn't have enough time to make a solid identification. It may have been a pelican; we *were* in central Florida, after all. But it could as easily have been the sculptor's mescaline-tinted vision of Mickey Mouse. Or maybe Walt Disney through the eyes of Tim Burton.

Let's call it abstract.

I chanced one more look to confirm the shooter's position then ducked again. I calculated some angles myself. This would not only be risky because I was opening myself up, it would take some damned fine physics and geometry. Even if I put the rounds in the spots I thought could work, I'd have to empty an entire magazine of 19 rounds and hope for one hit. But at least it was something to try. The guy would drop behind the car when I started firing, and if I sprawled far enough to my left his buddy on the right wouldn't be in a position to see me.

All of this was guesswork. Which, on many occasions, had gotten me killed.

My decision was made when they both let loose with another burst of at least 10 rounds each. Sometimes in my line of work you just get plain sick and tired of getting shot at. This was bullshit. It wasn't even my kind of case in the first place. I'd been loaned out from Q2 simply because there wasn't a pressing national emergency for me to work on. Whether I survived or got killed again, Quanta was gonna get an earful about this.

As soon as they finished firing I took two deep breaths and dove to my left. Raising the trusty Glock 18, I emptied the entire magazine. Just as I'd counted on, the guy lowered himself behind the Lexus at the sound of the first shot. Except I wasn't aiming for him.

Let's go back to science for a moment. This thick, heavy metal sculpture was tailor-made for ricochets. And in this case it was my only hope. I varied the target point of each shot along that large, curved belly — or whatever it was — striking it along the bottom curve. That would, in theory, send a variety of ricochets down at just the angles I wanted.

I know, long shot.

But it worked. Hey, all I needed was one.

He let out a strangled cry and collapsed, his gun clattering to the pavement.

I knew this would get the attention of his partner, and I wasted no time. Replacing the magazine, I rose to one knee and saw, over the top of my half-wall, Shooter Number Two craning his head out to see what had happened.

This time it took a single round.

Lest you think this evened the score for Agent Ford, when this pistol party started there were *three* of these guys. The third, the one Ford considered the planner and leader, had fled on foot, leaving behind Heckle and Jeckle to shoot it out with me. That meant I had no time to recover and count my blessings.

And that was the second reason I couldn't just sit around. This guy could not get away.

Everyone within a block of our battle had scattered when it all began. Now I heard the distant sound of sirens and holstered the Glock beneath my light jacket. The cops would have plenty of questions regarding the carnage here, but I couldn't afford the time.

My prey had hustled down the alley behind the strip of touristy businesses lining the street. Okay, maybe hustled isn't exactly accurate. He'd *wanted* to hurry, but Agent Ford, in one of his last acts of service to the DEA, had managed to plug the guy in his left calf. It started as a bloody mess and couldn't have improved in the last five minutes.

That meant several things, all good for me.

Running into a business to hide would be stupid. Hard to

remain inconspicuous gushing blood. For the same reason, few taxi drivers would let you in the car.

On top of that, it wouldn't be long before he'd need to staunch the flow. The body tends to go on strike at a certain point.

And best of all, he sure was easy to track.

I broke into a quick jog, following the dark red splotches down the alley, seeing where a couple of times he'd staggered up to one doorway or another before continuing down the alley. After two blocks he'd cut to the right and crossed a small parking lot that opened on the far side to a park.

I didn't like the idea of a desperate, wounded animal among a crowd of people. And it didn't take me long to find him. I only had to follow the screams to the street in front of the park.

Things had gone from shitty to just bloody freakin' awful. Let us go *mano a mano* and my training hopefully gave me the edge. But once civilians were thrown into the mix, the job got exponentially more difficult. Damn this freak. He'd already been responsible for the deaths of nearly a dozen people in a sick manner.

Now I sprinted toward the commotion. People were running away in terror, with the exception of one woman who'd dropped to her knees, hands together in a pleading manner. My target had crossed a line you just never cross.

He held up a young girl from behind, his gun at her throat. The girl, maybe 6 years old, was crying, screaming for her mother. Mixed with the mother's cries, the blaring of sirens from emergency vehicles rushing to the scene of the patio shootout, and the general cacophony of sound from the stunned people nearby, it was a madhouse of sound.

The gunman had stepped into the road and halted an

approaching F250 pickup truck. He stood right in front of the grill, forcing the truck to stop. The driver, a young Latino man who impressively filled the truck's cab, glared out the windshield. He didn't seem like the kind of guy you wanted to cross, especially if you were scum who would threaten a child.

Before the driver could act on whatever impulse motivated him, I arrived on the scene and pulled out my gun. This got the attention of the shithead, who looked around at me and clutched the girl tighter. She shrieked even louder.

"What are you gonna do now?" I asked, stepping forward. I held the Glock at my side, ready to raise it in an instant but not provoking him.

"Drop your gun," he said to me. Turning to the truck driver he yelled, "And you, get your ass out of there. Now!"

The young man sat immobile, continuing to glare.

"What do you think can possibly happen here?" I said, taking one more slow step forward. "This is pure panic. You know there's no way out. So why do you want to scare the girl?"

"I'll do more than scare her," he said, his voice high and quavering. The adrenaline, mixed with the loss of blood, had to be wreaking havoc on his mental state. That could make a dangerous situation deadly. The police would arrive soon, but this was going down one way or another before that happened.

I chanced one more step, which brought me to within ten feet of him and allowed me to lower my voice. "I'll tell you what," I said. "You let the little girl go, and you can take me as a hostage. How's that?"

"Do you want to die?" he screamed, waving his weapon at me. "Do you?"

I shrugged. "I can't. It's kinda my thing."

"Screw you! Get back and drop your gun."

"All right. I'll put the gun down. You just let her go back to her mother. Is that a deal?"

With everything coming apart in his world, and the blood loss draining his energy, the frenzied gunman was having a hard time processing all the inputs. His eyes darted from me to the man behind the wheel of the F250 to the screaming, terrified mother and back to me. I dared one more small step and held my gun out to my side in the international sign of *I'm putting it on the ground.*

And that's when the entire dynamic flipped.

The little girl, unaware that she was probably only moments away from running back into her mother's arms, had a spasm of fear. She let out another wail and kicked one of her feet backwards as hard as she could. It caught the flustered gunman square in the nuts and he let out a grunt while dropping the girl. She landed on her feet and immediately bolted toward her mother.

In one of those moments that truly does seem to move in slow motion, I saw what was about to happen next. Purely reacting out of his own fear and confusion, the lowlife recovered from the nut shot and raised his gun toward the fleeing girl.

If I'd been closer I could've leapt at him. As it was, the girl was now much closer, so I instinctively dropped my gun and dived, tackling her as the crazed gunman's weapon went off. I felt the searing heat and pain as the slug connected, but lay on top of the girl, awaiting the killing shot.

Which would've come, I'm sure. This maniacal fiend had officially slipped into the nothing-to-lose stage that meant he was prepared to go down blazin'.

But he never had the chance to finish me off. As soon as that first shot rang out I registered another sound. The sound of peeling rubber. The sound of an engine roaring with everything it had, which in this case was about 400 horsepower.

The next sound would've been sickening if I hadn't wanted it to happen or hadn't been dealing with my own wound. It was the sound of a large pickup truck driven by a large man running over a shithead with a gun.

I rolled to my side to let the girl escape to her delirious mother. I couldn't roll onto my back; there was a .38 slug lodged in my ass. And it hurt like hell.

Opening my eyes I saw a pair of cowboy boots next to my face. The owner knelt down and I recognized the truck driver. He looked at the blood dripping from my pants onto the ground and said, "What's your name, man?"

"Eric. What's yours?"

"Felipe."

"Well, thank you, Felipe," I said, grimacing.

He nodded as if he ran over people every day. Turning toward the mangled body beneath his truck he said, "That guy was an asshole."

CHAPTER TWO

W e were nearing the end of a strenuous workout, my first since returning from Florida. My shirt was soaked with sweat and my breathing was more like labored gasps. Not to mention the aches I felt along my chest and upper arms as a result of blocking as many blows as I could.

Which made it all the more disheartening that my sparring partner looked like she'd just finished a hard day of online shopping.

Her name was Quanta and she oversaw the domestic spy agency I worked for, known simply as Q2. There is no Q1 or Q3. In fact, the name began as something of a joke but, since no one could think of anything better, it was accepted with a shrug. Quanta, after running two similar organizations overseas, had been brought in to oversee the team of field agents, of which there were only 4, including me.

She liked to keep her agents in shape by beating the hell out of us with her own brand of martial arts, which I describe as a sort of Taekwondo meets Jedi Mind Trick. As usual, the beat-down took place in the elaborate garden on the grounds of her home. Quanta rarely went to the actual headquarters.

"Listen," I said between gulps of cold, January air. "I know you're kicking my ass, but do me a favor, will ya? Don't *literally* kick my ass. It's just now feeling back to normal."

She stepped back and assumed a neutral pose. "Swan, do you think an opponent would grant your wish?"

"Honestly, Quanta, I don't care. But I took a piece of lead in my butt cheek for a case I shouldn't have been on."

"Oh. So now it's up to you to decide when or where you work? The DEA asked for help and you had nothing going on at the time. Sending you out to stay in field shape is better than having you sit around getting fat and lazy."

"How about you just cut me some slack for another week or two?"

"You won't be here for the next week or two." With that, she walked past me toward the sliding glass door that opened from her kitchen. I used her exit to bend over, hands on knees, trying to recover. I didn't like to do that when she was watching. I've never come close to beating her, but there's still pride.

After a minute I walked into her kitchen and helped myself to some sort of juice in her fridge. It was purplish, I know that much. Quanta would be off meditating for a few minutes, so I took out my phone and used the time to kill off brain cells by surfing online. In the back of my mind, though, I considered her parting line. It had to mean I was back on assignment. A real one.

When you're an agent for Q2 you understand that those assignments have three primary characteristics:

One, they involved serious domestic threats against citizens. These are threats the government would prefer be kept quiet. Can't have every nut job's evil plan spilling out over social media. Believe me, you don't want to know a lot of the shit we stop. You just don't.

Two, they required a certain amount of espionage and sleuthing. That makes me part spy and part private eye, and those aren't the same things. Normally I would never use a word like 'sleuth,' but I devoured a lot of Hardy Boys and Nancy Drew books as a kid. Yes, Nancy, too. Shut up.

And three, the missions had a high probability of death. Usually the bad guys got to do the dying, but often *we* bit it, too. Since there's not exactly an endless supply of super agents you can pick off the tree, normally that would be a big problem.

The issue was solved thanks to a woman named Devya Nayar. She was the scientist at MIT who took the concept of Frankenstein, merged it with the science advancements gleaned from the work on artificial intelligence, and produced something we call reinvestment.

The quick explanation goes like this: My thoughts, my memories and experiences, and my personality — all the things that make me *me* — were digitally stored in something akin to a super-computer. If the body I was using got whacked, then my essence, that digital version of me, was downloaded into a new body and I was back on the job.

We got the bodies from convicts serving a life sentence. Without telling them exactly *why* we wanted their body, Q2 paid their family a cool $2 million in tax free money and they agreed to aid science, or serve humankind, or whatever noble phrase would make them feel better about taking the off-ramp from life in a cell.

It's all very weird but it worked for the country's security. I've been killed multiple times so I've experienced several different bodies. Many of them I didn't care for, but some were damned impressive. The one I had now — with the exception of that bullet wound currently chapping my ass — fell into the latter category. This dude worked out.

Maybe another reason why Quanta had loaned me out to the DEA. She didn't want to waste one of our better physical specimens just waiting around for a psycho to come along and threaten Uncle Sam. Now I guess a psycho had showed up.

Once she'd finished meditating in a plant-filled atrium in the center of her home, Quanta joined me at the big round table in the kitchen. She placed an electronic tablet between us, swiped to an image, and, without any preamble, started right in.

"His name is Steffan Parks. He's in his mid-50s, unmarried, and currently unemployed."

He looked his age. A slight graying around the temples, the hair pulled back into a tail. He sported facial hair, too, a goatee and mustache. One look suggested he might be the kind of 50-something hippie who'd refer to it by its old-school name, the Van Dyke. His eyes were semi-dulled, as if disinterested in anything except his own thoughts.

"What does he normally do?" I asked.

"He's a scientist. And not just a run-of-the-mill scientist." She swiped to another image.

I gave a low whistle. "Holy shit. Is that the Nobel Prize ceremony?"

"It is. Parks won the Nobel for chemistry about twenty years ago."

"Let me guess," I said. "His career has gone downhill since then."

Quanta shrugged. "Yes and no. After winning the prize he left the University of Chicago and started a company with one of his former associates. For the first few years he did remarkably well, mostly because of government contracts. Lots of those."

"What field?" I asked.

"Water. He was awarded the Nobel for his work in desalination, which has always had lucrative potential. In just a few years it's possible that one in every seven people on Earth will live in a region where water is scarce. Removing the salt from seawater is one way this could help."

I tapped a finger on the table. "Remind me what's kept desalination from taking off. Is it cost?"

She nodded. "Cost. Energy consumption. Some people worry that the process removes other important mineral elements besides the salt. Assorted other speed bumps."

"But the process is sound," I concluded.

"Oh, it works. The critical component is making it work in a way that's safe and efficient for the nearly one billion people whose lives either currently depend on it or will soon."

I got up from the table and fetched a refill of the mystery juice. I was afraid to ask my eclectic boss what type it was. I didn't want her to ruin it.

"Okay," I said. "So this guy wins the biggest prize in science, leaves his cushy university gig, and goes out on his own. Convinces the government to pour money into his company, probably lives the high life. But you're showing all of this to me because something has gone wrong. Jump to the nasty part. Why is Parks suddenly considered a knave?"

Quanta gave me the scowl she reserved for times she thought I was making fun of her. Which I kinda was. I just thought her pet term for the worst villains — her *knaves* — was funny.

"Four years ago several government programs began cutting off their funding to his company. There were allegations that his work didn't exactly hold up under peer review. One competitor lodged a complaint about falsified data, and there were other problems.

"Parks fought all of these claims, and for a while it looked like he'd get back on track. But then one of his developments, one that had been anticipated for many years, was unveiled. And it failed. Two other programs cut their allocations to and things inevitably snowballed."

I swiped back on Quanta's tablet and looked at the photo again. "Then?"

"Then it got uglier. A former colleague who knew Parks when they were in Chicago gave an interview where he questioned if Parks was even deserving of the Nobel Prize. He was vague, but he insinuated that Parks had ridden the coattails of others and maybe claimed certain things that either belonged to others or were questionable."

"Wow," I said. "How the mighty fall."

"Or how the mighty lash out," Quanta said. "In this case, with malice."

"I'm obviously hearing all of this because someone is dead. Let me guess: the dude who questioned him winning the Nobel."

She reached out for the tablet and swiped forward a few frames, then turned the screen toward me. "This man. His name was Leon Haas. Taught chemistry at the University of Chicago, including the years that Parks was on the faculty. And yes, his interview was widely circulated and it was surely an embarrassment for Parks, who was already reeling from his company's troubles.

"Three years ago Haas also left the university to open his own lab. He moved with his wife to Santa Fe where he purchased a company called Marquart Labs. He kept the name.

They, too, received some government funding in the area of water research, although their specialty was in filtering and recycling.

"When Parks fired back in some journals about what Haas had said, he often cited the fact that Haas was merely a competitor hoping to siphon away business at the expense of a former colleague. Parks used the term *professional envy* more than once."

I grunted. "So he tried to discredit the guy who discredited him."

"And it didn't work. From what we've gathered it only made Parks look worse. And then Mr. Haas was found at his lab."

"How was he killed?"

"According to the original inquest, poison. And not just Haas. One of his lab assistants, as well. At first investigators didn't consider an outside source for the poison."

"What do you mean?"

"The lab in Santa Fe worked on some of the foulest water sources you could find. That was their mission, after all, to cleanse the most contaminated water and make it potable. That meant they worked with a lot of chemicals, experimenting with countless combinations. So the investigative team started under the assumption that Haas and his people simply failed their safety protocols and managed to poison themselves."

I smiled at her. "But, again, you're talking to me because someone didn't buy that explanation."

"Few did. But the loudest of the non-believers was Haas's wife. She claims Parks threatened her husband a month before he died. And she says it's ludicrous to think someone of Leon's education, training, and experience would be so foolish as to accidentally kill himself with shoddy oversight. She's the one who reached out to the police, who contacted the FBI, who contacted us."

I studied the photo of Haas, then flipped back to Parks. "Anything concrete that could tie Parks in? Or is he merely a suspect because of the bad blood between them?"

Quanta sat back and sipped her water. "After his largest grant was terminated, Parks submitted a proposal to the Pentagon. It outlined a method of compromising an enemy's water supply and introducing a microscopic toxin that would be difficult to detect and yet prove fatal. The military, of course, rejected the proposal right away."

"Of course," I said, hoping my knowledge would impress the boss. "The Biological Weapons Convention of 1970."

"Very good, Swan. Although it was 1972, but yes. The United States is one of more than 100 nations that have agreed to ban production of biological and toxic weapons. The proposal from Parks would clearly be in violation."

"Although I'm sure there have been some behind-closed-doors experiments—"

She cut me off. "We're not here to talk about theories of that nature. We're here to talk about Steffan Parks."

Properly chastised, I gave a small shrug. "All right. But the more I think about what you said a minute ago, the FBI wouldn't have reached out to you if there wasn't something they considered an imminent threat. So what's the scoop?"

Quanta paused, then leaned forward again and swiped a couple more times on the tablet. She found a page she was looking for and pointed. "Haas's wife wasn't satisfied with the coroner's inquest, so she hired an outside pathologist. This is an excerpt from his report."

I scanned the document. Most of it was incomprehensible,

a lot of medical jargon and abbreviations. Then I found a paragraph toward the bottom.

I read aloud: "Includes traces of tabun." I looked up at Quanta. "I know that word. It's a nerve agent, right?"

"Extremely toxic. Developed by Germany just before World War II as a pesticide and then used as a biological weapon. And . . ." She held her glass up. "And it mixes easily with water."

"The plot thickens," I said.

She set the glass down. "The reason Q2 is involved is because Haas's wife claimed Parks made some wild comments when he threatened her husband. She said he called Leon and berated him for the interview. When Haas not only refused to apologize but actually doubled down on his accusations, Parks uttered something about 'screw you' and 'screw this whole country.' He told Haas that lots of people would be sorry. His parting words were, 'You'll be the first, but you won't be the last.'"

"So he's planning to strike back for all of the slights he's suffered."

"And," Quanta added, "he has the resources. His proposal to the Pentagon included some vague instructions. But they included tabun."

Whoa. I studied her face for a moment then said: "Guess I'm going to Santa Fe."

Quanta returned the gaze. "First thing in the morning."

CHAPTER THREE

I actually had a date with my wife, which was rare. Not because we didn't enjoy it, and not because I'm a cheap bastard, but because my life is mostly on the road. I think Christina's okay with that; she treasured her alone time, and with me she got plenty. I texted her and made plans to meet at one of our favorite Italian places where the servers would only interrupt you to take your order, bring your order, or tell you the place was on fire.

Before I could feed my fettucine fantasy, however, I had to make a stop at Q2 headquarters. Quanta's assistant, an overly-serious woman named Poole, would have travel details and other information. I hadn't been crazy about Poole when I first met her, but during my mission to stop a freaky family from wiping out the country's power grid I developed a newfound appreciation for the tall, lanky Poole. It was still my goal to get her to laugh at something, anything, but I'd concluded she was at least remarkably efficient.

I parked in the underground garage of the drab building

and took the elevator up to four. Poole was in her office, peeling an orange.

"Oh, hello Swan," she said, dumping the rind into a trash can. "I have a packet for you."

"You know I'm a sucker for a good packet," I said. "Have you had time to scrounge up anything else on Steffan Parks?"

"Actually, yes. Hold on." She swiveled around in her chair and retrieved a manilla folder. It was a lot thinner now than it would be once Poole got busy. "His last reported full-time address was just down the road from here, in Dover, Delaware. But reports show that he abandoned the property a couple of months ago."

"Abandoned?"

She nodded. "He just left it, furniture and all. Made a phone call to his mortgage broker and told them they would find the keys and garage door opener in the mail box. A sheriff I talked to said he went with the broker just in case there was trouble, but the home was in absolutely perfect condition. Even a vase full of fresh flowers waiting on the kitchen counter. Just no Mr. Parks."

"How polite to call and let someone know."

Poole didn't know how to respond to that, so after a momentary pause she continued. "He also walked away from some pending legal issues, all stemming from his company shutting down. His attorney wants desperately to talk to him, but no one knows where to find him or his girlfriend."

I raised my eyebrows. "Girlfriend? Okay, this is new. What's her story?"

"Very similar to his. She's also a former employee of the University of Chicago and left the same time Parks did. We understand that she didn't invest in his company, but did behave as a full partner."

"So they're business *and* personal partners," I said. "Makes car-pooling easy. But she's now missing too."

"Yes. Her name is Jayanti Pradesh. Goes by Jay."

"Of course she does. She's also a scientist?"

"And comes from a family of respected pioneers in physics and engineering. I've found quite a few references to her mother and an uncle. They've both been published many times. Not so much with Jayanti. I get the impression she was something of a disappointment for a high-performing family in the field."

I flipped through a couple of pages in the file. "It's hard to live up to expectations when your parents are already stars. Look at all the children of the Beatles." I glanced at Poole. "You know who they are?"

"I don't listen to a lot of music, but I've heard of them, naturally."

This made me smile. I tried to imagine the strict, stiff Poole at a concert, down in the pit, banging her head and throwing her hands up in the air.

That would never happen on its own. What if I took her some time, just as an experiment?

"All right," I said. "If Jay the girlfriend is missing, too, then we might assume she's part of the poisoning plot. And if she's a bit of an underachiever then she might have her own warped motivation."

I found a couple of pages in the file that caught my eye. It was a copy of the rather lengthy email exchange between Steffan Parks and a senior official at the Pentagon. Starting from the initial contact at the very bottom and rolling up through each of the replies it detailed the attempt by Parks to interest the military in his — using his words — 'hydro-incursion technique.'

In other words, his plan to poison the well for America's enemies. It didn't go into specifics, but seemed to treat the proposition as an almost patriotic duty. Never mind the grisly consequences for an innocent population; Parks suggested the plan could achieve 'near 100 percent effectiveness.' In other words, it would kill everyone: men, women, children, soldiers, civilians, probably even pets.

What I found interesting was the response from the Pentagon official. At first he just strongly declined the offer. But when Parks pushed the issue and questioned the integrity of the official when it came to protecting the country, the official dropped one particular word: *Monstrous*.

Because, really, that's what the plan was. It was monstrous to imagine poisoning an entire country's water supply. But this was the level Parks had sunk to. Either he had become crazy due to the hardships he faced in his career, or he'd always been nuts and had simply managed to mask it. Or simply hid behind the work of others, which is what Leon Haas had claimed. And, oh by the way, had been killed for saying.

I set the papers in my lap and gazed at nothing for a moment. There was a tickling feeling telling me this was much more dangerous than I'd first assumed. We had a crazy scientist who'd been not only sanctioned for his shoddy work, but publicly humiliated. *That* was the thing that stood out in my mind. The ridicule.

It's one thing to fail; we've all done it. But the shame is in proportion to the depth of the plunge. In this case, to go from acclaimed Nobel Prize winner to failure brings with it a degree of pain few of us would be able to comprehend. Once a wunderkind, then a laughingstock? It would screw with your mind.

Apparently it had with Steffan Parks. Two people were

dead already. How many more would it take to even the score? We could always hope he was satisfied by eliminating his most-vocal critic.

But what if he wasn't? What if he saw no reason to stop at two? What if he intended to make a grand show of his work, his deadly tabun-laced toxin that could disseminate quickly through an entire city's supply? Or state's. Or . . .

As usual, the rational side of my mind denied that anyone would go to this length just to assuage a personal slight. But over the years I'd seen a lot of vicious, inhuman displays by people who had no rational governor on their fury. And in an age where mass killings were considered a scorecard, when each psychopath felt challenged to increase the body count in order to stand out on the round-the-clock news services, it made things much more dire for the rest of us.

Some people put very little stock in gut feelings, but I practically lived by it. And my gut told me that Dr. Parks was capable of horror on an unprecedented scale. It was perhaps a good thing that this case had quickly filtered down to Q2.

Poole had respectfully waited during my comatose assessment. Shaking myself back to life I looked at the next sheath of papers in the packet. My itinerary. "Thank you for not making the flight too early tomorrow, Poole," I said.

"You're welcome. I also reserved one of your favorite cars."

I stood up and smiled. "Poole, what special treat would you like me to bring you from New Mexico?"

Her puzzled look returned. "I don't know what they specialize in."

"Then it'll be a surprise. Thanks for this," I said, holding up the packet. "I'll be in touch."

IT HAD SNOWED EARLIER in the day but now the skies were merely overcast with the classic Washington, D.C. gray. Late-afternoon traffic chewed up some of the seventeen hours I had until my plane left Dulles, but I tossed my keys to the valet attendant at the restaurant just a few minutes late for my six o'clock date.

Christina was there, absorbed in something on her tablet while she held a glass of wine. She looked up as I approached and broke into the smile that had mesmerized me from the first moment we met. I bent over and gave her two kisses, then sat down. I stole a sip from her wine and nodded in appreciation just as the server set down an identical glass in front of me.

"I knew you'd like it," Christina said, taking back her own. "I also ordered the caprese for us to split."

"This is why I married you," I said, placing the napkin on my lap.

"Because I order well?"

"You order well, you're an absolute wildcat in bed, and you don't mind me coming home with a new face and body sometimes."

We clinked glasses and each took a sip. "Speaking of which," she said, "when do I get to try out a new model again? This one is getting stale."

"Oh, hush," I said. "When the lights are out all you register is my sparkling personality and dazzling moves anyway."

"I don't know," she said. "This body didn't register as much as the last one."

I made a face at her. "Stop comparing. You'll give me a complex."

"That'll be the day."

This was routine chatter for us, a way to defuse what would otherwise be an incredibly awkward situation between husband and wife. There couldn't have been five women in the country who'd tolerate being married to an active Q2 agent, and I'd found one of them. Christina Valdez accepted the fact that her husband was gone for most of the year and would often show up with a new identity after being killed in the line of duty.

I rationalized her sacrifice by remembering that she embraced all the time she spent alone. She was a world-class chef who'd vowed to never marry after a few difficult relationships early on. I came along and gave her the best of both worlds: a relationship that also provided the independence she craved.

The only way it would work is if we shared a common snarky attitude toward life. That was a perfect match.

Christina also had the comfort of her own home. We had adjoining two-bedroom condos on the 7th floor of the upscale Stadler Building. She could decorate hers the way she wanted, I kept up mine, and we installed a hidden panel between the two units that allowed us to visit back and forth without going out into the hall. It was truly a dream setup, especially for her.

Sure, we were common-law, but to us we were married, and that was all there was to it. Q2 generally didn't allow agents to develop intimate relationships like marriage, so we'd stayed secret as long as possible. Recently Quanta had let me know I was shitty at keeping that particular secret. So my boss knew about the arrangement, but no one else. Not even Christina's family.

She told me that was for the best, for *my* sake.

"Thank you for taking off work tonight," I said as the caprese salad arrived.

"You leave tomorrow? Where to?"

"Santa Fe. Any recommendations from my chef wife for dining there?"

Stupid question. She rattled off four of them, then pulled out her phone to text them to me.

Over the next two hours we enjoyed a spectacular meal, some more wine, then shared a dessert and finished with limoncello. By 8:30 we were home, just as another light dusting of snow began.

We spent the night on her side of the dual condos, and I did my best to register well. Who knew if she'd ever see this specimen again?

What a strange life.

CHAPTER FOUR

Poole was true to her word. The rental car awaiting me in Albuquerque was nearly identical to the Mercedes SUV she'd arranged on an earlier mission. I made a quick stop at a Q2 safe house and picked up some of the tools I might need for this assignment, including a trusty Glock 18, my weapon of choice these days. Two minutes after ringing the doorbell I was back in the Mercedes and on my way out of town. It was almost 7 p.m.

The drive from Albuquerque to Santa Fe generally took about an hour, although I was in no rush and enjoyed the quiet time. My mind drifted back to a case that had brought me to New Mexico a year earlier. That one included a wild chase down back roads and ended with me barely escaping with my life, while at the same time planting a perfect shot through the heart of one badass creep. He'd killed four people and was preparing to off at least four more, all in service to someone who I *wished* I'd been able to take out.

Yes, the creep's employer was my ultimate knave, the one and only person I obsessed over. The one man who never failed to cross my mind at least once a day, even if briefly. Like right now. The man who'd personally cost me someone dear. The man I vowed to track down someday in order to extract my own brand of Eric Swan revenge.

His name was Beadle. He was a master knave, if there was such a thing, and he was damned near impossible to find. Hired out by the super-wealthy, be it individuals, corporations, or countries, Beadle was ghost-like in his movements. I'd encountered him face-to-face only a couple of times, although it was possible it had happened other times that I had no memory of, during the stage I called *lights-out*. That's the time between my last upload of information and the time I get snuffed. Those memories aren't stored anywhere. So I could've crossed paths with this shithead more times than I think. I have suspicions.

Anyway, New Mexico was one of those settings where Beadle's handiwork had been on display, but not his face. It was aggravating.

There are several rules that go along with working for your country's most ruthless agency, the one tasked with defusing the most savage threats and eliminating the most heinous villains. The one rule I consistently broke was the one about not carrying around grievances from past cases.

Man, did I break that rule. My grudge against Beadle was supersized. One day I'd find him and finish him.

But not tonight. Tonight was all about motoring into the quaint little artsy town of Santa Fe and getting some rest. Tomorrow I'd begin tracking down Steffan Parks. Beadle was quietly returned to the back burner.

After stopping at a small market to collect some bottled waters and snacks, I found my hotel, a three-star lodge within walking distance of the historic plaza that sucked in tourists like a black hole. I texted the requisite *I'm here safely* message to Christina, then fell asleep to an old Robin Williams movie on HBO.

AT 8 O'CLOCK the following morning I got in a three-mile run, which, at 7,200 feet of elevation, certainly taxed the lungs. The sun was out, but merely provided encouragement in the below-freezing temperatures. Then I showered and partook of the hotel's free breakfast buffet.

At 10:30 I was escorted into the office of the sheriff who'd overseen the deaths of the two scientists. He was exactly how you'd picture an old-west sheriff: tall with a paunch around the middle, graying hair, and no patience for Washington bullshit. His name was Tonkin.

"What do you want, Mr. Swan?" he asked, holding a very large mug of coffee.

"Eric is fine. This is mostly a courtesy call to introduce myself and let you know I'll be investigating the deaths at Marquart Labs."

"I was told that much," he said. "I'm still waiting for someone to explain Washington's concern with this case."

"All I can say is that the person we suspect is responsible for these murders, Steffan Parks, may not be finished."

"Here in Santa Fe, or elsewhere?"

"Likely elsewhere. But that's not the kind of information we want to get out there. No sense in causing a panic if we can take care of our business quickly."

He looked unimpressed with my business. This was the part of my job I loathed: working with local law enforcement. Don't get me wrong, I had all the respect in the world for them. They just hated having to share their hard work with some schmo from the Feds and it always made me feel like a dinner guest with a cold sore.

I said, "I'm told you were sent most of the information on Parks. Have you been able to dig up any information on where he may have stayed while he was in town?"

Tonkin didn't need to consult a folder. "As far as we can tell he wasn't registered at any hotel, nor did he stay at a room-share. There's no record of him spending *any* nights in Santa Fe. No record of him staying anywhere in the state, for that matter. The only thing we have to make him a person of interest is a claim from the wife of the head of the lab. But we have no fingerprints, no signs of trespass, nothing to tie in Parks at all. So you can see why I'm curious about your line of investigation."

I nodded. "And I appreciate that. This person of interest, Parks, worked on exactly the kind of toxin that killed both people at the lab. He had some bizarre vendetta against Leon Haas, we know that for a fact. As far as we can tell, however, the other victim was collateral damage."

The sheriff visibly stiffened at this last sentence. I kept going.

"I'll be talking with Mrs. Haas and another employee of the lab who was away when this happened. I might also need to talk to the county coroner. I just didn't want to intrude on your territory without checking in."

"Well," he said, drawing out the word. "I'm told to cooperate with you, so I'll do that. But I only have so far I'll go with this type of cooperation. If I feel like you're making life difficult for people I'll shut you down. Are we clear on that?"

I had no idea how I could make life difficult for any of the survivors, but there was something just under the surface bugging Sheriff Tonkin. Maybe he didn't like feeling subjugated on a case, maybe he just didn't like federal agents on a general basis. Or maybe he just had gas. I didn't know, and mostly I didn't care unless it interfered with my assignment. To get through this meeting, however, I let him know we were clear.

He gave a big, slow nod to show that we had a well-negotiated treaty between us. Then he gave me directions to see the coroner, and shared the home addresses of Leon's widow, Stacey Haas, as well as David Torres, the last surviving employee of Marquart Labs. He'd call ahead and let both know that an independent investigator would be calling on them that afternoon.

I wanted to wrap up this uncomfortable meeting as quickly as possible, so I thanked him for his time and the information. He stood to shake my hand but his face maintained the distrustful look.

"Since this case remains in my open file, I'll ask that you stay in touch with me," he said. "And if you happen to find that this Mr. Parks *is* in town, you'll let me know. I would like to be the one who makes the arrest, if you don't mind."

He held on to my hand throughout this exchange. I played what seemed the obvious card, given the sheriff's interest. "This is not just a case of someone committing a crime on your watch," I said. "This is personal to you."

"Oh, it's personal, Mr. Swan," he said, finally releasing his grip. "The young assistant at the laboratory, the *collateral damage* you referred to. Her name was Amy Elkington." He sat back down. "She was my niece."

So I felt like an ass driving away from the sheriff's building. It wasn't the first time I'd said something stupid during a case, but that didn't remove the sour feeling. As a Q2 agent you just got numb to the concept of collateral damage. Once you'd seen and dealt with dozens of dead in the line of duty you sometimes forgot they were mothers, fathers, brothers, sisters. Or nieces.

I already hadn't been welcome when I'd walked into Sheriff Tonkin's office and I sure as hell didn't make things any better by minimizing his personal loss, regardless of the fact that it was unintentional. Now, behind the wheel of the Mercedes and following the GPS directions to the home of Leon and Stacey Haas, I questioned my degree of humanity.

And that wasn't the philosophical whimpering of a chagrined man, nor was it the first time I'd wondered about it. My wife had brought it up more than once. Not in a mean-spirited way, but simply because she was curious.

When you're consistently brought back from the dead, how could it not diminish your appreciation for the sanctity of life? It crossed my mind that I'd begun to blur the lines between traditional life and my specialized, freakish version. Then, when something like my encounter with Sheriff Tonkin happened, I'd snap to — briefly — and make empty promises of trying harder to not take it all for granted.

It never lasted. And it wouldn't last this time, either.

I tapped on my phone with the intention of calling Christina, hoping that just the sound of her voice would ground me again. But I shut it back off without completing the call. Something about that screamed *neediness*; using my vulnerable, mortal wife to make me feel less freakish.

For a moment I'd been so deep in thought that I'd forgotten where I was going. Then I received a text message from the sheriff's office letting me know that Stacey Haas was home and expecting my visit. Checking the GPS I saw I was within a mile of the house, and pulled into a parking lot to check in with Poole.

"Anything new on Parks?" I asked.

"No, he's disappeared," Poole said.

"Not surprising. The authorities in Santa Fe don't show him ever being in town; no hotel room, no credit card transactions. If he did show up here to do some dirty work, he was completely underground."

"We have, however, pinged Jayanti Pradesh," she said. "She was scheduled to speak at a conference in Scottsdale until everything went south with their company. She excused herself as a speaker but it looks like she still showed up at the conference. We're not sure why."

I mulled that over. Scottsdale was less than 500 miles from Santa Fe. Could Jayanti and Parks have carried out the poisoning job, then hustled across the border to Arizona? Didn't seem out of the question at all. A leisurely eight-hour drive would mean no airline records. Our mad scientist could easily be there with his girlfriend.

"All right," I said to Poole. "I have a couple of people to interview here and then I'll let you know what the next step is."

"Please upload this evening if possible," Poole said. "It's been a few days."

"Yes, mom," I said with a smile and disconnected. Of course, she was right. Even without anything substantial, it was foolish to go very long without uploading a record of all my experiences.

I didn't expect to get much from the employee who'd been away when Leon Haas and Amy Elkington had been killed, and I expected even less right now from Haas's wife, Stacey. In truth, I felt like an oaf intruding on her time of mourning. But if Parks had more grandiose plans of revenge, neither of the interviews could wait.

The Mercedes nosed into a posh neighborhood of typical Santa Fe-style homes. Each had a xeriscaped yard, a three-car garage, and what looked like a separate building, known as a *casita*. On a summer day there might be families out enjoying the sun, but with the cold winter weather the area was quiet, everyone tucked indoors, beside a roaring hearth.

I found the Haas residence and parked on the street. Gathering myself for what would be a difficult conversation, I walked up to the door and rang the bell. Nothing happened for almost thirty seconds. The sheriff's office had said Stacey Haas was expecting me. I rang the bell again. This time I heard footsteps just before the door swung open.

It took everything I had to not utter an exclamation of surprise. Stacey Haas stood in the doorway, looking up at me with a weary expression. She was medium height, in superb shape, and dressed casually.

She was also the woman I'd almost married back in college.

CHAPTER FIVE

Okay, I should probably correct that last statement. I hadn't almost married her. But at the time I'd thought that I would. I'd even gone so far as to bring it up. Once.

Back then her name had not been Stacey Haas; she was Stacey Bromley, a young biology major from a wealthy family in Pennsylvania. I'd been smitten, and if I'd thought *she* was, well, that notion was quickly dashed when she'd laughed at my suggestion of wedded bliss. My head was packed with scads of romantic images of a picket-fence future. Stacey Bromley had incinerated all of it, telling me she couldn't imagine ever being married. The truth, at least as far as I could tell, was that she couldn't imagine marrying *me*.

All she wanted, she'd claimed, was a career and the lavish perks that came from owning something of substance.

She offered to remain friends after laughing at me. I quietly declined and skulked away, humiliated.

It was the last time I'd seen her. Now I stood on her front porch in Santa Fe, New Mexico, hopefully without my tongue hanging out.

"Yes?" she finally said, probably weirded out by my stare.

"Mrs., um, Mrs. Haas," I said. "My name is Swan. I believe Sheriff Tonkin's office told you I'd be stopping by?" We had at least one thing in common: neither of us went by the name we'd used in an earlier life.

She studied my face, and for a fleeting moment I had a wild notion she could tell who I was — or, rather, who I'd been. Something in the eyes? No, that was nonsense lifted directly out of pop songs. These were convict's eyes I'd merely borrowed. I stood there, trying not to flinch, until she finally nodded.

"Yes." That was all she said. Rather than invite me in verbally, she stepped aside and held the door open. I walked past her into a modestly-furnished home that belied its ritzy exterior and neighborhood. It was comfortable and homey. Almost eerily quiet. She offered me something to drink and I accepted a glass of ice water, mostly because I needed something to fumble with while my brain played hopscotch.

She indicated a love seat for me while she sat down in a plump chair and leveled another curious gaze at me.

"What can I do to help with your investigation?" she asked. "I thought the sheriff covered everything. Is there something I've missed?"

It was strange, hearing her voice again after twenty years. It was the one I'd replayed in my head for ages before finally moving on. For the first time in my career I found myself floundering at conversation, something that generally came easy for me. I wished that I'd looked up a photo of Leon Haas's wife before driving out, at least to be prepared.

Get it together, I told myself. Focus.

"Mrs. Haas," I started, and she said, "You can call me Stacey." Which would be a challenge at first. As Mrs. Haas she was unknown to me; as Stacey she was a former lover. I decided to avoid names altogether.

"First, let me add my condolences to those you've already received. I know it's not easy to sit and answer questions right now. I promise I'll be brief." She gave a small nod to go on. "You were not in Santa Fe on the day your husband died, is that correct?"

"You mean on the day my husband was murdered. No. I was in Albuquerque, meeting with a potential new legal attorney for the lab." Her tone, although calm and professional, had plenty of bite to it.

"You were with another of the lab's employees, David Torres."

"That's right. David was originally a chemistry student who worked with Leon, but he was better suited for the business side of things. We were transitioning him into something of a business manager, so it was important that he go with me. We left at nine that morning and got back late in the afternoon, about 4:30."

"And it was David who discovered your husband and his two assistants."

She took a breath. This was the worst part of my job. "Yes. When we got back to town I dropped him off at the lab and he ran inside. I thought Leon would be here at home, so I didn't go in. We'd planned a dinner with friends. I'd only made it a few blocks from the lab when David called me. I thought . . ." She took another long breath. "I thought maybe he'd left something in my car. But he . . . he told me what he'd found."

I gave her a moment, then said: "Again, I'm sorry. The reason I'm here is to ask you about your husband's relationship with Steffan Parks."

At the mention of the name she got up from her chair and

stalked toward a sliding glass door opening onto a patio. Her back was to me, but I could tell she was shaking. "Steffan Parks is a despicable human being. He and my husband used to be friends, you know, until Leon turned up enough evidence to question a lot of the papers Steffan had published. When he confronted him, hoping to work through it and simply repair the mistakes, Steffan lost it. He practically shoved Leon to the floor."

She turned back to face me. "My husband, Mr. Swan, could not have been more thoughtful and understanding about the whole situation. He gave Steffan multiple opportunities to correct his work, but instead that bastard flung charges at Leon that *he* was the fraud. Eventually it got to the point where Leon's integrity was on the line. So he published the piece about the Nobel work, to set the record straight, mostly to protect his own legacy in science. And, well, that drove Steffan mad." She crossed her arms. "He killed my husband for it."

I paused again out of respect. Then: "I understand that Parks called your husband a few weeks ago. What can you tell me about that?"

She eyed me, once again sizing me up. "You're not with the Santa Fe police or sheriff's office. Who are you?"

I took another drink from my water and then told a small lie. "I'm with a special division of the FBI. We're investigating Steffan Parks and his possible role in this."

"*Possible?*" she cried.

"Until we have enough evidence to officially declare his involvement, yes. Don't get me wrong, he's Suspect Number One, and we'll proceed with the investigation under that assumption. What about that call he made to your husband?"

Stacey Haas crossed her arms. "He threatened Leon."

"In what way? Did he say anything specific?"

She shook her head. "No. Just the usual rambling rant many of us were used to from that monster. He's quite fond of making grandiose speeches. Leon used to say that Steffan Parks could turn a coffee order into the Gettysburg Address."

I held up a hand to interrupt. "You said *many of us were used to*. You've had personal contact with Parks?"

"Not professionally, but through my husband. I originally met Leon at the university, and since the two of them often got together to talk science I spoke with Steffan several times. Even back then he gave me the creeps."

"Did your husband do anything about the threat? Did he contact the police?"

"No. He thought it was all just talk. Actually, the phrase he used was *theatrical ravings of an overwrought ego*."

"What about you? At the time did *you* think his threat was genuine?"

She stood still for a long time, obviously thinking about her answer. Then she said, "On some level I was concerned. But I thought Steffan was more likely to sabotage Leon's work than to physically harm him. So no, to answer your question. I didn't think it was real in this way. Neither did Leon. And now look what's happened."

Through the fog of having to interview a former girlfriend as a total stranger, I tried building a picture of the disgraced Nobel Prize winner. Bold, prideful, or, as my grandmother would've said, full of *puffery*. And apparently dangerous when cornered. After rocketing to the top of his field he'd been not just embarrassed, but humiliated. And, from what I knew of the scientist clique, reputation was damned near everything. Once that was tainted it was nearly impossible to regain stature. Trust was difficult to rebuild.

I had to adjust my thinking. It's too easy to imagine a

scorned scientist getting revenge by whacking you with a slide rule. Not only was that an insulting trope, it was dead wrong. Literally. We were talking about a man who'd created a lethal toxin capable of killing entire populations — and then gone off the deep end. Steffan Parks, far from a sulking egghead with taped-up glasses, was more like a brainy specter of death.

A specter on the loose and perhaps not fully sated by his first kills. After all, the United States government had shunned him, too.

"We're also interested in a woman named Jayanti Pradesh. Do you—"

"Yes," she said. "I know Jay. She's a bigger fraud than Steffan."

"How so?"

"Just a spoiled rich girl who couldn't live up to her family's legacy so she glommed on to the work of others. Tried to establish an image by association." Stacey gave a short, bitter laugh. "Only this time she hitched her wagon to the wrong horse."

"I understand that. But what I'm most interested in are her qualifications. She *is* a competent scientist, no?"

Stacey shrugged. "Competence is relative. I mean, compared to who? But yes, she knows her way around a lab."

"I guess what I'm getting at is—"

"Could she be intricately involved with the poison formula that Steffan created?" She nodded. "Yes. Jay knows enough to be involved."

I was running out of questions where Stacey could reasonably help me move the investigation along, and yet I was reluctant to end the interview. Don't misunderstand: this had nothing to do with any unresolved feelings or a surge of reminiscent romance. I'd more than moved on from my major college relationship, and I loved my wife.

This was, pure and simple, curiosity. Curiosity about a woman who'd once made it clear she had zero interest in getting married, who'd placed career and prestige above matrimony, and who'd subsequently walked down the aisle with a fellow faculty member, one who was her senior by almost 15 years. I mean, it could've been exactly the conclusion I'd reached all those years ago: She wasn't necessarily opposed to marriage, just opposed to marrying *me*.

And I wasn't even a globe-trotting, risk-taking, face-changing secret agent back then. I was relatively attractive, in great physical shape, an athlete with a sparkling personality, and . . .

Holy shit, what the hell was this? Self-obsessed much?

Who gave a rat's ass why she'd made a sudden left turn? She'd found happiness in the arms of an academic and I'd taken a different journey. Not to mention I never would've found my own happiness with the sexy chef.

No matter how evolved we think we are, and no matter how content we may be with our lives, the magnetism of the great *'what if'* is never really quenched. We'll always wonder about the forks in the road we didn't take, and puzzle over the reasons we didn't take them.

I happen to be fascinated by the many-worlds theory, although I've personalized it. In my version I live in an infinite number of universes in which I've taken every path, made every choice, and lived every consequence. It just gets ridiculously complicated when you factor in all the bonus lives I've experienced and the multiple bodies I've occupied. I'm my own freaking multi-verse.

So yes, the strange coincidence of circling back and reconnecting with my original past, the one from my initial body/lifetime, was kinda blowing my mind and I didn't want the show to end.

But now Stacey Haas was standing there, her arms still crossed in the universal defensive posture, and again staring at me like she was trying to place me. That weirded me out, too.

It was time to go. I stood up and thanked her for the information and observations, then offered my condolences a final time. She was ready for me to leave her house, but not until she made sure I understood the gravity of what I was fighting.

"The toxin that Parks has developed," she said as we reached the front door. "Do you have any idea how it works?"

"I know it's a powerful poison, and I know its origin," I said. "Why don't you paint a picture for me?"

"It's more than just a standard poison. Once it enters the bloodstream it races to all of the major organs and begins to attack them from the inside. Almost like an acid. It takes less than three minutes from the time you ingest it until you go into shock and die. And in those three minutes you suffer the most gruesome pain imaginable, worse than any torture device that's ever been used throughout history. Leon told me it unleashed a living hell on the victim. He said you'd scream in agony until your brain was overwhelmed."

She looked out the open door into the cold, gray sky. "Six weeks after he described this to me he suffered through it. Those were his last moments on Earth." Turning her face to once again look up into my eyes, she added: "Find this monster, Mr. Swan. And let me know as soon as you do. But find the monster."

I walked to my car without looking back. Once buckled in I saw that Christina had tried calling. I dialed her back.

"How's Santa Fe?" she asked.

"Charming as always, but cold. And very interesting. I just discovered that the victim's wife is my old college girlfriend."

"No shit," Christina said. "Has she gotten fat?"

"No, if anything she's in better shape now. Shed the freshman fifteen and never looked back, I guess."

"Good for her. I'll bet that was weird."

"Babe, it goes into my top ten of weirdest days ever. And you know I've had a few of those. What about you? What's the special tonight?"

That wasn't a bullshit question just to pass the time. I was intrigued by her cooking and her processes, and she always obliged with answers, whether I understood them or not. After talking about the restaurant we made idle chit-chat until I got a call from Quanta. You don't let those go to voicemail. I told Christina I'd call her back later.

"Yes, boss."

"You need to contact the sheriff again. There's been another incident."

"Incident" I asked. "Another killing?"

"Yes. That other Marquart Labs employee. David Torres. He's dead. Poison."

CHAPTER SIX

If you've seen any of the popular television crime shows you're familiar with the routine when you encounter a victim. The funky jumpsuit, mask, gloves, the works. All of these precautions might look like they came straight out of *The Andromeda Strain*, but they serve their purpose. Anymore a crime scene is ripe for making mistakes, the kind that could lead to an acquittal on bullshit technicalities.

Not only that, but compromising a crime scene could destroy critical evidence, the kind prosecutors depend on.

In this case the precautions served a dual purpose. Not only did we want to prevent contamination of the evidence, we didn't want the evidence to chew up our insides and turn us into screaming wraiths with blood oozing out of every opening.

I couldn't say for sure yet about the oozing blood part, but after Stacey Haas spelled out the grisly death dance my imagination added lots of garnish.

David Torres lived alone in a duplex about a mile from the

lab. He was single, a meticulously-detailed science student-turned-administrator who'd worked with Leon Haas since graduating from the University of New Mexico, just down I-25 in Albuquerque. His half of the duplex was decorated in a traditional southwestern style that seemed to be required by law in New Mexico. I maneuvered into my jumpsuit, then stood aside in the entryway as a technician walked past carrying a cat in a pet carrier. The freaked out fur-baby was being taken to a specialized vet to get checked out.

There was a cluster of activity going on in the small kitchen, which is where I assumed the body had been found. I saw the bulky shape of Sheriff Tonkin talking with someone I assumed to be the coroner. All I saw were the sheriff's eyes above his mask, and they were intense. The coroner was listening and nodding, then pointing down and saying something I couldn't hear over the bustle. I waited until two other people left the kitchen before easing in.

Sure enough, curled up on the floor near the sink lay the body of a man in khaki pants and an untucked shirt. He was contorted in a manner that implied agony, and I did indeed see evidence of blood mixed with what had to be other bodily fluids that had escaped during the death throes. There was a sickly smell hovering over the scene and I forced back a gag reflex. I'd seen dozens of corpses in my work, including the many I'd personally dispatched to the morgue, yet I never acclimated to the scent of a crime scene.

Tonkin glanced up and took a moment to identify me as the unwanted Fed in town to complicate his life. He indicated with his head to follow, and we walked into the garage where we lowered our masks.

"I take it we're dealing with the same toxin?" I asked.

"Looks like it. There was an opened bottled water on the floor next to him. It's on the way to a lab for tests right now." He shook his head. "Poor guy."

I saw that beneath his gruff exterior Sheriff Tonkin really cared about the people under his watch.

"I was coming out here to talk with him at some point today," I said.

"Then you could've died just as easily if he'd offered you something to drink."

This was true. I'd accepted a glass of water from Stacey Haas; who's to say I wouldn't have happily sipped from a bottled water here?

"Two ways this could've gone down," I said. "It's possible all three of the employees at Marquart Labs were targeted from the beginning. It's also possible that they initially only wanted Haas and your niece was unfortunately in the wrong place at the wrong time. Maybe now they felt like they had to eliminate Torres from talking about something he knew or saw. The trouble is, we don't know for sure Torres brought this water home from the office where it was compromised, or if someone snuck in here and tampered with it when he wasn't home."

The lawman pursed his lips. "Sounds like we're dealing with villains of a caliber that don't often wander through Santa Fe."

"If you knew the caliber we were talking about, Sheriff, it would cause you sleepless nights." I looked back toward the door to the house. "Who found him?"

"The woman who lives in the adjoining place heard him through the wall. It wasn't pleasant. She came over and banged on the door for a while then called us."

I thought again about Stacey's description of the poison's effect. Her final words to me had been '*Find the monster.*' Anyone who understood a body's reaction to this toxin and could intentionally administer it to innocent people was beyond a monstrosity. They were pure evil. Sick, demented evil. Just the kind of people I found myself chasing after on a regular basis.

We reapplied our masks and went back into the house. I looked around a bit but never expected to find any clue that would tie in Parks. If there'd been no whiff of him elsewhere in town then it was unlikely he'd left anything behind at this crime scene. Plus, it may not have been Steffan Parks at all, but rather his assistant and lover, Jayanti Pradesh.

I left the jumpsuit and other investigative gear with one of the deputies and walked back to my car. As I pulled away from the curb I saw a white Audi screech to a stop and a woman jump out. It was Stacey. She must've heard about the murder and raced to the scene. Just an emotional reaction, I'm sure. My heart went out to her, but I didn't stop. As I drove off I watched her in my mirror, being held up by another deputy. I turned a corner and sped away.

Two minutes later I was back on the line with Quanta. I filled her in on the murder of Torres and my chat with Stacey Haas. I did *not* share details of my personal connection to the widow. No sense giving the boss any reason to think I was distracted.

"There's no sign of Parks anywhere in town," I said, "so all we have to go on is his hatred for Leon Haas and the threat reported by Haas's wife. But we do have that mention of Jayanti Pradesh in Arizona."

Quanta processed that for a moment. "Parks knows by now we're on his trail. He wouldn't be foolish enough to show up at a high-profile conference with his girlfriend. Still, unless you have loose ends in Santa Fe, you should probably go."

IT WAS about a 7-hour drive in good weather so I allowed for a little more. That would have me at my hotel in Scottsdale around 11:30 or midnight. Cruise control and a good playlist made the time pass quickly while allowing my mind to roam. I refused to dwell on my intersection with an old flame, especially one I'd probably never see again. Instead I tapped a finger on the steering wheel to a Beck song and mulled over the assignment as it had played out so far. Sheriff Tonkin had my number and would reach out if something else turned up.

Mostly I was curious about how the poison had found its way into those coffee cups. Had it been there for a day or more? Or had a third person been there that morning? Certainly not Parks; I doubt Haas would've let him in, given their bad blood. Jay Pradesh, perhaps? Under what pretense could she have wormed her way in? Seemed a long shot, and yet it made the most sense at the moment.

During one of my breaks at a truck stop I called Poole. She was out of the office but answered her cell.

"Hey, do me a favor, please," I said. "Have the sheriff's office in Santa Fe send you the complete list of visitors to Marquart Labs over the past month."

"Everyone?"

"Yeah. I want to see who's been there recently, whether just as a guest or as a visiting scientist."

"All right," Poole said. "But what good would it do someone to visit a month ago? The poisoning happened this week."

"Right. But if someone poisoned the coffee that morning, it

might be someone who'd already visited, so it was natural to let them back in without any security concerns."

"Got it. Okay, I'll have that for you by tomorrow afternoon. You're en route to Scottsdale?"

"Roger that."

"I know it'll be late when you get in, but please do a backup before you go to sleep."

I groaned. "What about first thing in the morning? We can keep our fingers crossed that I don't die in my sleep."

"Okay. But it's been too long. I'm sorry to nag."

"Just doing your job. And believe me, I don't want to lose all the stuff I've learned today. Some of it was, um, personally interesting."

"Like what?" she asked.

I'd gone too far and had to pull back. "Oh, you know I'm a science nut. All of the biology involved. It's just interesting." That sounded lame but almost believable. "I got your text with the hotel information, so thank you. I'll touch base with you tomorrow."

I went back to my playlist and drove on through the darkness of the southwest desert. The weather cooperated and I made good time, checking into my hotel near Gainey Ranch around 11. Exhaustion had set in, physically and mentally, and I was conked out by 11:45.

THE SOUND of bird call just outside the window woke me up a few minutes before seven. It was a brisk morning in the low 40s, so I went for a quick three-mile run, then took coffee back up to the room. After showering I decided I'd put off the upload long enough and gathered up the necessary gear.

Being an agent of Q2 means you not only put your life on

the line, you actually lose it on a fairly consistent basis. Only movie star secret agents cheat death; those of us working in the real world get popped. In order for the investment program to work properly, I needed to upload all of my recent experiences on a regular basis. That way, if I got killed we could download my knowledge, my memories, and this charming, witty personality into a new body and I wouldn't have to play as much catch-up.

The only drawback was that uploading took about 90 minutes, and I couldn't do it during sleep. In order to upload I needed decent wifi speed — which I had here at the hotel — a rather serious chemical that should never be used for anything else, and a couple of gadgets we'd disguised as ordinary travel-kit items. On one hand it's so corny as to be painful, but on the other hand no one had ever snooped through my deodorant or shaving cream.

Now I pulled everything out, put the Do-Not-Disturb placard outside the door, made myself comfortable on the bed with my reading material of choice during the process — a good ol' rag magazine, this time Cosmo — and popped the pill.

For what's gained through the process, and, by extension, what's ultimately *saved*, the time sacrifice isn't that bad. But I've still pressed Quanta to get that genius behind the whole thing, Devya Nayar, to compress the time to less than five minutes. Or, if that was out of the question, at least figure out how to accomplish it while an agent slept.

That convenience was still out of reach. For reasons way beyond my realm of understanding, the human brain goes into a different mode while sleeping and it jacks with the upload process. So, for the time being at least, I had to carve out almost two hours and find something to entertain me while I was semi-doped. Reading about Hollywood stars and pop music idols fit right into that state of mind.

When it was finished and I'd preserved all of my memories and experiences from Santa Fe, I packed everything away, changed clothes, and set off to find Jayanti Pradesh.

CHAPTER SEVEN

I like to think of myself as a scientist wanna-be. I may not be a specialist in any particular field, but I know a little bit about a lot of things. Astronomy, physics, chemistry, biology, electronics. It's a result of my lifelong habit of learning. I'm a curious creature. Some have said I'm also nosy, but that's different.

Regardless, while a science conference might strike the average person as a complete yawn-fest, I thought it was pretty cool. Now, to be truthful, it didn't stop me from thinking that many professional scientists were big dorks. As I walked toward the check-in desk I had to stifle a few chuckles when I saw major Poindexters huddled together in very animated conversations. Yes, I can be a jerk sometimes.

Through her deep connections, Quanta had reserved a conference badge for me under the name Edwin Phillips. I bristled at the name Edwin and figured that was Quanta's little way of messing with me. I resolved to tell everyone to call me Ed.

My cover was as a recruiting specialist for the Department

of Defense. That was vague enough to get me into conversations without having to go into too much detail. And the DoD credentials opened doors to speak with science-types hungry for government funding. It also kept Q2 from having to create a large online presence for this guy Edwin. I'd be able to move around easily.

After checking in and getting my goodie bag and name badge, I wandered up and down the halls, glancing at the conference program, wondering where Jayanti would turn up. I had a photo that Poole had texted, and I casually stole a glance at every female face I passed. So far no sign of her. Parks was a long shot, but I kept my eyes open for him, too.

It was the final day of the conference and they'd saved the keynote address for the farewell luncheon. Every attendee would be there, so I'd pretty much decided that's where I'd run into her.

But then she was right in front of me.

Jayanti Pradesh stood in a cluster of five or six people, all chatting amiably, sharing ideas and anecdotes, and probably a fair amount of professional gossip. I wondered how she handled the fact that her boyfriend was being whispered about throughout the scientific community. From what I could see right now she wasn't bothered by anything in the slightest.

As I stood off to the side I compared my photo image with Pradesh in the flesh. She was short, barely over five feet, and slight of frame. Her long, dark hair was coiled up into a knot, and she sported two sizable moles on her face, one to the side of her mouth and another between an eyebrow and her temple. She laughed easily, with dazzling-white teeth and eyes that danced with delight. I could see why Parks was attracted to her. Jay Pradesh was a natural beauty.

It was time to make a move. I strolled up wearing my own

smile and greeted the group. Each of them glanced at my name tag and registered my Defense Department connection. That would at least buy me a few minutes until they decided if I had something they wanted.

"Hello," I said. "I always seem to be late to the party. I'm Ed."

"Hello, Ed," said a woman whose tag identified her as Clara from the University of Texas. "You haven't missed too much, unless you get off on fluid dynamics. Too much of that at this conference, if you ask me."

"The last time I got off on fluid dynamics was in college. And that was in my dorm room."

Just like that, with a slightly-naughty but completely stupid quip I'd broken the ice and let them know they could open up with this particular government dweeb.

A man from Cal Tech spoke up. "What brings you to the conference? Looking for anything in particular?"

"Oh, only the best and the brightest," I said. "Last year space science was all the rage in our hallways and this year it seems to be focused more on traditional ground-troop defense. I'm sure next year it'll be something else entirely. What are you all working on these days? And what brings you to this particular conference?"

They went around the circle, each trying to sound self-assured yet humble about their specialties. I couldn't help but notice that Jayanti hadn't spoken a word yet, and seemed to look at me somewhat suspiciously. Granted, her boyfriend had been burned by the government. But eventually it was her turn to share.

"I'm not really here for the sessions. Mostly for the networking," she said with a polite smile. "It's been a long time since I've been able to catch up with old friends."

Such a non-answer. I wouldn't let it go. "But," and I made sure to squint at her name tag as if I had no idea who she was. "But Ms. Pradesh, when you're not expensing dinner and cocktails, what's your line of work?"

She waited a full five seconds before answering. "I've done some work with desalination."

"That's a very noble cause," I said with another smile. "Saves lives."

"We try," she said and turned to look at one of her companions, hoping for a bail out.

I refused to let her off the hook. "Where do you do this desalting? Your name tag doesn't list a school or a lab."

For the first time she lost the smile. "I'm between jobs at the moment, Mr. Phillips." She was irked at being pressed. Turning to one of the men in the group, she said, "I'm going back to my room for a bit. I'll see you at lunch?"

They all said goodbye and she made her exit. I made sure to not watch her leave, instead engaging Clara from Texas in some other inane chat. But I'd at least made contact.

From the Cal Tech guy I discovered the real place to make connections. There was a big happy hour party to close the conference, and supposedly everyone went. Nothing like scientists letting their hair down, and I don't mean that sarcastically. I told you, I was a nerd at heart. I would've wanted to mix and mingle even if I wasn't on the job.

But this would give me another chance to irritate the lovely Jay Pradesh.

I left the conference center and went back to my hotel. I saw no reason to sit through the lunch keynote; my target zone was now the evening party.

IN THE ROOM I reached out to Poole and let her know I'd spoken with Jayanti and expected to have more interaction in just a few hours. She'd accessed the conference attendance log and texted a file to me with each person's name and affiliation. I wouldn't be able to sift through all of it now, but it could come in handy if I needed to get the low-down on someone. I briefly checked out the four people Pradesh had been talking with, but nobody seemed overly interesting.

Although I recognized that I didn't really know who or what would constitute *interesting* in this particular setting. Other than Steffan Parks.

Poole finished by telling me she'd gone through the records of every visitor to Marquart Labs in the past month. No names jumped out, but she'd hold onto them for later cross-referencing if necessary.

I called Christina next.

"I miss you," I said when she answered. "Tell me how much you miss me, too."

"Desperately," she said.

"Why do I sound more sincere than you?"

"Because you're a better actor?"

I laughed. "What are you doing?"

"Freezing. I don't know what it's like in Arizona right now but here it's about ten degrees. I might get in the tub just to warm up. Got any bubble bath over on your side?"

"Yes. Lavender. Wish I could join you?"

Her voice turned tender. "Oh, you really are feeling lovey today, aren't you? Sorry, I'll turn off the snark machine."

"No, please don't. I'll think an alien has taken possession of your body."

We talked for another ten minutes, during which I could hear the tub filling. I truly was homesick for Christina; we'd had very little time together in the past few months. I'd even missed Christmas with her because of an island assignment that resulted in a bullet to the chest and a hospital stay.

Your standard pulp fiction spies always grab a little bedroom action while on their assignments, usually in the first couple chapters and then at the very end, sort of as a reward for risking their lives.

I'm devoted to my wife and I actually *give* my lives. Hollywood producers will never make a series about me.

After another round of sweet talk we hung up.

THE NAP HAPPENED without me planning it. When a sound outside the window pulled me back to consciousness I discovered I'd slept for almost two hours. The scientists' happy hour would get underway soon so I ordered room service, caught up on a little news and sports, then grabbed my conference badge and started back over. A plan for how to move forward with Jayanti Pradesh would be very helpful, and I had none. I figured it would come to me when I needed it.

The party was underway by the time I walked into the ballroom. A DJ was playing really bad tunes and a few mobile bars were set up around the perimeter of the room. I moseyed up to one and secured a Jack and Coke, hoping it would distract me from the burned-out little ditty about Jack and Diane.

Pradesh was nowhere to be found and it dawned on me that she might ditch the party altogether. I did, however, catch sight of good ol' Clara from Texas. She'd cornered a woman who wore the universal fake conference smile. She could use an assist, so I strolled up.

It took Clara a second and then she smiled. "Hey, it's our Pentagon man. Ed, this is Kathleen. She's from another of our fine institutions in the great state of Texas. I've tried to get her to leave Baylor and come to Austin, but she's stubborn."

Kathleen shook hands while her eyes thanked me for the interruption. After a quick exchange of pleasantries she made an escape. Clara leaned in and muttered, "Nice girl, but her work is shoddy. We'd never have her at UT." Then she tipped an almost-empty glass of white wine to her lips and gave me a wink.

"Maybe I should talk to her," I said. "With our budget at Defense we can usually only afford shoddy." We both gave the standard conference laugh. "Where are all your friends from earlier?" I added, sipping from my own cocktail and looking around the room.

"If Rick is being Rick, he's got someone up in his room right now. He only comes to these conferences to screw around on his wife."

"Oh."

She nodded knowingly. "Uh huh. And Marcus — he's the guy from Cal Tech — doesn't drink anymore, so I don't know if he'll come or not."

"What about your other friend? What was her name? Jamie?"

"Jayanti? She'll probably be here. Why? You're not like Rick, are you?"

"No. I love my wife."

Clara laughed as if I was kidding.

I said, "I was hoping to talk to her some more about that desalination program."

"Yeah? What does that have to do with national defense?"

"Help countries who are hungry or need fresh water and they're more likely to become allies and in turn help us with defense."

"Ah." She finished off the wine so I steered her toward one of the bars to top things up. She kept talking. "Jay's an odd duck, too. Got hooked up with a guy who used to be a really good scientist but became a star. And you know what that means."

"He can charge more for lectures?"

"That, and he can become a certified asshole. Which he did."

This was the thread I'd been looking for. "Tell me more about the asshole."

"Name's Steffan Parks. Guy actually won some pretty big awards when he was young and hungry. Since then he's not so hot. I hear he's not easy to get along with. Except with Jay. She likes him, for some reason." She lowered her voice. "Not that she's a great science whiz either."

It appeared that no one measured up in the eyes of the great Clara from Texas, which was all right with me. I was on the hunt for dirt anyway. "I've heard the name before," I said. "He's had a few contracts with us over the years. Not my department, though, so I don't know any specifics." I looked around. "Is he here, too?"

Clara scoffed. "He won't show his face until his rep cools off. Had a bit of a tough go lately. Then he went and got on the bad side of some little group he hung out with."

"What group is that?"

She scrunched up her face in concentration. "I can't remember the name off the top of my head. Something foreign. Maybe Latin."

I glanced around the room and tried to act only marginally interested. "What is it, a social group?"

Clara scoffed. "I don't know how much they socialize. From what I gather they just bitch. Some of us have a completely different name for them. We call them the POS. Stands for Pissed Off Scientists."

We shared a laugh, but this, I realized, could be important. I took a long drink of my whiskey just to slow down the conversation. Then: "I'm glad I came to this party. I'd love to know more about this unhappy little group."

"Why?" she asked.

"You'd be surprised at the number of tech advances that came about because someone was pissed off. Necessity might be the mother of invention, but discontent can be ridiculously profitable."

Clara laughed. "Lucky for you, here's a guy who can tell you all about it."

I followed her gaze to a man approaching with a bottle of beer wrapped in a napkin. He was tall and painfully thin with equally spare strands of hair brushed across his head. His clothes had the look of being slept in, but I guessed he simply wasn't overly fussy about their care. Something about his face, though, particularly his eyes, told me he wasn't a stereotypical nerd. He just gave zero shits about conventional standards.

"Jonas," Clara said. "Come meet Ed. He's here to woo some of us to Washington to help the government get right with science. Ed, this is Jonas Aiken."

I shook his bony hand, which was damp from having carried around his beer. His badge said Aiken Inc., which told me nothing. He nodded a greeting.

"Ed's curious about that group I've heard you mention," Clara said. "You know, the angry scientists society, or whatever it is. I'm going to the ladies room so you can tell him all about your little fun club."

As she walked away Jonas took a long pull from his beer and tried to size me up.

I said, "I think Clara was kidding when she told me it's sometimes called Pissed Off Scientists."

He gave a polite chuckle, which came out deeper than I'd expected from such a thin frame. His voice was the same. "Oh, Clara's an interesting character. Yeah, I've heard that some people use that phrase, but that's not the name the group itself uses."

"And what name do they use?"

He hesitated by taking a sip of beer. "Why are you interested in them? It's just an informal group of people. Nothing really organized."

"Just sounds like the kind of people who might be motivated to look for something new to inspire them."

He shrugged. "Oh, I don't know. It started out as a monthly bitch session. Sort of the old *We don't get no respect* kinda stuff. Fortunately, as time has gone by, it's been a bit more productive than that."

I was getting a good read on Jonas Aiken. He walked around in his nerd uniform, but he was nobody's fool. I liked him.

"Well," I said, "when my buddies and I get together we sometimes have a quick session we call *shop bitch*. Gets it out of the system. Why should scientists be any different?"

"Is there a specific reason why you're curious?" he asked.

"Clara just mentioned a guy who I guess used to be in this little band of bitchers, and then became a pain."

He smiled again. "That could be an extensive list. Who were you talking about?"

"Steffan Parks."

The smile faded, and Jonas took yet another drink of his beer in an obvious attempt to cover the change of temperature. He looked around the room and said, "Yeah, well, Steffan is not the most popular member of the community these days. *Any* scientific community, for that matter."

I was going to have to pull information out of him. But my gut told me I stood a better chance of picking up a nugget from this guy than anything Jayanti might divulge. In fact, unless it was under duress I had the feeling Ms. Pradesh would divulge *nada*. Time for a spontaneous change in tactics.

"Look," I said. "I'm not much of a party animal, and on top of that I'm starving. How would you feel about grabbing a steak? We can put it all on Uncle Sam's tab."

He gave a slight smile. "Even though it may not look like it, I never turn down free meals."

Then he set his beer down on a table and added, "Besides, I think you're really just poking around to see if Steffan Parks is going to kill a lot of people."

CHAPTER EIGHT

In high school I had a buddy named Ron who was notorious for eating everything in sight and still looking like one of those stick bugs.

Jonas Aiken was the second coming of Ron. I watched him demolish a large house salad, a 16-ounce ribeye, and multiple helpings of au gratin potatoes. The server refilled the bread basket twice and looked at me like I was the guilty party. Who would suspect Poindexter sitting in the other chair?

By the time the entrees arrived we'd maneuvered past my fake identity. I'd satisfied his curiosity by simply explaining that I worked with a government agency tasked with protecting citizens from bloodthirsty assholes.

"I'm not surprised you're poking around about Steffan," Aiken said.

"If he was that bad why didn't you report him to someone?" I asked.

"What would I report? That a guy was exceptionally angry at being humiliated and talked a lot of trash about people?"

"Never any specifics?"

"No, not really. I mean, we all knew he'd worked on some pretty dangerous stuff, but so do a lot of us."

"That's a pretty explosive combination," I said. "Pissed off scientists with deadly chemicals."

He waved that away with a handful of buttered roll. "You've probably been pissed a lot. And I'm guessing you carry a gun. How's that for a combination?"

I started to open my mouth and make some smart remark about how it was different because I didn't walk around with a huge chip on my shoulder. Then I thought about my personal grudge with Beadle. I stayed silent and let Aiken keep going.

"This group you're asking about; they're not an official society or anything like that. But when you've had funding eliminated, or you've had your conclusions proved wrong after years of hard work — *years* — it doesn't just sting. It cuts deep. And there's no one in the general public who'll feel sorry for you. Hell, they never pay attention of *any* kind, even if your studies eventually save their life."

Aiken poured a refill from the bottle of red on the table. "So commiserating is part of it; you mingle with people who understand. And for some, like Clara, that's where it begins and ends. But Clara would never understand. She's so cloistered in her safe little UT laboratory, not really doing much. And that's why she doesn't get it. Clara would never stick her neck out on the kind of project that lends itself to heavy review and, consequently, potentially heavy criticism. She plays it safe. Not every scientist does that."

"Like Steffan," I prompted.

"Yeah. But Steffan began to make noise that went beyond bitching. He never came out and directly threatened anyone. At least not that I knew of. But once I heard him say something along the lines of, '*They'd be better off having me on their side than fighting against them.'* I'm sure he was referring to the Pentagon, because you guys shunned him."

He set down his wine glass and looked at me. "Has Steffan hurt someone?"

"What's the term the police use? He's a *person of interest*."

Wiping at his mouth with the fancy cloth napkin, Aiken nodded. "I liked him the first time we met, long before he became a fancy prize winner. That rewired him somehow. Made him think he was not only brilliant but perfect. It's hard for someone with that attitude to accept defeat. Or to handle criticism."

I'd heard plenty about Parks and his temper. The time had come for someone to give me tangible information to catch up with him. "I appreciate your insight into Steffan Parks," I said. "When's the last time you saw him?"

He considered the question. "About four months ago? Yeah, that's right. He showed up at a talk on fluid mechanics not far from my office. Asked if he could drop in for a few minutes. I was already turned off by him at that point, but for whatever reason I said okay." He paused. "That was a meeting that did not go particularly well. I had to ask him to leave."

"Why?"

Aiken picked up the menu and flipped to the dessert page. I'm telling you, the guy was a bottomless pit with the metabolism of 200 hummingbirds. Anyone else with this appetite would weigh 450 pounds.

Finally he said, "I got the feeling he was recruiting me for some project that would involve his work on poisons. When I pressed him for details he shouted at me — actually yelled — that he needed to know who his friends were. Which makes no sense. Why can't you be a friend and still want information?" He shrugged. "I think he wanted blind devotion, and why the hell would I offer that to anyone, let alone a borderline nut case. I don't know anyone who'd agree to work with him these days."

I poured a refill on my own glass of wine. "Is there anyone who might know where he's doing his work?"

"*I* know. Well, not specifically. But he's definitely doing something in Arizona, probably around the Phoenix area. There's a lot of the tech support he'd need."

"How do you know this? He told you?"

Aiken shook his head. "Not directly. But while he was trying to convince me to join his work he mentioned that it would be convenient for me. That I wouldn't spend much time away from my family." He took another bite, then under his breath added, "Not that that's an issue these days."

I understood the subtext perfectly. Jonas Aiken was on the outs with his wife. I wondered if that played into his decision to either work — or not — with Parks.

I downed my wine in one gulp. Then I excused myself from the table under the guise of a bathroom break, but instead went out the restaurant's door. Walking past the valet stand I called Poole. She answered on the second ring.

"He's around here," I said. "Probably Phoenix or one of the 'burbs. I'll try to get more details, but according to another of the eggheads, Parks is probably based within a few miles from where I'm eating an overpriced steak."

"That's odd," Poole said. "Nothing shows up on any records. Not in Arizona, at least."

"I can't explain that. And maybe it's an intentional dodge on his part to throw people off. He might hint to people that he's nearby just to create a web of confusion. He may be in Minneapolis for all we know, but for now it's the best intel we have. Let Quanta know."

"Upload tonight, please."

"Will do," I said. "Also, while you're at it, get some background on this source of mine. Name is Jonas Aiken." I spelled it for her and also mentioned Aiken, Inc.

WE ENDED the call and I stood for a moment, looking up at the winter night sky of the American Southwest. I caught sight of Orion and it's famous belt breaking through the glow of city lights. I knew I was on the verge of something breaking big, and just another hour with Aiken could do it.

I made a real bathroom stop on the way back to the table, where Jonas had just taken the first bite of some sort of chocolate cake.

"I didn't think you'd mind," he said through a full mouth.

I stared down at my half-eaten steak and asparagus and chuckled. "Knock yourself out." I picked up my glass of wine. "Let's go back to something you said at the party. About Parks killing a lot of people. Tell me how he would do that."

Aiken dabbed away a smear of frosting below his lower lip. "I couldn't say for sure what delivery system he might use. But I know enough about tabun to realize how dangerous he *could* be. Assuming he's crazy enough."

"For the moment let's assume that. What would be your best guess for distribution?"

He pondered this. "Steffan created an off-shoot of traditional tabun. Now, in its original form it could be transmitted through direct contact with the skin, or through mixing in a liquid. But it's also deadly in a gaseous state. So someone could breathe it in, like the old-style mustard gas used in World War I.

"If I understand Steffan's work," he continued, "he tried to develop a toxin similar to tabun but one that was much more difficult to detect. And that meant some trade-offs. His invention was most effective when camouflaged within another agent, like a liquid. He gave up the airborne element to create a more potent poison."

"He told you all of this?"

"Not all of it. Some of us were able to piece together the rest after he was rejected by the government. I mean, when the Pentagon says your way of killing people is too ghastly, you know it's pretty bad."

I chewed on this for a minute. "If he wanted to poison a water supply — hypothetically, of course — how would he go about it?"

Aiken finished off the last crumbs of his cake. "A city's water supply is highly contained and regulated. You can't just walk in and dump a bunch of arsenic into a vat and presto, death and mayhem. So — as you say, hypothetically — if Steffan really wanted to use his invention, he'd look for a way to contaminate the supply after it had been through most of the quality checkpoints." He thought about that for a second. "Which would also eliminate the diffusion issue."

"Explain that," I said.

"No matter how much work he does on it, Steffan won't have thousands of gallons of this toxin. He'll have a pretty good supply, but not enough to poison an entire system. It's a question of dilution at some point. Pour a thimble-full of poison into the ocean and it does nothing. But mix that same amount into a pint of beer . . ."

"Right," I said.

"So if you're thinking he'd try to wipe out the whole country or even an entire city, that's just not practical. It would take an incredible amount of toxin, tons of planning, and lots of cooperation from people on the inside."

"What about a subdivision? Or a few subdivisions?"

"Sure, he could do that," Aiken said. "Maybe even a little larger. But you get the picture."

It was a grisly picture. Three or four subdivisions may not be the same as a city, but you're still talking thousands of dead, perhaps tens of thousands. And my mind leapt ahead; unless he was caught, Parks could repeat the procedure down the road. Ten thousand now, another ten thousand in a year, and so forth.

Now I saw proof of why this had become a Q2 special. The FBI would definitely be involved, but this was a case where the knave needed to be taken out immediately.

Aiken said, "Of course, this is all conjecture. It's just something I've thought about since Steffan went off on his rants about the government."

"No, I appreciate your insight into this," I said. "Our job is to be prepared. You've helped us become better informed. So thank you."

He pushed his dessert plate away. "This was thanks enough. I don't get to eat like this very often."

I doubted that.

We parted ways in front of the steakhouse after I collected his contact information. Checking the time, it was still relatively early. I could head back to the party and hope to make contact with Jayanti Pradesh. Word had it the conference attendees would keep things going until midnight.

But I couldn't afford to lose the data I'd picked up since my last upload, either. I'd promised Poole another backup, and decided to fit one in. I'd have to trust that Pradesh, who'd made it clear she was only there for the social aspect, would stay late.

On the way to my room I made another quick call to Poole and explained this to her.

She sighed. "All right, but still tell me everything you found out from Jonas Aiken. I can start doing some checking. And when you get back to the party activate a Series-8 for the rest of the evening, please."

I agreed, and proceeded to detail everything from my talk with Aiken, finishing just as I got to my hotel.

The upload took 78 minutes. Not bad.

I PULLED into the conference center parking lot at a quarter past ten. Reaching into my coat pocket I fished out one of the business cards I'd picked up at the safe house in Albuquerque. The Series-8 was heavier than a normal card, but not enough to create suspicion. It was a technical marvel, acting as a voice transmitter once activated. Through the years I'd used them plenty of times; sometimes they worked like a charm, other times they ended up in a trash can.

Tonight it would be in my outer coat pocket, eavesdropping on every conversation I had, and sending a recording back to Q2 headquarters at the same time. Real secret agent stuff. Made me wish I had a pen that shot tranquilizer darts.

As I'd hoped, the party was still in full effect. On the right I saw Clara engaged with three cornered listeners; I made sure to turn left. After picking up a cocktail I gazed around the room, cringing at the sound of Whitney Houston's *I Wanna Dance With Somebody*. The DJ vigorously nodded along with the beat, looking like a strutting Mick Jagger.

"So even government people can let their hair down."

I turned to see where the cheesy line had come from. It was Jayanti Pradesh.

She sipped from a glass of white wine and studied my face. "Of course, you're not dancing. Maybe you only let it down so far."

I held up my cocktail. "Depends on how many of these I've had. So far not enough."

This brought a smile and she indicated her own drink. "I've had far too many of these tonight. But that's the problem; I'd rather drink than dance. Of course, I'd rather do anything than dance."

Was she flirting with me? I couldn't tell for sure. Either way, I put on a great performance to mask my absolute shock at the conversation itself. Glancing down at the name badge which was slightly askew I made a show of trying to make out her name in the strobe-infused lighting. Of course, in her state she may have thought I was just staring at her breasts.

She stuck her hand out. "We almost met earlier. I'm Jayanti. What's your name again?"

"Ed. Ed Phillips."

"Hello, Ed Ed Phillips."

"I see you're almost empty. Need another?"

"Plying me with alcohol won't work."

I took a small drink from my whiskey. "What won't work?"

"I won't sleep with you."

"That's okay. I love my wife."

She laughed. "And I can't work for the government, either."

"Why not?"

"Bad record."

"Really?"

"Uh huh. Too many speeding tickets."

She was clearly enjoying the situation. I started to toss in one of my own smart-ass comments when we were interrupted by a couple of very intoxicated men, asking Jayanti to join them on the dance floor. She declined and graciously accepted their quick pecks on the cheek. They jostled their way toward another woman.

"This is getting old," Jay said. "I'm staying here at the conference center. Let's take our drinks up to my room and talk about our nation's defense."

I smiled at her. "Ms. Pradesh, I told you. I—"

"Don't flatter yourself, Ed Ed. I just want a quiet place to talk."

She seemed pretty drunk, and none of this made sense. But as random and as curious as it was, how in the hell could I turn down this opportunity?

I could only imagine what Poole was thinking as she listened to this exchange two thousand miles away.

CHAPTER NINE

More than a few fictional spies are known for their prowess with the opposite sex. Never mind that the premises behind these exploits are patently ridiculous. SuperSpy meets woman at craps table and fifty frames later they're smoking a cigarette in bed and making cutesy talk. This, in the minds of the authors and screenwriters, displays the intersection of a spy's charm and his virility, and somehow adds to the mystique.

Real life for a government agent is much different. Yes, there's sex to be had, as much for a spy as there is for a bartender or a bus driver. We all just meet in different settings, but rarely in a casino. And we never score within fifty frames.

Which meant that everything happening right now was not only pure fiction, but fiction of the sort that isn't ashamed of being so obviously fake. In other words, Jayanti Pradesh knew that I knew this was bullshit and she just didn't care. She wanted me in her room and there were three possible reasons.

One, she wanted to kill me. But I'm pretty handy at defending myself, no matter how many times Quanta has kicked the living shit out of me. The odds of Jayanti matching my boss's skill level were slim so I wasn't overly concerned with getting kicked to death.

There was always poison, the modus operandi of Jay and her boyfriend, Parks. But if our analysis was correct, I'd be vulnerable if I consumed food or beverage from her hands. I doubted she'd surprise me with a poison dart from the tube of a blowgun. Although that would be dramatic as hell, and one of the few ways I've yet to be killed.

Of course, Pradesh could just whip out a gun and shoot me, the preferred method of many killers. Unimaginative and downright bourgeois, but pretty damned effective.

No way she'd risk a loud gunshot in a hotel room, however. I was packing heat myself, if it came to that.

The second reason she might be luring me upstairs was purely investigative on her part. Perhaps she thought it a mighty big coincidence for a Defense Department schlub to stroll up at a conference right after her boyfriend had lost a major contract and then responded by murdering his old friend. She'd had all day to communicate with Parks, and it wouldn't be unreasonable to assume their intuition had suggested a deeper dive into this Ed Phillips character and what the hell he really wanted. It might take only ten minutes for her to be satisfied that I was a harmless bureaucrat and send me on my way. After all, she'd been emphatic that sex was off the table.

There was a potential third reason and I latched on to it. What if Jayanti was an unwilling participant in the monstrosities committed by her mentor and lover? It was certainly possible that she was a starry-eyed apprentice who'd grown appalled at the crimes and yet was hesitant to turn in Parks for fear that she'd be guilty by association.

Why hadn't she spoken up sooner? How could she let his

heinous behavior reach this point before contacting authorities? What if these thoughts were running through her head?

Now, with the help of numerous servings of house white, she may have finally summoned the courage to tentatively reach out for help. How I behaved in the first few minutes could determine just how much intel she dished.

I didn't want to handicap these three possibilities, maybe out of superstitious fear that resting too much hope on option three could jinx it. The best play was to hope for number three, be mindful of number two, and be prepared for number one.

As we left the ballroom I stopped at the bar and slipped the young bartender $40 for a two-thirds-empty bottle of Jack. I held it at my side as we made our way down the long hallway and up the elevator to her room on the fifth floor. Neither of us spoke until we were inside.

"I need the ladies room," she said. "Fix yourself a fresh drink. I think there are mixers in the kitchen, or you might just have to drink it straight."

I was definitely choosing straight. She probably wouldn't have tampered with the items in the mini-bar's fridge, but why take the chance? Instead I rinsed out one of the glasses, filled it with ice from the room's small freezer, and poured from my own — safe — bottle. There was an opened bottle of white wine in the fridge, so I filled a glass for Jayanti. Setting the whiskey and wine on the suite's coffee table, I gazed out the window at the twinkling lights of Phoenix and Scottsdale. I needed to gather my thoughts; at no point in the day or evening did I imagine this scenario. Being caught off-guard pushes all the advantage chips to the other side of the table. I didn't like that.

Remembering that Poole would be listening to the recording, I muttered, "As you've heard, I'm in the lair of the lioness. I'll call you when I'm back in the car."

A minute later Jayanti opened the door from her bedroom. I watched her reflection in the window as she fell onto the overstuffed sofa. She lit up at the sight of the wine glass. I chose the large chair next to the couch and we clinked glasses.

"Thank you for leaving that horrid party," she said, taking a sip. "I can be social in small groups, but I don't care for *that* social. Does that make sense?"

"I'm the same way. I much prefer one-on-one." I didn't want to rush anything, but there was also no point in dallying. She'd invited me here to talk. I took a drink, letting the straight whiskey have its usual, calming effect. "Do you really want to talk about national defense, Ms. Pradesh? Or is there something else on your mind?"

She smiled. "First, it's Jay. And second, yes. But not yet. I'm still wired from the loud music. My God, why do they have to play it so loud at every conference party? What if people just want to talk about science?"

I returned the smile. "You mentioned your specific field earlier, I believe. What was it? Desalination?"

"You have a good memory."

"It's why I'm here, you know. Get to know the people who can help the good ol' U.S. of A. You also said you're between jobs. What made you leave your last employer? And please don't tell me you didn't feel challenged."

Jayanti was a cool customer. She held her wine glass up to the room's light, pretending to inspect the contents. It was clearly a stall tactic. "People aren't allowed to feel unchallenged?"

"If it's the real reason, sure. But when 90% of people use that expression it becomes background noise. Like *thinking out of the box*, or *paradigm shift*. Of course, the biggest load of shit is *I want to spend more time with my family*. Those people always have the next job within a week or two. I guess I'm just expecting more."

"Expecting more from me, or from people in general?"

I paused, then let a grin spread across my face. Taking another sip of whiskey I looked at her over the top of the glass. "You don't like answering questions, do you? I noticed that this morning."

"I . . ." She stopped and stared down at the glass in her hands. For a moment I felt something akin to sympathy wash over me. The pained look on her face, the way she sat on the couch, looking almost scared. Almost vulnerable. She slowly spun the tall wine glass between her fingers, either deep in thought or simply worried about what she was about to say. I remained silent, enjoyed my drink, and waited to see what spilled out of her.

A full minute went by before she spoke again. "Ed—"

"What, no more Ed Ed?"

She didn't break a smile. Her brow took on the classic furrow of someone unsure of how to proceed. "I do need to talk to you about something, but I can't just tell you everything. I have to do it my way. Slowly." She looked up at me. "Is that okay with you?"

This was looking more promising by the minute. "Tell me what's troubling you."

"It's just . . ."

She finished her wine, so I stood up to refill it at the room's small bar. "We're in no rush. You tell me whatever it is you want to say." I set the fresh glass in front of her and sat back down. "Does this have something to do with one of your jobs? Maybe your last job?"

Her voice was now very low. "Yes."

"The people you worked with? Did you have some trouble with them?"

She just nodded. Apparently this was going to be a full-blown fishing expedition. That was okay as long as Steffan Parks could be hauled into the bottom of the boat.

I didn't want to drink anymore because I needed all of my wits for what lay ahead. At the same time I couldn't let her think I was here for any other reason except friendly support. I took a couple more sips and decided to wait her out again.

Her phone vibrated inside the purse next to her, but she ignored it. For a moment I thought she was going to cry.

"The person I've worked with isn't the same man he used to be," she said, still quiet. "You work for the government, right? So you've probably heard of him."

"What's his name?"

"Steffan Parks."

I feigned some mental check of a rolodex, acting as if it took me a while to make a connection. "I think I've heard something about him, but I don't know details. He's an award-winning scientist, I know that much. He did work in the same field as you?"

"He's done a lot of different work in fluid mechanics. Mostly in a military capacity."

"Oh," I said, raising an eyebrow. "So this is why you wanted to talk with me."

"Mostly," she said.

"What's the problem?" She didn't answer, so I reached across to her and placed a hand on her forearm. "Honestly, Jay, if you're in some sort of trouble, or if this Parks guy is doing something he shouldn't, I can help you."

A single tear began to track down her cheek. "I don't know if you can help, Ed. In fact, I know you can't. Not anymore."

I smiled. "Not anymore?"

She surprised me by throwing her glass against the wall, where it smashed. She stood up and let out a gasp of frustration. "I'm sick of it!" she yelled. "I'm sick of the killing. So much killing."

"What?" I said, standing up beside her. "Whoa, slow down. Here, sit back down." I pulled her back onto the couch, and now sat next to her. "What killing are you talking about?"

She rubbed her hands together, maybe embarrassed by her outburst. "People. People who crossed Steffan. People who didn't respect him. Or respect me."

I took a deep breath, then another. The air in the room grew heavy, thick. I swallowed, which had become difficult. "But what killing?" I asked. "Who has Steffan killed?"

She turned to look at me and took my hands into her own small grip. Her eyes bored into mine. But the tear was gone. In its place was a slight glimmer. A look of . . .

What *was* that look?

"Steffan killed people in Santa Fe," she said and tightened the grip on my hands. I tried to take another deep breath, wondering what was coming next. But the breath fought back.

"He's going to kill more," Jay said. "And there's nothing you can do about it, Mr. Government Man. Because you're dead now, too."

My mind raced, and a bolt of fear shot through me. My breathing was now not only difficult, it was painful.

"You'll be dead in another minute, Ed Ed," she said, her ultra-bright teeth flashing in a smile. "Your bottle from the bartender was fine. That was a great plan. Very safe. But . . ."

She let go of my hand and pushed me so that I lay against

the back of the couch, struggling to breathe. But over the last few seconds breathing had become the least of my worries. Pain exploded within me, bursting from every possible point of my body. My face contorted beneath the agony. Every nerve was under heavy attack.

She leaned against me and whispered just loud enough for me to hear over my own terrified shrieks. "Silly boy. You didn't think of *everything*, did you?"

I tried to speak, but the pain grew so intense that spasms shook me. I let out a cry, then another. Jayanti shoved a pillow over my face, muffling my agonized screams. My body was too stricken to fight back. I'd gone rigid, my legs kicking over the small coffee table and my arms now stiff and straight.

The pain became so horrendous my mind lost the ability to comprehend anything going on around me. I lost the connection with my other senses. The only thing my brain could focus on was the unrelenting torture.

Seconds later I raced down a dark tunnel into blissful peace.

CHAPTER TEN

Quanta and Poole sat across from me at the conference table, papers and tablets interspersed with water bottles, a bag of awful snack chips I'd heard were healthy, and my own half-empty soda bottle.

For my boss to leave the sanctity of her garden home and make the trek to HQ, one of two things had to happen. Either a situation reached a super-critical stage, or an agent had royally screwed up.

In this case it was both.

While the two women huddled in conversation about some detail in a report, I took stock of my new body. The specimen I'd left dead in Scottsdale was one of the best I'd ever used, but this model was at least above average. I think my incessant bitching about sub-par choices could've finally filtered through the ranks.

I was now a shade over six feet tall with a physique rather common to inmates who had little to do except pump iron and shank cell-block snitches. Part of my right ear was missing, which, although unattractive, provided an air of *Don't-screw-*

with-me that might come in handy. The middle finger on my left hand was also disfigured, the skin mottled and scarred. While I had no idea what had caused that particular injury, it provided a unique visual when flipping the bird.

The nose was a tad large for my taste, but Christina had a thing for the classic Roman schnoz. I'd get confirmation later that evening.

Acclimating to a new body is something fewer than ten people on Earth had ever experienced. Somewhere a spreadsheet detailed all my various bodies and the men who'd sacrificed them for my use.

I'd send a thank-you card if I could, but their consciousness lay in stasis, a void of darkness where time ceased to exist. Their essence was uploaded like mine, but, rather than investing it into another body, theirs was kept in a specially-designed and highly-secretive hard drive. All they'd ever been, all they'd ever experienced, all their loves, losses, and limitations, were kept within something resembling a dark shoebox, with only an occasional blinking light to register that a human being waited inside.

Theoretically they could exist in that digital coma for centuries, perhaps millennia if properly cared for.

Is that immortality? If I uploaded your inert consciousness into an external hard drive and left it until the galaxy grew dark and died, would you technically be an immortal being? Or does it take actual thought and activity to qualify?

I was told the longest I'd waited in my own shoebox for a fresh body to inhabit was five weeks. During that stay there was no sensation of time whatsoever; one moment I was finishing an upload on a hotel bed in Idaho and the next my eyes were opening on a table in the basement of Q2 headquarters in Washington. Every single second in between was gone.

And listen, it's the strangest goddamned sensation you could imagine. The first two times it happened I panicked, which was natural. You reach to unplug from your upload and you're suddenly thousands of miles away, staring up at a tiled ceiling in a lab, cold, completely disoriented, and often with a raging headache.

After accepting that I'd become a new person, I was always debriefed. Quanta or Poole would explain, to the best of their abilities, what had happened. If details were sketchy it was because I hadn't stayed in touch with headquarters as much as I should've. Lately I'd been better, at least texting Poole with my plans and movements, just in case something happened.

And that didn't even necessarily have to involve a bad guy. Theoretically I could simply get hit by a bus and start the whole process over again, including the debriefing and other items that required attention.

This morning, before walking in to this particular meeting with Quanta and Poole, I'd taken care of two things.

The first was my required meeting with Q2's psychologist, a guy named Miller who I liked and trusted. He'd made sure things were firing properly in my head, which was his primary job. But he'd also probed further into a concern I'd expressed during our last meeting.

"Still think you're evolving into a monster?" he'd asked.

"I'd say I've plateaued," I said. "Mr. Hyde is being kept at arms length for the time being."

"How do you explain this plateau? If each new download into a body is really corrupting files in your brain, as you told me, why would that be on hold?"

For a moment I almost said, *So I can get out of here and back to work*. But I knew better.

"I've thought about that. It probably has to do with the quality of the receiving brain. Some are better equipped to handle the download."

He didn't say anything for a few seconds while he just looked down at his notes. Then, making eye contact, he said, "It's not like you to sidestep a question like that."

"You think my answer was bullshit?"

"No," he said. "It may be entirely valid. We're obviously all still learning about the process. I'm saying it's bullshit regarding the specific line of discussion we're having. It's a copout."

It was my turn to pause. I decided to go on the offensive.

"If we're going back to this topic, I'd like some data that could help me process everything."

"Such as?"

"Such as Agent One."

I'd known this would catch Miller off guard, but to his credit he kept a neutral look on his face. He was good. I knew that inside he'd been pushed back.

I don't know what the first Q2 agent's name had been, or what had happened to him. In fact, nobody — including Quanta, I suspected — knew where he was or what he was doing. The only thing I knew for certain was that he was a loose end, and that produced a lot of angst within the organization, as you might imagine.

Agent One, which was the name I'd attached to him, was missing, but had not died in the line of duty. His last upload was kept in a secure vault for security reasons. There was much more to the story that I might never learn.

"What does he have to do with this?" Miller had finally asked.

"I consider him to be the poster child of corrupted files. If it's happening to me, perhaps there are similarities in behavior."

"Swan, if there were similarities in your behavior — to that extent — you wouldn't be active right now."

I shrugged. "To that extent, sure. But markers for future behavior? Am I a test subject because I've maybe shown a few of those?"

He gave a low chuckle. "If you're asking if you're a guinea pig, the answer is yes. All Q2 field agents are guinea pigs until we develop more historical information. But you're not a test subject the way you're implying."

"And you'll never tell me anything about Agent One? Even if it might help me?"

"If I thought it would help you? Yes. But I haven't made that determination. Not even close."

I'd turned away and chewed on that, not just at the time, but throughout the rest of our session.

After meeting with Miller, I'd sat alone in a small room and listened to the Series-8 recording of my time with Jayanti. Imagine listening to the sound of your own execution. Then imagine listening to one of the most agonizing, horrific deaths ever conceived. It was brutal and disturbing.

But I listened to the whole thing twice, going over everything, from Jayanti's contact with me at the party, to the invitation back to her room, and the short discussion we'd had. I paid particular attention to the last few minutes of the conversation, absorbing Jay's odd behavior, the way she meandered back and forth between regret for her actions and the thrill of taking out "Mr. Government Man."

After a torturous minute where my insides were eaten away as if dissolved by acid, and when I'd finally sighed my death gasp, she'd giggled. Actually giggled. I replayed that part a few times, mostly out of total disbelief.

I'd assumed Steffan Parks was a complete psycho; now it appeared he'd found his perfect match.

Quanta, at last satisfied with the report she'd been discussing, turned her attention to me. I prepared for the questions, which would not be pleasant.

She said, "Have you figured out how it happened? I think it's pretty obvious."

"Yeah. Bitch poisoned the ice cubes I happily added to my Jack. That's the only possible way."

"You never thought to just get ice from the vending area down the hall?"

"Honestly? No. I thought even doing the whole BYOB thing was over the top in terms of caution, but I did it anyway." I shook my head. "Think about it, Quanta. Jayanti Pradesh went from meeting me for the first time to killing me in about 12 hours. Why? Just because I wore a Department of Defense badge? Does that seem right to you?"

Quanta laced her fingers on the table. "So the question is: What made her feel so threatened that she had to take you out?" She turned to Poole. "Thoughts?"

"Well," the top assistant said. "It's *possible* she's programmed to take out anyone from the Pentagon or Defense Department, just to be safe. Seems absurd, but then she and Parks have become quite fanatical. If this is truly one giant vendetta against the United States, it's not out of the question they'd resort to something this extreme."

She paused, then added: "But is it just coincidence that Eric showed interest in Steffan Parks to a couple of people at the party and a few hours later Pradesh killed him?"

"The obnoxious Clara from Texas and the bottomless-pit, Jonas Aiken," I said.

"Right."

I thought about this. "Both expressed no love for Steffan Parks."

"Could be an act."

"Or they could've said something to someone else, maybe innocently mentioned that I'd brought up Parks. And *that* person could've alerted Jayanti."

Quanta stepped in. "Regardless of what precipitated the killing, it confirms that Pradesh is just as dangerous as Parks. She's not just his co-worker and girlfriend; she's a verified murderer."

"Does this vault her into knave status?" I asked, fighting back a smirk.

She ignored this. "What does your gut tell you about Aiken?"

I reined in my sarcastic nature and played it straight. "Struck me as a pretty genuine guy. Nerdy scientist, but not out of touch with the real world. Understands relationships and how they fluctuate."

"And his relationship with Parks?"

"Seems to echo what everyone else says about him. They got along at first and then Parks went nuts."

"And did that seem genuine?" Quanta asked.

I opened my mouth to say yes, but hesitated. This was one of those instances when I was thankful to have taken the time to upload an experience. If I'd rushed back to the party from my meeting with Aiken, I wouldn't have preserved the *feeling* of our dinner chat. That feeling swirled right now, like silt in an ocean tide, looking for a place to settle. I didn't have sediment to paw through yet; I had murky water.

But a picture began to take shape. It hadn't registered at the time, maybe because I was engrossed in squeezing as much information out of Aiken as I could get. Now, however . . .

"He was *too* genuine," I said.

"What does that mean?" Poole asked.

"I should've realized it over dinner. Look how much this guy spilled to someone he'd just met. Yeah, I was supposedly a government official, but still. Aiken wasn't interested in grant money. He never asked me once about what I was looking for at the conference, or how he could help. But I asked one or two innocent questions about Parks and suddenly Aiken is laying out an entire backstory that's sure to not only hook me like a tarpon, but practically guarantee I'd try to get more out of Jayanti."

Quanta mused over this.

Poole fidgeted. "So you're saying Aiken is part of it?"

"Maybe not. Maybe he's just an over-sharer. But, there was a two-hour gap between my talk with this guy and my return to the party. Plenty of time for him to brief Jay, either on the phone or in person."

"And he approached you at the party, right?" Poole asked. "Clara may have introduced you, but he put himself in position for that introduction."

"Yeah. And remember what he said to me in the first few minutes? *I think you're poking around to see if Steffan Parks is going to kill a lot of people.*"

"If what you're suggesting is true," Quanta said, "then this could be a bigger conspiracy than we thought. This group of disgruntled scientists — you never did get the name of the organization, right? Aiken might be a card-carrying member. And if they're involved, we could potentially have a much larger problem on our hands."

I shook my head. "I doubt we're dealing with a sizable cabal. For one thing, it's too hard to keep that under wraps. That's why the whole *fake-moon-landing* silliness collapses. You can't count on a large group of people to keep their traps shut. Not for long, anyway."

Quanta sat back. "But a small team could include Parks, Pradesh, and Aiken. Maybe one or two more."

The idea made sense. All along it had seemed unfathomable that one guy, even with a trusted partner like Jayanti, could pull off something of the magnitude we were investigating. Killing a handful of people? Sure. But poisoning a large population? That shit was straight out of a Marvel movie.

Of course, I always did fancy myself Iron Man without the suit.

I looked at Poole. "What did you dig up on Aiken and his company?"

She spent the new few minutes filling us in on Jonas Aiken, from his unremarkable studies at the University of Arizona to his first job at a chemical manufacturing company. Worked there almost ten years until he had a falling out with the owner over company direction. After that he moved around to various companies and labs, essentially flying under the radar. He'd opened his own business three years ago, primarily as a consultant. Again, nothing stood out.

Until Poole came to the end of her report.

"Based on everything we've just talked about, this would seem relevant. Aiken's business has not done very well. There are numerous creditors with their hands out, and his contracts have dried up.

"He's applied for multiple grants through the years, and used to get his fair share. But two years ago he lost out on funding for a major project. It went instead to a team at

Arizona State University, supposedly based on a recommendation by Aiken's former boss."

I thought about this. "Okay, sure, he'd be pissed. But that's the whole idea behind the Pissed Off Scientists, or whatever their code name is. They're disgruntled scientists who feel they've been professionally mistreated. Where's the relevance you mentioned?"

She'd been tapping on a tablet. Now she turned the screen toward me. It showed a PDF image with an inscrutable amount of small print.

"What am I looking at?"

"This is the application Jonas Aiken filled out for that large grant, the one he was ultimately denied. The fact that his old boss supported one of the other teams probably isn't the most important thing about this. Look at the names at the bottom of the application."

I scrolled down. Right beside the signature of Dr. Jonas Aiken was a co-applicant.

Steffan Parks.

"That son of a bitch," I said. "All that talk about how Parks was insane and how he distanced himself. He was *working* with Parks."

Quanta looked at the screen. "At least two years ago he was. But probably the worst thing Aiken could've done was include him on the application. Parks was already radioactive, professionally speaking, when this was submitted."

On one hand, all of this struck me as absurd. Here we were, thinking that Aiken could be involved in a plot to kill people, all because he'd been snubbed.

But then I remembered the talk with my former girlfriend, Stacey Haas, the widow of the man who'd scorched the career of Parks. She said Steffan's poison unleashed a living hell, and she implored me to "find this monster" before he could murder thousands. She had no reservations about the kind of man we were dealing with.

Jayanti Pradesh was clearly on his team. It wouldn't be a shock to find there were more, each of them disconnected from reality and morality. Each ready to strike in retaliation for their grievances.

I pushed the tablet back to Poole's side of the table and fixed a determined look on Quanta. "Get me on a plane tomorrow, back to Arizona. Mr. Aiken needs a visit from a dead man."

CHAPTER ELEVEN

I had nine hours until my flight departed Dulles. I intended to spend most of that time in some form of physical contact with the gorgeous Christina Valdez. I was in a state of mind where even if she wanted to get a glass of water I'd tag along and hold her hand.

The professional killer with a soft streak. That's me.

We accomplished quite a bit in the short time we had, if I do say so myself. Of course, the first 15 minutes were spent in the usual way whenever she got her first look at a new body of mine. Her critical eye looked me over the same way I'd seen her chef's eye sizing up a cut of meat, figuring out what she could do with it.

She could do a lot.

Afterward, we lounged in the oversized bathtub on my side of our split-living arrangement. We'd filled it with almost-brutally-hot water and an insane amount of bubbles. We fell into a stretch of five minutes where we didn't speak at all, just sipping our wine and letting the bath salts work their magic.

Christina broke the silence. "Do you remember Antonio?"

"Oh, I love it when you think about other men during these intimate moments."

She flicked a soapy stream of water at me with her foot. "Do you remember him?"

"The server with the really tiny hands?"

"That's Dylan."

"Right. Drops a lot of plates."

"Antonio's the bartender. I told you he laughs at everything, whether it's funny or not."

"What about him?"

She dipped back until her face was barely above water. "He wanted to know why I never had kids."

"As long as he's not getting too personal. What'd you tell him?"

"I told him I had nothing against children, I was just never in the right space to have them."

"You didn't tell him that raising a child with a professional killer could be frowned upon?"

She laughed. "A daddy who looks different every time he comes home? No, it turns out he was doing research."

One of her feet began to slide up and down my leg. "Okay. I'm listening," I said. "Distracted, but listening."

"Antonio and his wife were curious if I'd be a surrogate mother for them."

Her foot continued to stroke my leg below water, but I'd leaned forward, pushing away a hill of soap suds congregated around my chin. "No shit."

"That's exactly what I said."

I let it sink in a while longer. "And . . .what did you tell him?"

"First, what do *you* think about it?"

This had officially become the most interesting bath we'd

ever taken together, and we'd had some doozies. I kept my eyes locked on hers.

"Babe, it's obviously your call. But I think it's an incredible honor to be asked. If you want to do it, I'll support your decision. I mean, I probably wouldn't be around for much of the pregnancy, but I'd support it."

She smiled at me. "That's sweet. And I agree, I'm completely touched that they asked."

"So what did you say?"

"I told him how honored I was, and said I'd think about it."

I reached out beneath the suds and found her hand. Christina and I had talked many times about children, and the feasibility of anything like that happening in our unique — and downright bizarre — situation. Neither one of us had ever been gung-ho to become a parent, and yet we weren't completely opposed to the notion, either.

Ultimately my job made the decision simple. I couldn't raise a child like this, home for brief snatches of time before flying off to kill people. Christina would make an outstanding single mom, but never felt a strong enough urge to make that happen. Our homes remained quiet and perpetually free of toys and stains.

Occasionally I felt a pang, wondering if I'd made the wrong decision. Okay, a *lot* of wrong decisions, but this one in particular. Would we both regret the choice later? Then I'd shake away those thoughts and chide myself for slipping into that mindset. Our life together was complete. We didn't even need a dog.

We'd been silent for another long stretch of time and something needed to punctuate the exchange. I finally said, "You'd grow a wonderful child. It'd come out smelling like one of your sauces, but that would just be a bonus."

This drew the smile I'd hoped for. "Thank you for being okay with the idea," she said. "I'll think about it."

MY FLIGHT to Arizona the next morning turned into a flight followed by a two-hour drive south. While I'd been soaking in the tub, Poole had tracked Jonas Aiken from Phoenix to a hotel in Tucson. No obvious reason for the visit that we knew of, but he must not have wanted anyone to know he was there. He'd paid for the hotel in cash to avoid a credit card transaction.

But the guy was a rookie; he'd used his phone, which pinged a couple of towers around Tucson. With the help of the area FBI office Poole discovered Aiken booked — under his own name — at a Hyatt Place. The guy might be perfectly legit and pure as snow, but if he wanted to be clandestine he needed to take an online course.

It was early afternoon and nearly 70 degrees, a nice improvement over the upper 30s I'd left in Washington. I cruised down I-10 in my BMW M4, another nice find courtesy of Ms. Poole. The music selection for this drive was a shuffle of artists who make the kind of stuff that quickens the pulse and prepares you for confrontation.

I don't know if the bands in question intended this reaction to their songs, but it worked that way for me. All it took was a solid three-song set from Spoon and I was ready to play dirty with the shitty scientist.

While the music pounded the interior of the car, I thought about the last few minutes of my conference with Quanta and Poole. What they told me added a new twist to the case.

Until recently we'd believed we were dealing with only a couple of crazy scientists out for revenge. One believed his reputation had been cruelly maligned, the other felt disrespected as a scientist because of her family's legacy. But now there was a new element.

They'd hired muscle.

The Series-8 recording of my murder in Scottsdale ended not long after the actual deed. You could hear Jayanti speaking with someone on the phone, but it was muffled, from a distance. Soon afterward it came to a stop entirely. Jay had cleaned out my pockets, looking for any sort of information, and the business card mic wound up in the trash, the fate of every business card since Don Draper dropped out.

But Q2 acquired the hotel's security video. It showed two men, pushing a wheelchair, arriving at the door of Jayanti's suite an hour after the killing. Minutes later my corpse was rolled out of the room, staged to look sound asleep, blanket and all, and taken out of the building.

The best guess was that my body was disposed of somewhere in the desert, either buried or left for critters to devour. No one seemed worried about fallout; in fact, they'd become wildly brazen. Kill the government man, chuck the body, then casually disappear into the night.

Good. I wanted them overconfident.

The salient new component was the hired help. Both men were large, well-built specimens, the kind you'd see on WWE. Poole would work on identification.

Steffan Parks, it appeared, had joined the major league of villains. He'd hired goons, ready to handle the dirty work and free him up to simply wreak havoc on innocent civilians. This might seem elemental to some, but it changed the dynamic. Parks knew he was a hunted man, and now he'd invested in protection.

This added a new complication. At some point I'd come face-to-face with the help.

Your tax dollars at work.

Once in Tucson I stopped to stretch my legs and grab an energy drink, just to add a dash of caffeine to my already-heightened state. I took the opportunity to call headquarters.

"I'm here," I told Poole. "About two miles from the hotel."

"Okay. Aiken's in room 237."

I grunted a laugh. "The Shining room."

"I'm sorry?"

"You know, the book? The movie? *The Shining*? The dead woman in room 237?"

"Stephen King?" she asked.

"Never mind, not important. Any other news on Parks or Jayanti?"

"No," she said. "They're back underground."

"All right. If Aiken's in his room I'll check in again with you soon. If you don't hear from me it means I'm having to hunt for the guy. Hopefully he'll make this easy for me."

"I'll be here."

Of course she would. Poole was married to Q2. I had no idea what her compensation was, but in the last few months I'd decided it should be huge.

I pulled into the parking lot of the Hyatt Place and began my prep routine, similar to a pilot's pre-flight checklist. They made sure all the plane's switches were in the right place; I made sure my killing gear was ready and my mind was right.

The Glock was loaded with my usual 19-rounds, with a spare magazine tucked neatly into my jacket. I didn't anticipate firing a single shot, but I hadn't planned on getting poisoned, either.

As for my mind, during the drive from Phoenix I'd considered the various ways I could play it with this guy. It would be fiercely direct. No monkeying around, no playing a part, no friendly chit-chat. The bastard had cost me one of the best bodies I'd had in ages, so I'd play rough in order to coerce him into helping me find that other dick, Steffan Parks. Through extension that would lead to a certain giggling femme fatale. I had a score to settle with her, too.

But it started with Aiken.

I waited until a family with two fussy children stormed into the hotel with an inordinate number of bags for four people. While that circus played out at the front desk I slipped past and made for the stairwell.

The second floor was quiet. I walked up to room 237 and gave an officious knock, waited five seconds, and knocked again.

The peephole grew dark and from the other side of the door came a curious voice. "Yes?"

"Mr. Aiken, I'm Reggie with Hyatt guest services. I'm so sorry, we made a billing error with your reservation. I'm delivering a $50 dining certificate at any of our restaurants as a courtesy."

I'd used this same line before and it never failed to open doors. Nobody in America turns down free food. And it would be impossible for Aiken, with his voracious appetite, to pass up.

Sure enough, the door swung open. Jonas Aiken was barefoot, dressed in jeans and a polo shirt, and happy to get his meal ticket. "Wow," he said. "That's very generous."

I smiled. "We like to keep customers happy." Then I pushed my way past him, and in one move closed the door with my left hand while pulling out the Glock with my right. It gave him no time to utter so much as a gasp.

The barrel of the gun settled nicely under his chin. "Hello,

Jonas. I'm here because you're behind on your student loan payments."

His eyes darted between my face and the gun, and he finally managed a sound. It came out like a child's slow windup before a crying fit, a sort of *eh-eh-eh*. He may have wet himself. He wouldn't be the first in a situation like this. In movies people act like real badasses at gunpoint, lots of balls and bravado. They say all sorts of cocky things.

But in the real world even Chuck Norris would whimper with a semi-automatic weapon shoved against his throat.

Wait, scratch that. Everyone *except* Chuck Norris.

I used the gun to steer him backwards. It was a standard guest room, with a queen bed, love seat, chest of drawers, and a small work desk. Aiken was a sloppy guest; clothes lay scattered across the bed and the floor, with a towel draped over the television. The bathroom light was on, revealing a mess of toiletries, more towels on the floor, and a magazine lying in front of the toilet.

"Damn, Jonas, maybe I should've identified myself as housekeeping. What a pig. I hope you tip well."

I'm sure none of this coalesced in his mind. It's hard to concentrate with a gun pressed against your larynx. The jabber was really for me. It's fun pestering victims.

Pushing him down onto the love seat, I cleared a space on the bed and sat facing him, the Glock leveled at his chest.

"It's good to see you," I said. "I've heard so much about you and your weasel ways. Just kidding about the student loans, by the way. Nobody pays those back."

His eyes continued to stare at the gun. He licked his lips. "Who . . . what—"

"Yes, excellent place to start," I said. "The who is Steffan

Parks. The what is how pissed he is at you right now. He sent me to straighten things out."

"Why?"

"Great, now we add why. You're really good at this. The why is because you didn't get enough information about that government asshole before you called Pradesh. Parks wanted to know more. And let's skip the where, because the answer to that question is right between your eyes." I waved the gun to make things clear.

He looked up at me and stammered. "But . . . but . . . no . . . that's bullshit. I got everything I could. I couldn't have asked him any more. Do you know how suspicious that would've been?"

I looked up at the ceiling and released a long, slow breath. "Oh, Jonas. Thank you. That's exactly what I needed to hear."

Aiken couldn't have looked more confused if I'd been wearing Mickey Mouse ears.

Returning my gaze to his face I said, "I don't work for Parks, dipshit. But thank you for confirming your part in the murder. You saved us *sooo* much time here. I hate all of the *Where's Parks?* and you saying *I don't know what you're talking about*. Ugh, so tedious. And it saved me having to put a bullet in your knee to get you to talk. See, you're helping everyone here, even yourself."

His face was pure defeat.

"So," I continued. "Now that we've established you as an accessory to murder of a federal agent, we can get down to business."

His voice was almost a whisper. "What business is that?"

"For starters, what are you doing in Tucson?"

"Hiding."

I laughed. "You suck at hiding."

His voice shook. "Look, I had no idea anyone was going to be killed, and that's the truth. When I found out, I got scared. I didn't think I'd be connected in any way — I mean, I wasn't even there when it happened — but I was still freaked out. So I left town for a while to lay low."

"Does Parks know you're here?"

"He must. I told Jayanti I had to get away. She said he'd be in touch."

"That will be very helpful."

"Why?" he asked.

"Because you're going to take me to Steffan Parks."

"But I don't know where he is."

I gave an exasperated roll of my eyes. "Just when I thought we were really moving along here. I guess I have to shoot you after all." I pointed the Glock at his right knee.

His hands went down to cover himself and his voice took on a high-pitched squeal. "No no no! No, I mean it. I don't know where he is. I'm telling the truth."

For effect, I pushed the gun up against his knee. "Look, dude, you think I'm a cop? Wrong. I'm someone who really doesn't care if you hobble for the rest of your life, or, for that matter, if you bleed to death in a Hyatt. I need information, and I need it now. Why don't you tell me what you *do* know."

He swallowed hard and adopted a placating look. "I . . . I know where he *probably* is. Does that help?"

"What if I *probably* cripple you?"

"It's all I know," he said.

I hesitated, then pulled back the gun. "All right. Where is he probably?"

"San Antonio."

"San Antonio? As in the Alamo? The River Walk, over-priced margaritas? *That* San Antonio?"

"Yes."

"Why?"

"He needs some sort of phone app."

I almost laughed. "Jonas, are you pulling my lariat?"

"What? No. He has to make a trip there at some point, and it's probably now."

"This phone app; it's part of his plan?"

Aiken put a hand up, palm facing me. "Listen, whoever you are. I will help you the best I can, but you have to help me in return."

"Help you? You got someone killed in Scottsdale, shithead. I've helped you already by not splattering your brains against the ceiling."

"Yes, okay. Fine. You could kill me. But I'm willing to cooperate. That has to be worth something."

I shook my head. "You really are a weasel, aren't you?"

But the truth was, I did need his help. I had to track down Steffan Parks pronto, and if that meant a trip to Texas, then it was time to rodeo.

And it looked like I'd have a companion with me the whole way.

CHAPTER TWELVE

There have been more than a few movies made about reluctant partnerships. De Niro had one in the 1980s called *Midnight Run*. There was the classic with Eddie Murphy and Nick Nolte, *48 Hours*. Sandra Bullock and Melissa McCarthy in *The Heat*.

Even FBI agent Clarice and Hannibal Lecter in *Silence of The Lambs*. That on-screen dynamic is still electric no matter how many times I see it.

There was no electricity between me and Jonas Aiken.

I'd be traveling almost 900 miles with not only someone who was involved, however remotely, in a plot to murder innocent people, but the guy who'd triggered the process of my *own* murder. I wasn't happy about it, but this was't about my happiness. It was about finding Steffan Parks before he could poison thousands of people.

We could wait around for Parks to contact Aiken, but who knew if and when that would happen. If Aiken was right about an important transaction taking place in San Antonio, then that was our destination. We couldn't fly; that's a nightmare when you're basically kidnapping someone. It's not like I could sit in coach with a gun stuck in his ribs.

We'd drive. That's roughly 12 to 14 hours, depending on stops. I could go long stretches without having to pull over, but what if Jonas had a puny bladder? I wanted to leave right away, so that meant we'd also stay the night somewhere along the way. That would be fun.

There was another reason driving was preferable. It provided an opportunity to question Aiken about the sick mind inside Steffan Parks. Maybe some insight into Jayanti. Not that I wanted to become besties with either of them; it just helps to understand the animal you're hunting.

After confiscating his phone I watched Aiken shuffle around the hotel room, gathering his things. He moved like a man who thought he'd be dead as soon as I got him outside, so I convinced him he'd live through the night.

As soon as the last pair of socks was tucked into his bag I raised the gun. "Get out your wallet."

"What? You're robbing me?"

"Take out 20 bucks. Now."

He grumbled, reached into his wallet, and held out the bill.

"I don't want it," I said. "Put it on the nightstand. I told you that you'd need to leave a big tip for housekeeping, you filthy pig."

Just before opening the door I pushed him against the wall. "Let's get the nasty disclaimer out of the way. I don't expect to repeat this over the next few days. Do anything to cause a scene, or try to bolt, or anything stupid whatsoever, and you will die. You just will. I'm good at killing and I have no conscience. Plus, I'll get away with it. Do you understand all of this? Is there anything I need to make more clear?"

"No. You're a bloodthirsty killer. I get it."

I laughed. Like a lot of people, once he got over his initial pants-wetting fear, Aiken redirected his emotions into surliness. I really wanted to smash the Glock across his smarmy face, but instead opened the door and shoved him into the hall.

When we got to the car his bag went into the trunk of the M4 and we buckled up for the first leg of the trip. I planned to spend the night in El Paso and handle the final eight hours the next day. The good news was that we'd be on one interstate highway, I-10, the entire drive. And if I remembered correctly, the speed limit along the desolate stretch of West Texas was 80.

Texans are in a damned hurry to get there, wherever there is. And so was I.

As soon as Tucson's lights faded in my rearview mirror I called Poole. I had the phone up to my ear instead of using the car's speakers. Aiken didn't need to hear the other side of this conversation.

"We're heading to San Antonio."

"We?" she asked.

"Jonas is comfortably reclined in the passenger seat, behaving himself."

"What's in San Antonio? Parks?"

"We'll see. He has business there. I'll text you when we stop in El Paso. Anything for me?"

"Positive ID on one of the men who removed the body from the conference center. Name is Cox, Darnell Cox. Former military, former deputy sheriff before he did time for assault with a deadly weapon. I just sent you the file."

"And the other guy?"

"Nothing yet. No match on prints, no facial ID. Still working on it."

"What about the evil girlfriend?"

"Walked out of the hotel and left the scope of security cameras on foot. We're assuming she was picked up by someone, maybe Cox. But for now she's gone again. That's one thing about Parks and Pradesh: They're very good at disappearing."

With a little good fortune — which was overdue — and the help of my current co-pilot, I'd be able to at least unearth Parks.

I ended the call and looked over at Aiken. He was sullen, staring out the passenger window, watching the scenery roll by as twilight painted the desert. On some level I felt pity for him. He'd devoted his adult life to academia, which was fine when you toiled in the minor leagues. But the bigger players, the ones who slurped up the largest grants and government investment dollars weren't in it for fun. It was serious business, with more than cash on the line. Reputations often determined where the funds went; once yours was damaged, you were crushed.

That was the impetus behind the mysterious group he'd described, and explained why they felt the need to associate. Throughout history maligned groups have banded together, finding strength not only in numbers but in a shared sense of injustice. Aiken had felt it, probably found solace in it at first. And he probably never dreamed that one day it would snowball into something sinister and deadly.

So yeah, part of me felt bad for the guy. Things go off the rails, and sometimes they accelerate and devolve into something far removed from the original path. Aiken got caught in the undertow.

Not that I completely forgave him for sending me to an agonizing death. Bastard.

Instead of the usual loud music I enjoyed on road trips, I

left things quiet, allowing both of us to think. I wanted to plot my strategy, and Aiken was probably wondering how much he'd need to cooperate to save his neck. The longer I let him stew the greater the chance he'd realize just how screwed he was.

We drove into the rising half-moon, and as darkness descended the night sky came alive. Away from city lights it was a beautiful show. I set the BMW on cruise and relaxed.

"Shoot straight with me, Jonas," I said, breaking the silence. "When you told Phillips that Parks had an office in Arizona, was that complete bullshit?"

He kept his gaze out the window. "Complete. I don't know where he works."

"How much of anything you said at dinner was true?"

"Oh, bits and pieces. Enough to seem willing to talk." He paused. "I wasn't lying about disliking Parks. I think he's basically insufferable. But he used to be a pretty big deal. It didn't hurt to have his name on a grant proposal."

"So you just used his name."

He turned to look at me. "And I'm the first person in the history of business to do that, right?" He scoffed.

"But then his reputation went south, and quickly," I said. "It burned you in the process."

No reply.

"What's the target for his poison plan?"

"I don't know. I never really grasped exactly what he was up to until recently."

"How many people is he targeting?"

"I don't know that, either. It has to be something significant, though."

"Why?"

He let out a long, pained breath. "Because he's sick and

feels like his revenge should match his highest achievement in terms of scale."

I furrowed my brow. "You mean his terrorism has to be on a scale with winning the Nobel?"

"Sounds stupid, but if you knew his mind . . ." His voice trailed off.

Aiken was telling the truth, I was sure. The question was why he'd helped Parks in the first place. So I asked him.

This generated a much longer pause before he said, "Just a stupid mistake. A horrible lapse in judgment."

Now he was lying.

"Horse shit," I said. "Listen, you're getting handcuffed to a bed tonight, which isn't ideal but at least puts you in a bed. If you'd prefer to sleep handcuffed to the bathroom sink, just keep treating me like I'm stupid."

"I still haven't heard what legal protection I'm getting for all this," he said. "I told you—"

"And I told *you* that I kept your skull intact instead of blasting it into the 3rd floor. That's what you get for now. I have a hall pass from very powerful people, and it says I can dump your skinny corpse out here in the wilderness at any time if I believe you're jerking me around. You're pissing me off, Jonas, and that's not something you want to do. Now why did you work with Parks when you knew he was crazy?"

Another heavy sigh. "I didn't agree to help Steffan. I agreed to help Jayanti."

I took my eyes off the road to stare at him. "What does that mean?"

"It means . . . look, I'm tired and I'm starving. And on top of that I don't feel like talking right now after everything that's happened. Can we just get some food, and get to a hotel so I can sleep? We've got a long-ass drive tomorrow, and you'll have all day to hear the sordid story. Is that okay? Or do you need to kill me and dump my skinny corpse?"

He went back to sulking, glaring out his window. I left him alone until stopping for gas at the Flying J in Lordsburg. I wasn't hungry, but Aiken grabbed a handful of the unhealthiest shit you can get at a truck stop. He'd polished off the M&Ms and half the package of mini-donuts within minutes.

It took another two hours to finish passing through New Mexico and we did it in complete silence. I didn't feel like sharing my playlist with him. Too personal.

El Paso is in Texas but it's still the Mountain time zone, so we rolled into the outskirts at ten o'clock. I found a room with two queen beds at a passable motor inn.

Once inside I locked the door and checked the bathroom. It had a window, but barely; it was one of those squatty rectangles near the ceiling. As thin as he was, even Aiken would have a difficult time squeezing through.

"I've got some calls to make," I said. "Behave yourself. Watch TV, or do whatever a chemical scientist does to pass the time."

I opened the curtains to allow me to see into the room from outside. But just to be sure I took the room's clunky telephone and unclipped the handset. It would go outside with me. This brought a disgusted grunt from Aiken, but he positioned himself on the far bed and curled up facing the wall.

Outside, I leaned against the BMW's hood and texted Poole, as promised. Short and sweet, I gave her the name and location of the motel and said we'd be back on the road at seven a.m. That would get us into the Alamo City by mid-afternoon.

After that I calculated the time in Washington and hoped that Christina would still be up. She was.

"Where's my secret agent tonight?" she asked.

"I'll give you a hint: Marty Robbins."

"I have no idea who that is."

"An old country singer," I said. "His big hit was called *El Paso*. I think the Grateful Dead did a version, too."

"Who are *they*?"

"Stop playing around."

She laughed. "Yes, I know the Dead. My father took me to see them when I was 12. I never forgave him. Although I do like the Ben & Jerry's ice cream flavor, Cherry Garcia. So what are you doing in Texas?"

"Drinking a Dr. Pepper, chasing villains, making the country a safer place to live. Actually just a quick stop. I'll be in San Antonio tomorrow."

"Oh, yum. Chile Rellenos."

"That's my wife, the chef. I'm partial to the Whataburger, myself." I paused while a car with its radio blasting through an open window rolled past. "How was work?"

We spent five minutes catching up. It was after midnight in Washington, so she chatted while getting ready for bed. I pictured her moving about her side of our dual living space. Suddenly I was homesick.

Assignments for a Q2 field agent came in spurts. There would be times when I was on the road, killing and getting killed, 90 days out of 100. Then there might be a stretch where I stayed in the D.C. area. That usually involved additional training, often in tech updates, but also the requisite ass-whooping at the hands of Quanta.

During those precious weeks at home I practically suffo-cated Christina. It was strange because I'd never been so head-over-heels. Sure, there was the college affair with Stacey Bromley-now-Haas, but that, upon reflection, was just me being young and stupid in the ways of love. An infatuation, or, as a friend of mine once called it, the love mulligan.

And, to be honest, once I got a new assignment I think Christina was quietly relieved. Don't misunderstand, she loved me and I knew she was happy to be married. But she also appreciated the freedom my job provided. She got a nice helping of matrimony with a side of privacy.

While I leaned against a rental car in El Paso, keeping watch through a window as a misguided scientist curled up in the fetal position.

Christina yawned. "Babe, I have to go to sleep. I'm sorry."

"It's okay. I'll call you again when I can."

We said goodnight. Then I leaned back and looked up at the West Texas night sky, slightly faded by the nearby city lights but sharper than what I could see in Phoenix. Times like this gave me a tinge of regret. For a few minutes I'd question my career choice, wondering if there was something else I'd be perfect for. Something that wouldn't have me scurrying around the Western Hemisphere, stomping out bad guys and eating lousy food.

But the feeling would pass. The loneliness and insecurity would dissolve, leaving me with the realization that there *wasn't* another job perfect for me. It was *this* job. I was good at it, despite the occasional blunder — like getting poisoned.

And I did enjoy it. Professional athletes try to explain the exhilaration of winning a championship, and we've heard about the runner's high. It was something similar for me, a surge of endorphins at the conclusion of a major assignment, especially those that included a close call. It was living on the razor's edge between calm and catastrophe, and it powered me.

I pushed away from the car and was about to walk back inside when my phone vibrated. It was a text from the always-diligent Poole, burning the midnight oil.

Darnell Cox, the goon hired by Parks, had been found.

In San Antonio.

Things were about to get real.

CHAPTER THIRTEEN

The breakfast burritos were small and heavy on the potato, which always struck me as cheap filler. But the green chili was excellent. I ate both of mine as soon as we merged back onto I-10, while Aiken, true to form, devoured three. Confinement did nothing to dampen his appetite.

It was a chilly morning, temps in the low 30s, and the day began overcast. I'd scraped a thin layer of frost from the windshield and had the seat warmers on low. But we'd be driving into the sun and the forecast promised a dramatic improvement by the time we reached the San Antonio hill country that afternoon.

As the miles swept beneath us I considered the news about Cox. His appearance pretty much confirmed that Parks was in Texas for his appointment, or would arrive soon. The good news was that, although Parks and Pradesh were meticulous about staying below the radar, Cox was as bad as Jonas. Poole sent me his hotel information, an inn within walking distance of the historic Riverwalk.

I'd brought Jonas along for the ride because I thought he

might come in handy tracking down Parks. Having the hired gun in town was even better, and knowing I could focus on the downtown area saved time.

The location made sense. For decades San Antonio relied on tourism and the military for revenue, but now they were on the hunt for fresh income streams. Lately the city had lured tech companies from the sprawl of Austin, and many of these offices were clustered in newly-renovated spaces. I was confident that, with the help of Poole, I could zero in.

In the light of a new day an air of curiosity replaced Aiken's defiant 'tude. Instead of glaring out the passenger window he seemed interested in the trip, and eventually started questioning me.

"You know," he said, "you pulled me out of Tucson at the point of a gun. But I never saw any kind of badge."

I smiled. "I've always found the barrel of a gun much more of an inducement than any ID."

"So who do you work for? I assumed it was one of the national security departments. NSA or something."

"Jonas, my employer isn't important. I've told you enough. I have the power to operate in the best interests of the country without worrying about interference from any local agency. Is that good enough for you?"

"I don't even know your name. What am I supposed to call you?"

"I like *Pharaoh*. But I'll settle for Eric."

"What are you going to do with Steffan?"

"Stop him. To what extent I do that will be up to him. If he cooperates, he'll be taken into custody. If not, I'll ruin his day."

He contemplated that as he drank from a container of

orange juice. In a voice that was trying much too hard to be nonchalant he said, "And what about Jayanti?"

I glanced at him. "All right. I've been patient. I've let you sulk like a child for four hundred miles. That's over. Now, you told me you weren't involved with this because of Parks. So what the hell is your connection with Pradesh? What made you help her?"

There was no answer for a long time. I waited for him to find the words.

"I met Jayanti at a science conference a year ago. We had similar backgrounds in our studies and she was very interested in my work with chemical relationships. As it turned out, I was very helpful in the projects she was involved in with Steffan. So we met often."

"That's it?" I asked. "You do a few calculations together and suddenly you're willing to become a criminal for her?"

"Not exactly." He paused. "Some of those meetings were late into the evening, and, well . . ."

I nearly spit out the coffee I'd been sipping. "Holy shit. You *slept* with Pradesh?"

When he just stared through the windshield I couldn't help it; I laughed hard.

"Damn, Jonas. I wasn't prepared for *that*." I shook my head and chuckled again. "You nerdy types are a randy bunch, aren't you? She's sleeping with Parks. And you're married."

He still didn't say anything.

"So walk me through everything. You have sex with Jayanti and then what?"

It was obvious this discussion was the last thing he wanted. But he finally cleared his throat and said, "She was cool about everything at first. Even talked Steffan into signing off on a proposal of mine, adding his stature to the program. But it wasn't long before she asked me to help him with some things *he* was working on. Of course I did; I mean, if you're invited to work beside a Nobel Prize winner you don't think twice.

"I didn't understand exactly what he was trying to accomplish at first. The work he gave me was the kind of stuff that was buried in the middle of a project, so I didn't know for a long time what his ultimate aim was. And I certainly never understood his motivations. And then, when they became a little more clear, I knew I didn't want to be a part of it. I told both of them."

It began to make sense, and I finally understood. "They blackmailed you."

His voice was low. "Yes. Professionally and personally. Steffan threatened to spread the word that I was deeply involved with his biochemical plans — which I wasn't, but from my association with him it would look like I definitely was. And Jayanti had all sorts of texts and photos that she said she'd give to my wife."

"These are some wonderful people you've hooked up with," I said.

He turned to me. "Look, Eric, or whoever you are. When all of this started I had no idea it was this bad. I knew Parks was angry and borderline-crazy, but I never thought Jayanti would be part of something that included murder. So I went along. I didn't like it, but I went along. And then the more I helped, just a little bit here and there, the deeper I was in it. Okay?"

"Doesn't forgive a goddamned thing, Jonas. All it does is explain it."

After that we cruised in silence for a while. I felt him steaming from the passenger seat, a mixture of anger, despair, and plain embarrassment. Well, the damned fool had brought all of it onto himself.

Jayanti Pradesh had turned into quite the villainess. And yet I found myself with a confusing cocktail of emotions about her. Don't get me wrong: She'd killed me once, would do so again without a moment's hesitation, and she was part of a conspiracy to murder thousands. She was a very bad person.

At the same time, I couldn't help but feel something bordering on admiration for her. She'd been frustrated in her attempts to pursue a legitimate scientific career, but had never wavered in her desire to win. She'd used her association with Parks to further her career, sure, but she'd also carried her weight with his programs and his business.

She'd managed to convince Aiken, a man with talent and a solid reputation, to betray not only his marriage but *all* of his ethics.

It had been child's play for her to get me, a well-trained and experienced secret agent, up to her room where she poisoned me with something as simple as ice from her room's fridge. It had all seemed so easy for her.

How could I not have a grudging respect for everything she'd accomplished? I could hate her intentions and still applaud her abilities.

It was going to almost pain me to take her down, which might easily involve a bullet.

This wasn't the first time I'd deeply admired an adversary. Two years earlier I'd actually apologized to a wily character named Chester Fuller moments before putting a kill shot into his brain. The sequence of events went like this:

Shot to the chest, which got him to drop the rifle pointed at me.

Apology.

Finishing shot through his forehead.

That guy was about as evil as they come, having snuffed out 11 people and with plans to make it triple digits — and yet in another universe we could've been friends. Stylish as hell, great sense of humor, and a mind sharp enough to pilot a Fortune 500 company if he'd been so inclined. Instead, a wire had come loose somewhere and he'd turned to murder.

I liked Chester. It was too bad I had to kill him.

There was also a reluctant respect for the asshole called Beadle. Look, there wasn't a goddamned good thing about him, but I'd never managed to take him out and he'd offed me more than once. That has to induce *some* kind of approbation, whether you like it or not. He was a pro, one who'd bested me. I hated him and admired him at the same time. One day, Beadle. One day.

The only time I broached this subject with Quanta — the ability to loathe and yet respect the slime we're charged with eliminating — she'd surprised me. I'd expected a scoff. Instead, she grew quiet for a time before revealing one of her own stories. Nobody knew much about Quanta's resume, except that she went from premier agent to overseeing two different country's programs before taking over Q2. I had enough wisdom to keep my mouth shut when she opened up.

It was a long story, but I can sum it up. Quanta tracked a man who befuddled the secret service of three separate European nations, a man who put a bullet into her back. While recovering, she hatched the plan that would ensnare him. She told me that when it finally went down, she almost mourned the end of the hunt.

Might seem nuts to you. Might seem nuts to *most* people. Made total sense to me.

Our job is to find and erase the worst people. Those people, it just so happens, are generally smart enough to rise above the level of petty criminal and wanna-be gangster. To capture *our* attention they have to be. Probably not much different from admiring Tom Brady even though you might hate the rival Patriots.

And now, once again, a knave had wormed her way into that category. Jayanti Pradesh may not have accumulated the kill totals of the biggest badasses — yet — but in this game, style points do count.

We stopped in Fort Stockton to gas up and stretch our legs. Aiken hit me up for a few dollars so he could grab two bags of junk food and a fountain drink big enough to bathe in. As promised, the sun had broken through. Before getting back in the car we sat on a picnic table next to the convenience store, soaking up the rays, and I watched him eat combinations of Funyuns and Bugles. That was new to me.

I tried it. Strangely good together.

Between mouthfuls Aiken said, "What happens to me when this is over?"

"That depends on a lot of things," I said. "How much you're able to help. How deep you were into everything in the first place. How many people die as a result of your contributions. How much you get on my nerves."

He gave a hint of a smile. "They say couples shouldn't take vacations, especially road trips, until they've known each other a while. We've barely met."

I pulled a handful of Bugles out of the bag. "Tell me something. This little club of angry scientists. Is that really a thing, or was that a smoke screen, too?"

"Yeah, it's real. Totally informal, of course. But there are get-togethers. Happy hours, stuff like that. No minutes recorded, if that's what you mean."

"So I've been thinking about that. If enough scientists feel slighted, or even humiliated, could something like this Parks project spring up again? I mean, you guys may be socially awkward, but a lot of you seem capable of a Biblical-sized shit-storm."

The smile disappeared and he looked down at his crusted fingers. "A year ago I would've said no. The whole conceit of a mad scientist was just Hollywood selling tickets. But now? With the pressure on science to keep up with the escalation of technology? A population that talks about noble causes when it's really just every man and woman looking out for themselves?"

"All right," I said. "So I'm tired of calling them everything but their name. What is it?"

He kicked at something on the bench of the picnic table, then looked at me.

"They call themselves the Arcetri." He pronounced it Ar-Chet-Tree.

"Sounds impressively Italian. Is it for real or did you just see it in The DaVinci Code or something?"

"Oh, it's real. But the wrong Italian. Not DaVinci. Galileo."

I raised an eyebrow, but didn't interrupt this time.

"Galileo was way ahead of his time," Aiken said. "Helped push science along when it was criminally held back by the ignorance of others. His discoveries, his writings, his *ideas*. Just incredible. He was a man way ahead of his time.

"The church, which had all the power in the 17th century, tolerated most of his work and his theories. But in 1633 they were challenged by one of Galileo's books that dared to claim the Earth wasn't the center of the universe. It orbited the sun. And that contradicted the interpretation of holy scripture. It was heresy."

"He was put on trial," I said.

"The church demanded that he recant his observations and theories, that he disavow any notion that did not place God's beautiful planet Earth at the center of everything. And if he didn't, he'd be tortured until he did."

Jonas fell silent for a moment, stewing in the indignity suffered by one of his scientific idols. Then he said, "To add utter humiliation to it all, after he was forced to take back all of the science he'd proven, they still found him guilty. They sentenced him to house arrest until he died."

I'd heard most of this, and shared Jonas's resentment.

"So the name?" I prompted.

Aiken closed up the bags of junk food. "The home where Galileo stayed until his death, Villa Il Gioello — *The Jewel* — is in an area of Florence called Arcetri." He faced me again. "Arcetri represents, in a symbolic way, all of the ignorance and humiliation that people of science have endured for millennia."

Two large trucks whipped by on the highway, loud enough to necessitate silence from us for a few moments. I used that time to digest this story and the explanation it provided.

I certainly didn't like what it implied.

"So this group of contemporary scientists, the Arcetri — they're basically inspired to address thousands of years of mistreatment. And they'll use their knowledge to lash out through violence, if necessary."

He looked grim. "Not just the mistreatment of the giants who came before us. But to address the *corruption* of science today. You know, it's not enough to create a life-saving vaccine, or to develop a gadget that tends to your every desire.

No, it's about monetizing everything. And if you can't get your product to market before the other guy, you're screwed. You lose your funding, you lose your status, and you damned well lose your career. Because some other enterprising young MIT graduate will beat you to the punch, file the patents, grab the available money, and leave you holding the beaker."

I waited a moment before responding. "So that's a yes?"

This time, when the smile returned it was rueful. "It's a scary yes. Men and women who have devoted their life to science, years of school, pouring everything into it — and then get raped by the system? Hell yes, some of them will go rogue."

"They won't use their power for good."

"No, they won't. Parks may be the first; I don't expect he'll be the last."

He offered the chips again but I waved them away. I'd lost my appetite.

CHAPTER FOURTEEN

"Did you know Ed? The guy from the Defense Department?"

The question caught me off-guard. We'd chewed up another fifty miles, mostly in silence, and it took me a moment to realize Aiken was referencing my former identity. I allowed myself another few seconds to process how I should answer it. *Yeah, I knew him; he used to be me* wouldn't exactly work.

"He was a good man," I said. "Loyal. Worked hard. Very generous. The most popular guy in the department. Helped anyone who needed anything. Left behind a beautiful wife." I paused, then added, "His wife found out about his murder on her birthday."

All right, I'll admit that might've been overplaying it a bit, but I'd never been in this position before, and it was fun to torture the little asshole. Plus, the look on Aiken's face was priceless. His mouth was shrunken and tight, lines creased his forehead, and he blinked several times as he stared ahead. He was churning with guilt, and it dawned on me that this was an angle I could milk. Jonas hadn't really participated in killing me, but he knew there was still blood on his hands, even if only by association.

"I know you have a thing for Jayanti," I said. "But you can't stand by and do nothing when you find out she's a cold-blooded killer, can you? Especially when a grand jury might reasonably decide your contribution to the events are enough for an accessory to murder charge. Doing nothing, when you could help, could easily be deemed enough for an indictment and probably a conviction."

After letting all that sink in for a moment, I kept going. "Do you have a way of contacting her?"

He shook his head. "She and Parks both work exclusively on burner phones they purchased months ago. I know Jayanti doesn't use one for more than a week, at most. When I talked with her at the conference she gave me the temporary number she was using. When I tried a couple days later she'd obviously moved on to another one. So, no, I can't reach her. I have to wait for her to reach out to me."

"Are you expecting that?"

"I'm not expecting it, but I wouldn't be surprised to hear from her. Her needs come in waves. I might go a month without hearing from her and then get a flurry of messages in one day."

"And you don't feel used?"

He turned to look at me. "What an asinine question. No, I don't feel *used*. I feel useful. There's a difference, you know. Or maybe you don't."

I shrugged. "If you say so."

With a snort, he leaned away from me and crossed his arms. "Haven't you listened to anything I've said? I played the game. I worked hard, I helped my company *and* my country. I directed my intellectual capacity to help — no, don't make that face. That's what I did. And in return I got screwed over. More than once."

"Sounds like you've memorized the Steffan Parks manifesto," I said.

"Hey, he's crazy, I'm not denying that. And what he's planning, if it's really what I think it might be, is criminal. I don't endorse that. But his *reasons* for wanting to lash out are spot on. Those aren't crazy."

He fell silent for a moment, fuming. Then he added one last shot. "You know, the reason we might have a major catastrophe on our hands is partly because of that same condescending attitude you're exhibiting right now. Parks put up with it for years. And remember, it started long before he ever dreamed of doing something like this. It began when he was trying to contribute to the country's defense. I think *anyone* who had that much shit thrown in their face over and over would want to strike back. So maybe you should modulate your tone a bit."

It was a damned good speech. There may even have been some elements of truth mixed in. But it would do no good to needle him any more, so I let it go. Besides, in my position it helped to allow a small victory here and there. Ultimately it might lead to him opening up about something critical. In fact, I was counting on it.

I also realized this was at least the second or third time Aiken had vehemently defended the position of the scientists in the Arcetri.

At two o'clock we passed a sign stating we were a hundred miles from San Antonio. I wanted to push straight through, but my bladder protested. I exited at another convenience center and we both went inside. While I used the restroom he poked around the aisles, looking for something new to pollute his body. I came out to find him clutching two bananas and a bottled water.

"You're shitting me," I said. "That's it?"

"No, I have other stuff at the counter. Add these to the stash, will ya? I have to pee, too."

I carried this latest handful to the front to pay for everything. Already bagged were Pringles, some sort of jerky, and a small box of Chips Ahoy. I started to explain that it was all for my friend, but in the end didn't care enough what the cashier thought. I threw in a couple of protein bars for myself and walked out to the car.

Back on the road I discovered that Aiken had calmed down again. Food seemed to do that for him. He munched on the chips and cookies and asked random questions about what I did for the government. I sidestepped most of it and directed questions back at him.

"You know something, Jonas? When you talk about Parks it's pretty vicious. Even the agent you got killed in Scottsdale, Ed Phillips, told us you really bashed him. I think it threw us for a while. That's quite an act."

Aiken gave a slow nod. "The craziest part is that it's all Steffan's idea."

I glanced back at him. "It's his idea for his followers to crucify him?"

"Yeah. He even has a name for it. Damnation Deniability."

I laughed. "It's a mouthful. What exactly does it mean?"

"It means that the best way to throw off suspicion is to not only deny association with him, but to rip him apart. The more you can damn him — not just his work but his personality, his style — the less it looks like you'd ever lower yourself to work with him."

He reflected for a moment. "Now that I think about it, Damnation Deniability is maybe Steffan's own little inside joke. He's been trashed so much in the last few years that he's putting the bad rep to good use."

"Okay," I said. "In a strange way it makes sense. Now, without getting upset, tell me what you know about Jayanti's relationship with Parks. We know they were romantically linked; at least *physically* linked. I'm not sure how much romance was involved. But if he assigned her to seduce you, they can't be that close."

"Why not?" he asked.

This threw me. "I mean . . ." I glanced at him. "He asked her to have sex with you."

"Yeah? So?"

I took my eyes off the road to look at him again. "You have no problem sharing her with Parks?"

He laughed. "I'm married. Should I have protested?"

"Oh. Right."

"What about you?" he asked. "You married?"

It couldn't hurt to tell him. "I am. Very happily."

"I'm happy, too," he said. "I didn't get into a relationship with Jayanti because I'm unhappy at home."

Call me old-fashioned, call me naive, call me any damned thing you want. This was just odd to me, but I didn't want to get too deep into Aiken's home life.

"Fine," I said. "But back to the original question. Other than loaning her out, how does Parks feel about her?"

He thought about it. "I guess he might love her. I've never asked. What does this have to do with anything?"

"Maybe nothing. But people react differently in various

situations if it's a strictly professional relationship compared to a personal one. And so far I haven't been able to figure out a damned thing about any of these relationships. His and hers, yours and hers, yours and his. It's the goddamndest love triangle I've had to deal with, and you're all involved in something that could kill a lot of people." I shook my head. "Just trying to make sense of the players."

"Good luck."

It was my turn to laugh. "Yeah."

"So about your wife," he said.

"We don't need to talk about my wife."

"But I'm curious. We have another hour or two of driving ahead of us. Humor me."

"You wanna sleep with her, too?"

"No. I know you'd kill me and dump my body, or whatever you said before. I'm just wondering how she manages to live with a guy who does what you do for a living."

A fair question. "Jonas, I wonder about that myself. She's obviously a saint."

"No, don't give me a stock, bullshit answer. You travel around the country or the world and I'm pretty sure you're involved in a lot of violence. Not exactly the best ingredients for a marriage."

I didn't answer, so he plowed on. "All right, here's an easy one. How did you meet? Can you answer that without shooting me in the head?"

I chuckled again. "God, you're nosy." After hesitating, I decided that talking about it might make Aiken feel like he could trust me.

"I wasn't looking for anyone, which probably helped. I'd been burned by someone in college and decided I didn't want to be in love anymore. Or at least for a long time." The face of

Stacey Haas floated through my mind, but Aiken didn't need details.

"So I did what plenty of young Americans with shattered hearts do. I joined the military. Took my frustrations out on the enemy."

"Ah," Jonas said. "So that's where you learned how to kill people."

I ignored him. "Years later I was in New York. An attractive woman asked me to dinner, so I said yes. I didn't know anything about her, except she was a friend of a friend. I wasn't expecting — or even wanting — anything to happen. It was just a chance to get out for the night and have simple human interaction.

"Anyway, this date of mine turned out to be a nightmare. She complained about the traffic; I mean, it was New York. She complained about the weather. Once we were in the restaurant she bitched to the hostess about the wait for the table because we had reservations. She gave the bartender a hard time about the alcohol content of her drink. And when we finally got to our table she took one look at the menu and demanded to talk to the chef."

"Why didn't you just leave?" Aiken asked.

"To be honest, I was having the time of my life. I mean, there's something about being around a person like that, someone you know you'll never see again, just watching how outrageous they can be. And she never once grasped what a pain in the ass she was."

Aiken was laughing now. "Okay, I see how this would be fun. But I don't see where your wife comes into this story. Don't tell me she was the pain in the ass."

"Oh, hell no. My wife was the chef."

He gawked. "What?"

"Yeah. My date demanded the chef come out and explain why certain ingredients were used and others weren't — no, I'm not kidding — and a few minutes later this beautiful woman in an apron is standing in front of us, asking what the trouble is."

"And you hit on her right there?"

"What? No, I was a gentleman. I probably had a smirk on my face while my date quizzed her about the menu, but I didn't say a peep. Just sipped my drink and looked around the restaurant."

The memory was making me smile, too. I could still see Christina, standing there with hands on hips, splotches of various sauce stains on her apron, looking with wide-eyed amusement at the very definition of high maintenance who sat next to me, bitching about the food before she'd even ordered.

I took up the story again. "But that's all it took. I stole a few glances at this drop-dead-gorgeous chef and knew I had to go out with her. So the next night I went back to the restaurant."

"Alone this time."

"Naturally. I sat at the bar and asked if the chef had a moment to come out. It took almost 20 minutes, but she came out, wiping her hands on a towel. I explained that I'd been there the night before with the walking nightmare, and apologized for my date's behavior. Then I asked her if I could buy her a drink later on to make up for the trouble ."

"You're smooth," Aiken said. "And she said yes."

"She said no. She didn't even wait around for me to make conversation with her. She thanked me for coming in again and went back to the kitchen. If anything she seemed annoyed that I'd bothered her during a busy time of the night."

Aiken stared at me. "But you're married now."

"We are indeed. That's another story. Maybe some other time."

I let silence descend as I passed a sign that said *San Antonio 82 miles*. I thought about my bride for a few minutes.

Then I thought about what was to come in the Alamo City, and Aiken's words echoed in my head:

I'm pretty sure you're involved in a lot of violence.

CHAPTER FIFTEEN

W e rolled into town and I consulted the directions on my phone. After exiting I-10 I took a few back roads, then parked on a residential street. We were two blocks from a Q2 safe house.

"You can't come with me on this stop," I said to Aiken. "And since I'll be gone for about 20 minutes, I need to make sure you stay put." I handcuffed him to the steering wheel. "You understand, I'm sure."

The disgusted look on his face was answer enough. I grinned and handed him the half-empty Pringles can from the back seat. "This should keep you happy."

A chill wind had kicked up and I walked around the corner and up the street with both hands in my pockets. San Antonio might be hot and muggy in the summer, but on a January day like this it wasn't unusual for temperatures to dip into the 40s. A school bus pulled up nearby and several chattering kids descended the steps and spilled onto the sidewalk. I gave a friendly wave to the bus driver and kept going.

The house I sought didn't appear out of the ordinary;

certainly nothing about the well-manicured exterior suggested that lethal government agents came and went on a semi-regular basis. I pulled open the screen door and knocked in one of our established codes, two taps followed by four. A curtain pulled aside, then the door was unlatched and opened.

A short, red-headed woman smiled at me from behind the screen. "Are you looking for someone?" she asked.

"Susan B. Anthony."

With the silly code business out of the way, she pushed open the screen and ushered me in, then locked everything shut behind us.

"Susan B. Anthony," I said with a laugh. "Did you come up with that one?"

"Can't take credit for it," she said and stuck out her hand. "Cole."

"Swan," I said, appreciating her firm grip. "I need an SL phone."

She nodded. "I can do that. In here."

I followed her through the living room into a kitchen that looked right out of the 1970s, complete with a formica countertop and green appliances. "This is hideous," I said.

"You should see the bathrooms. Have a seat, I'll be right back. Oh, there's beer and soda if you're thirsty."

While she left to get the phone I peered into the fridge and removed a bottle of my favorite Texas beer. I screwed off the cap and took a long drink, then sat at the small kitchen table. Looking around, I admired the way Q2 gave no indication whatsoever that this was a way-station for its agents. It looked like an average, ordinary middle-class home, albeit one in desperate need of a makeover. Through the sliding glass door a trim, neat backyard rolled up to a concrete patio with the standard table, chairs, and umbrella. I was sure a grungy barbecue grill lay off to the side, just out of sight.

I took out my phone and made a quick call to Poole. I let her know where I was, what I was doing, and asked if there was any news.

"Darnell Cox doesn't seem to have made contact with Parks. He's holed up in his room. Must be waiting for the boss to arrive."

"Good. I'm glad I beat Parks to town."

Cole returned as I took another sip of beer. She sat down across from me with a new cell phone and held out a hand. I gave her my phone and she went to work on the two gadgets, connecting them with a patch cord, while I continued my talk on speaker with Poole.

"What about Pradesh?" I asked.

"Nothing."

I grimaced. "Okay. And Santa Fe? Any updates there?"

"Autopsy results on David Torres, the guy found on the floor of his kitchen. Same poison used on Leon Haas and his assistant at Marquart Labs. We'd probably find it was also the same used on you, if we could ever find your body."

This caused Cole to look up from her work, her eyebrows raised. I chuckled and said softly, "It's a long story." To Poole I said, "Let Quanta know I'll be downtown in about an hour. I could use some backup, especially to watch Jonas for a couple of hours while I do an upload."

"Will do. I'll text you the hotel information and have someone from one of the other departments meet you there."

We hung up.

Cole kept tinkering. "So, poisoned, eh?"

"And really nasty stuff, too. I'm sure I suffered. Those are the bastards we're after."

She nodded, and left it at that. Good Q2 support staff knew when to stop asking questions.

"How long have you been stationed here?" I asked.

"Since late summer. It's a nice city. Good food, that's for sure. You'll like the river."

"I was there once six or seven years ago. I'm sure it's the same, only more expensive."

She finished up her work, disconnected the two phones, and pushed them across the table to me. "You're all set. Anything else? How are you on ammo?"

"Haven't fired a shot. Yet. Could be different at the river. Oh, there is one more thing." I reached into my pocket and removed Aiken's cell phone. "Will you please break into this and change the password? I'll need to see what he's up to. And can you add static to this model?"

"Piece of cake," Cole said, taking the phone from me. She pointed down the hall. "If you need to use the facilities, they're right down there. If you want, let me have your weapon, too, and I'll give it a quick cleaning and checkup while you do your business."

I handed her the Glock, finished my beer, and walked down the hall. I also made a note to let Quanta know that our San Antonio field staff was first-rate.

She'd been right about the bathroom. The walls were a pink hue and the toilet had one of those fuzzy seat covers on it. When I finished I washed my hands and then leaned against the sink and called Christina. It went to voicemail, so I left a short, sappy message. I missed her, and told her so.

Back in the kitchen Cole had finished hacking Aiken's phone, and was wrapping up the quick maintenance on the Glock 18. She wiped it down one last time and handed it back.

"You've been great," I said, shaking hands with her again. "Thanks for everything. Including the Shiner Bock."

"Good luck," she said. "If you need anything, let me know."

WHEN I GOT BACK to the car the passenger window was open a bit and Aiken was asleep. I picked a long weed from the ground and fed it through the opening in the window, right into his ear. He jumped, his hand catching on the shackle that held him to the steering wheel and yanking severely on his arm.

"Jesus!" he shouted and gave me a glare. I laughed and walked around to my side of the car.

"Real funny," he muttered, rubbing his wrist after I unlocked the cuffs. "What was this stop all about?"

"This," I said, and tossed the new cell phone onto his lap. "A late Christmas present."

"You're giving me a phone? Why not just give my own phone back to me?"

I started the car and pulled away from the curb. "Because this is the worst phone you could ever imagine. The kind a parent would want to give to their 8th grader. It will do two things: Send calls and texts to me only, and receive calls and texts from me only."

He looked at it. "That's it?"

"That's it. No other calls and texts will work, not even 9-1-1, so don't use it if you're caught in a burning building. It also has no Internet connection or anything else. You've heard of smartphones; this is perhaps the dumbest goddamned phone ever. But it's perfect for you and me. All you do to call me is hit 1. That's it."

Naturally, he had to try it. He hit 1 and my phone vibrated.

He hung up and tried punching in some other ten-digit number. The phone just glowed back at him, silent. "If I'm stuck with you on this trip, why do I need it?"

"Because," I said, "there may be times when you're *not* stuck with me. It'll be crowded down at the tourist trap and we might get separated in all the confusion. And if that happens, you need to be able to reach me. Trust me, you'll *want* to reach me. Because if someone else from my merry little band of badasses finds you, they won't be so kind and understanding as I am. Clear?"

He put the phone into a pocket and grunted. "Yeah, yeah. Clear as always."

We merged onto highway 281, heading south, toward downtown San Antonio. I figured it was time, during this home stretch of the drive, to set Jonas Aiken straight on a few things.

"You and I have had a great time together," I said. "But I hope you don't think you're out of danger. Not only do you have government agents on your ass, but if Steffan Parks catches you there's a good chance he'll want to give you the ol' funny water treatment. And you know what that means."

"Why? I haven't done anything. I've helped him."

I gave him a look of astonishment. "You're joking, right? You show up, unexpected, at his appointment in Texas, tagging along with a government agent. And you think he'll just say, '*Hey, what a surprise*!' Jonas, if he's not in a position to poison you he'll have his bodyguard slit your throat in about two seconds."

He sat in stony silence for a minute. "If Jayanti's there—"

"If Jayanti *is* there she might kill you faster than anyone. Remember, she knocked off Ed, another employee of Uncle

Sam, and you're the one who clued her in that Ed was interested in her. You think she wants you around to testify?"

Another moment of silence, and then Aiken turned to me. "See, it's things like that. What makes you so sure I told Jayanti anything? You act like you have all this inside information about me, but you weren't there. How do you know anything?"

I grinned again. "I'm omniscient."

He rolled his eyes. "Uh-huh. Omniscient."

"The point isn't how I know. The point is that you're a loose end. And you've seen enough movies; loose ends get snipped. So do two things if you wanna see home again: Stay close to me, and, if something goes wrong, use that phone."

"If you're dead, what good would it do me to call you?"

"Because we think of everything, Jonas. Well, almost everything. If I don't answer after seven rings, the call forwards to one of my friends. So just stay on the line, got it?"

He let out a quiet laugh. "God, you're a real secret agent, aren't you? Got all the James Bond toys and everything."

"Not quite. Never got the ejector seat. And our Miss Moneypenny has absolutely no interest in me."

In another 20 minutes we pulled up to the hotel. It was right on the river and only three blocks from where Cox was holed up. I didn't bother to warn Aiken about slipping away. We just got out of the car and strolled into the lobby while the bellman took care of the bags and the BMW.

The courteous young man at the front desk checked us in to our two rooms, gave me both keys, and pointed to a woman sitting in one of the lobby chairs.

"She asked me to point her out to you, sir," he said. "Said she's supposed to meet you?"

"That's great," I said. "Listen, can I order room service from you?"

He nodded helpfully and I rattled off a handful of things that every hotel's restaurant in this city would carry. I promised a fat tip for fast service, and also slipped 20 bucks to the desk agent.

With the important stuff out of the way, I escorted Aiken across the lobby. The woman, in her mid-30s with short, dark hair and a business suit that screamed Fed, stood up and reached for a badge.

"I was sent to meet you," she said and showed the ID. Sure enough, she was FBI. The name on the badge was spelled K-o-w-a-l-c-z-y-k.

I attempted the pronunciation. "Ko-wall-zik?"

She smiled. "On the first try, even. And this is?"

"This is Jonas Aiken. He's been really good so far. Haven't you, Jonas?"

He didn't respond.

"Don't mind him," I said. "He gets into this mood from time to time, but overall he's been good. Agent Kowalczyk, can you look after him for a couple hours? There's some work I need to do."

"No problem," she said, taking Aiken by the arm.

I handed her the key to Aiken's room and made for the gift shop to buy a trash magazine. What I wanted more than anything was a quick shower, some food, then a bunch of Hollywood gossip to pass the time while my brain was hooked up.

My room overlooked the water from the fifth floor. I peered out the window, watching hordes of people strolling both sides of the greenish-brown river meandering through the heart of San Antonio. Even with the cool weather business was booming. You couldn't walk 50 feet without encountering a bar, restaurant, or shop, and the ambience oozed happiness and frivolity. Whatever your cares when you arrived, the river would lift them up and carry them away — helped by a shot or two of tequila. I liked the place. I mean, I don't care for crowds or traditional touristy fare, but this had a pleasant quality.

When I stepped out of the shower the food was waiting. It's remarkable what the promise of a sizable tip will do to bump your order up in line. I savored the queso and guac with tortilla chips, and layered a fajita that would make Christina proud. Once sated, I stretched out on the bed, made all the connections necessary for the upload, and began reading about the Greek heiress flaunting her new bod on the beaches of Portugal with the guy who used to be in that boy band.

The time flew by.

At 6:30 I unplugged, ate a few more chips, and relished my break from babysitting Jonas. He seemed like a decent enough guy, but his fanatical obsession with Jayanti could potentially muck things up. I checked his phone to see if he'd received anything from her; all it showed was a text from his wife.

Of course I read it. It said: *The car is ready. Want me to pick it up?*

I texted back: *Yes.*

I scrolled back to see if an *I love you* was expected. Didn't look like it. I didn't see a single tender note between them. Their texts were nothing like the ones I exchanged with my wife. Were they the oddballs or were we?

My own phone vibrated with a call from Poole.

"I hope you have news," I said.

"Cox is on the move. He just left his hotel and he's heading toward the river. We're guessing that Parks has arrived."

"Perfect. Who's on him right now?"

"Name is Brockington. I'm sending you a photo right now so you can make a positive ID. He's a loaner from the Texas Rangers."

"Hey, that's cool. I wondered what they did during the off-season."

Poole's silence told me she totally did not get it. That wouldn't stop me from trying to make her laugh until the end of time.

"Link me with Brockington's GPS," I said. "I'm leaving right now."

Poole hung up. At the same moment another call came in. It was on Aiken's phone.

I answered it and immediately hit the star and hashtag buttons at the same time. This added a little something we simply called static. It scrambled the voice on our end so that the other person could barely understand us — you know, the typical bad-signal shit we're all used to with cell phones. The other person, however, came through loud and clear. Cole at the safe house had installed it in about a minute.

"Hello?" I said. Whoever was on the other end paused, wondering about the bad signal.

"Jonas?" they finally said.

"Yes," I said. With the intentionally-induced crappy sound there was no way they'd be able to identify me as anyone other than Aiken. "Speak up, I can barely hear you."

"Where are you?" the voice said.

I smiled. It was Jayanti, calling Jonas.

"Still in Tucson," I said. "Where are you?"

She paused, probably out of frustration for the sound quality. "I'm with Steffan. We have some business to take care of before we get back to Arizona. I'll need to meet with you."

"All right," I said.

"Listen, this call sounds like shit. I'll call you back in about an hour."

She hung up. I grinned again and walked back to the window. Pulling aside the curtain, I gazed at the mass of people shuffling along the Riverwalk. "So you're with Parks," I said. "Excellent."

CHAPTER SIXTEEN

I collected Jonas from his FBI handler, Kowalczyk. She would shadow us from the opposite side of the river, and the Texas Ranger, Brockington, would stay on Cox the whole time. The photo Poole sent showed a big, chicken-fried-steak-eatin' Texas Ranger. I liked having tough guys on my team for a change. Things were looking up.

In the lobby gift shop I bought a Spurs hoodie and a pair of sunglasses for Jonas. It would disguise him well enough, plus Steffan and Jayanti wouldn't be looking for him. As far as they knew he was still holed up in Tucson.

We pushed through the doors leading to the congested walkways and melded into the crowd. Even with the cooler weather San Antonio's Riverwalk was its usual lively self. Street vendors, bars and restaurants every few feet, tourist boats puttering by, crammed with out-of-town visitors who enjoyed watery excursions with snarky guides. It was a festive, convivial atmosphere, strangely at odds with my assignment.

I checked my phone's map and saw Brockington's dot moving basically toward us. The Riverwalk was set below street level, with stairways for entrance and exit about every block. After calculating trajectories, I took us over a pedestrian bridge to the other side of the water. If I had it right, Cox would be walking down the stairs from Crockett Street.

We were sheltered from the worst of the wind, but it was still brisk. I watched people bracing against the chill on the nearest tour boat, the pilot pointing out landmarks and assorted historical facts. When she indicated a building that once housed something or other I actually looked up at it like a dork.

One glance across the river revealed Kowalczyk, playing her part, pretending to read a guide map. She seemed competent and comfortable.

As we neared Crockett Street I tugged on Aiken's sleeve to slow him down. I spent a minute perusing the menu of an Irish pub. What that had to do with South Texas was beyond me, but I'm okay with Irish pubs anywhere. Their fish-n-chips looked great, and several of their patio patrons were already pretty well lubricated. If I wasn't on an assignment I would've happily joined.

Aiken bent toward me and said in a low voice, "What are we waiting for?"

Good question. I'd expected to see Brockington by now, and, by extension, Cox. I could only stare at the menu for so long before the hostess would think I was drunk myself.

I checked the tracking signal again and saw that the Ranger's position had shifted to a strange, out of the way spot and wasn't moving. Of course, Cox could've stopped. But if so, Brockington would be conspicuous just standing there. Something felt wrong.

"Let's walk. Slowly," I said.

Kowalczyk was looking at me over the top of her map. I

shook my head twice, then held my hand up to keep her in this spot. If Brockington did show up, she needed to be able to make contact. We couldn't *all* go barreling off to one secluded spot.

I figured we were about a hundred yards from the stationary GPS dot. At the end of the street was a turn to the left, a tributary of sorts, leading to a dark underpass. This part of the walkway was not trafficked at all; I assumed it led to some sort of maintenance area. There were no vendors, no shops, nothing. Just a concrete strip ending in shadow.

"Shit," I muttered. I didn't want to walk down there, but I was *paid* to walk down there.

Jonas picked up on the vibe right away. "I can wait here."

"Right. I'm sure you'll be waiting right here when I get back."

He nodded toward the underpass. "I don't want to walk in there."

"I don't either, pardner. But this is what we signed up for."

"*I* didn't sign up for anything," he said with a whine.

"Yeah, you did. As soon as you gave up Ed to your scorpion friend. That put you square in the middle of it. Let's go."

I took hold of his arm and he resisted, refusing to budge. So I leaned in close, my face within inches of his.

"Jonas, we've been getting along pretty well. Which means you might think I've grown a soft spot for you. So let me set you straight. If you don't move your ass right now I will start by breaking your nose and then see what else fancies me. *Capiche*?"

He glared back at me, but relaxed. We started down the path.

The wind had picked up a notch, blowing around assorted pieces of trash. It was colder than most of us expected for

South Texas. My jacket provided decent protection but I would've liked a pair of leather gloves. The wind also created background noise, which mingled with the sound of traffic passing overhead. This was good in that it covered our approach, but bad because it also covered any sounds from up ahead.

We got to the edge of the gloom of the underpass and stopped. The water, whipped up by the wind, lapped against the side of the walkway. It smelled slightly of sewage and other assorted filth. The whole scene concerned me. On top of it all, Brockington's GPS dot hadn't budged. It was within 30 yards.

Taking a deep breath, I pulled out the Glock, held it to my side, and moved ahead. My eyes adjusted quickly, and I realized it wasn't that dark. It was simply a big contrast from the glitz and glam of the tourist section of the river. Aiken scuffed one foot against the ground, which, within the tunnel we'd entered, seemed remarkably loud. If we'd had any chance of approaching unannounced, that was gone.

That's when I saw the form ahead. It was undoubtedly the shape of a person on the ground, lying on their side. My concern ratcheted up to alert status.

"Wait here," I said to Aiken. Then I walked over to the shape and knelt down.

It was Brockington. His crumpled form was oddly twisted, the way a large man would land if killed or knocked unconscious. A sickening amount of blood pooled around him.

He'd been made, obviously, and taken out. I felt for a pulse and found a weak one. Someone, likely Cox, had belted him but good. Damn.

I stood up and pulled out my phone, but before I could do anything else I heard footsteps coming toward me from ahead.

Out of the darkness walked two figures, a man and a woman. He was smiling, she was not.

"Good evening," the man said. His tone betrayed the fact that he gave no shits about the body lying on the ground between us. I recognized the hair, both the goatee and the tail. Finally — *finally* — I'd come face-to-face with Steffan Parks. He stopped six feet from me and casually clasped his hands in front of him.

I kept eye contact with him for a few seconds before shifting my gaze to the woman beside him. Of course it was Jay. She was bundled inside a full coat. The change from Arizona's warmth to the winter chill of Texas apparently didn't appeal to her.

Looking back to Parks, I said, "Hi. Would you guys know where to get a really good Alamo T-shirt? The ones in these shops are crap."

Jayanti's stare grew even more unpleasant, but Parks continued to smile. "Funny you should mention the Alamo," he said. "An historic place of death."

"And pee," I said. "Didn't Ozzy Osbourne urinate on it or something?"

"I thought he bit the head off a bat," Parks said. "Did he pee on the Alamo, too? What a bad boy."

"You know a few things about bad boys, don't you?"

The banter was the last straw for Jay. "Can we please finish this and go? I'm cold."

"I'm going with you." The voice came from behind me, and a second later Aiken brushed past and pulled down the hood of his hoodie. "Get me the hell out of here, too."

The smile on Steffan's face evaporated. Jayanti practically gaped. They both looked back and forth between me and Aiken.

"Jonas," Jay said. "What the hell are you—"

"This asshole kidnapped me and dragged me here." He took another step toward them and looked back at me. "And I do mean asshole."

Steffan rocked back and forth on his feet. "Well. This is unexpected." He squinted at me, which looked funny in a dimly-lit setting. "You're the third government agent to stumble into us. Including the gentleman currently disposed on the ground before you. Why couldn't I get this kind of attention from the government when I actually wanted it?"

"Because you presented them with something on a par with Nazi techniques?"

This didn't sit well with Parks one bit, and he practically snarled. "I won't trade quips with you. In fact, there's no reason for this conversation at all." His gaze shifted just over my shoulder and I felt a gun pushed into my ribs from behind.

"That'll be Mr. Cox," I said without flinching. "He'll no doubt kill me, which will be very annoying and put me way behind schedule."

Both Parks and Jayanti looked suitably confused by the comment. Cox, however, was nonplussed. He reached around and removed the Glock from my hand.

"And what about Jonas?" I asked. "Will Cox finish him off, too, or do you need to question him?"

"There's nothing to question me about," Aiken said, his voice an octave higher than normal. "This guy dragged me here and now I'm going back with you."

I shrugged. "Okay. That should be a fun trip for everyone. No concerns about security breaches or anything like that. Good."

Parks turned a cool eye toward Aiken. "Walk back to the

hotel with Ms. Pradesh." When Aiken opened his mouth to reply, Parks shook his head and added, "Just go. Now."

"Its about time," Pradesh said. She walked past without so much as a glance at me.

Jonas hesitated a few moments, looking like he wanted to say something else to Parks. But finally he gave a frustrated sigh and trudged off after Jayanti.

Steffan took a step forward, looked down at the unconscious Ranger, then back at me. "All of this has been so unnecessary. I didn't ask for much."

I scoffed. "Steffan, are you actually painting yourself as the victim in all this? You and your girlfriend killed an agent in Scottsdale and three more people in Santa Fe, including someone who used to be your friend. If you get your way you'll murder a lot more."

Behind me, Cox pushed the gun further into my lower side until it really hurt. But I kept going. "Tell me this, since you're about to kill me anyway. Where are you planning your little murder experiment?"

A slow smile returned to his face. "I think I'd rather let you die wondering about that. It can be your last thought. What a way to end a life. As a failure."

I chuckled. "Yeah, well, it won't be the first time. How about a hint? East or west of the Mississippi?"

He matched my laugh. "What's your name?"

"Eric. Look, if the meathead behind me shoots that thing the other agents just down the way are going to come running."

Parks pursed his lips. "Mr. Cox does his best work with a knife, Eric. He's going to cut your throat, dump you into this filthy river, and then do the same with that extremely large man lying at your feet."

He glanced over my shoulder at Cox, gave a curt nod, then walked up to my side. Leaning up to my disfigured ear he whispered, "West."

After that he smirked and walked on. As the sound of his footsteps faded away, I tuned all of my senses into the large problem behind me and waited for Cox to reach for the knife. He may have been good, he may have been trained well in the military and during his time as a deputy sheriff, but he wasn't a pro's pro, and he stood no chance if he didn't use the gun right now.

And, like all bullies, he felt the need to get in one last dig. Pulling the gun back a bit and leaning up to the same ear that Parks had nuzzled, Cox said, "Looks like someone tried to cut off one ear already. I'll take the other one. A souvenir." With a grunt he added, "You government types are too easy. This is gonna be—"

That's when I did it. With Parks out of the way, and this hired shithead caught up in his stupid tough-guy performance, I re-enacted a move Quanta had used on me with great success — more than once. In a flash I spun and used my left hand to chop his gun hand downward and the heel of my right to smash his nose.

The gun clattered to the ground and I struck again, this time a left into his larynx. He let out a sound that could've been *gack*, and stumbled backward. I expected him to drop to his knees. Anyone else *would've*.

But no. He steadied himself and gave me the angriest look I've ever seen on a human face.

It was my first chance to size up Darnell Cox. He was big in all three dimensions, a massive shadow in the already-dim light. "You've got to be shitting me," I muttered. "You're not a Cox; you're an ox."

He spat out a wad of blood, ran a hand across his face, then reached behind and pulled out the knife I'd heard so much about. It was certainly impressive, especially when he whipped it through the air toward my face.

I leaned back just in time, then avoided the next slash, too. I stepped back and summoned my training. The key elements came down to this: don't fall down, and don't get stabbed.

The thing I had going for me was that Cox had made his career as a goon simply through sheer size and stamina. He bulled through his victims. I probably could've punched him in the face 50 times and it would barely slow him down.

But guys like that often neglect to hone their real hand-to-hand skills. Between my military training and the frequent ass-kickings supplied by my boss, I was confident I'd have one of those pricey margaritas before the night was over.

But nothing was a sure thing.

The broken nose definitely hampered Cox the Ox. He swiped away another stream of blood, then tried a lunge. I easily sidestepped him and delivered another blow to his throat, followed by a shot to his kidneys. It felt like hitting a mattress.

With a growl he swung the knife again. I circled him, which gave me time to analyze the battleground. There was something about this area Cox had forgotten, and didn't see now in the poor light. So I moved back to my right, guiding him exactly where I wanted him. As soon as we were there, I feinted a move forward, which caused him to try another slash. That had him off-balance, and my sidekick to his chin worked perfectly. He staggered back a step.

And right over the prone body of another large man, Ranger Brockington, who'd slept through the whole thing.

Cox went down hard and, in trying to keep his balance, the knife clattered to the ground.

I bent down and snatched it just as my dance partner pushed himself up and, with a roar, leapt for me. From my kneeling position I executed my own lunge, driving the knife right up through that Simmons Beautyrest of a chest.

For a moment he was frozen, supported by the knife at the end of my arm. I slowly got to my feet, relishing the look of utter disbelief on his face. I drew the knife out and plunged it in again, this time into his oxen heart. Now he did fall, toppling backwards onto the pavement.

I caught my breath, hands on hips, and wiped perspiration from my brow. For such a cool night I'd worked up a nice sweat. That margarita would become a sure thing, along with a good shot of whiskey, to boot.

After checking one more time to make sure that Brockington was still alive, I turned back to Cox. Grabbing him by the arms, I grunted and heaved him over to the edge of the river. Rooting through his pockets, I lifted both his gun and mine, along with his wallet and phone. There was nothing else except change and Tic Tacs.

I gave him one last glance. "Guess we're not so easy after all, dickhead."

I used my foot to tumble him into the river with a large splash.

Then I called Kowalczyk to help me with the Ranger.

CHAPTER SEVENTEEN

In my line of work, any time there's a major foul-up — in this case a Texas Ranger who'd been assaulted and a prime witness/suspect abducted — it meant getting your ass chewed out.

With Quanta there was never shouting, and that's worse. In the military I *always* got yelled at, but I was prepared for it because my dad had been a shouter. After a while it's like a drug; your body becomes resistant and it loses any potency.

Mom, however, rarely raised her voice. She'd worked the disappointment angle, which is playing dirty as far as I'm concerned. Nobody can stand the idea of disappointing their mother.

That was Quanta's style, too. I'd successfully completed a good number of missions, but I'd also bungled my share. Most cases have an assortment of both. A spy's job is built on more of a risk/reward system than that of a Wall Street hedge fund. You want results, you have to stick your neck out. Consequently, I'd been through numerous replacement necks.

In fact, my boss would often point out I'd been through

more bodies than any other Q2 agent. I was told by Sherilyn, my favorite tech in our basement lab, that the count wasn't that close, either. When curiosity demanded I push her for actual stats she gently told me to piss off. We're not supposed to know anything about the other agents. Some day they'll explain why, but I suspect it has to do with Q2's first investment agent.

Things with him didn't end well — although I haven't heard *his* side of the story; we'd have to find him first — and now we're all pretty much sequestered from each other.

At the moment I was sitting in my San Antonio hotel room on a conference video chat with Quanta and Poole. My room service dinner sat on a nearby tray, mostly just picked at.

"So you went into a darkened, secluded area, confident there was trouble ahead, without backup," Quanta said. "And you dragged your potential source of information, Aiken, with you, even though he was known to be sympathetic with the other side. So that makes at least four potential adversaries, one of whom was a hired thug. How could that possibly go wrong?"

"He was one of the shittiest hired thugs I've ever encountered," I threw in. "But, then again, Parks isn't experienced enough to hire the best. Yet."

"That's beside the point. What outcome were you expecting?"

"The exact outcome I got."

Quanta fell silent, and I saw on the split screen that Poole was trying to become invisible.

"Do you want me to explain?" I asked.

"Oh, by all means," Quanta said. "I'm anxious to hear any explanation that could remove the stench from this situation."

I shifted in my seat, one of those uncomfortable desk chairs that hotels specialize in, even the 4-star chains. I had this explanation pretty well set in my mind; it was just a matter of expressing it so that I didn't sound nuts.

"It's like this. As you say, if Brockington was indeed out of commission, as I expected, then it was going to be four against one. I wasn't going to capture both Parks and Pradesh without the possibility of a gun battle, and in that case anything could happen, including the unfortunate death of Steffan Parks.

"To me, that was unacceptable, because he may have already programmed it so the poison is distributed at some pre-determined time. If he died, we wouldn't know when or where until Eyewitness News broke in with a bulletin. And the same thing might apply if we just apprehended him. He could sit there, smug, waiting for the poison to roll out."

"So far this explanation is nonsense," Quanta said. "Of course we need Parks alive. But you not only lost him and his partner, you lost one of the few people who might've helped us get the information."

"I didn't exactly *lose* him," I said. "I planted him."

More silence. Then Quanta shook her head. "All right. I'm listening."

"Aiken doesn't know enough yet. I think he can find out more. And then I'll find out from him."

I don't often see my boss laugh, but this was one of those times. It was the sarcastic variety.

"You think Jonas Aiken is going to soak information out of Parks, and then rush back to you to share it? Swan, he's probably already dead."

"I don't think so. I think he's pretty convincing. And the fact that he threw me to the wolves at the soonest possible moment also looks good for him. At the very least I think

Parks, who we already know is a genius at potions but a relative amateur at crime—"

"Not counting the bodies he's already piled up?" Quanta said.

"Well, yeah. But still, it's not his forte. I don't think he'll murder Jonas. At least not yet."

Poole finally spoke up. "Could you just send Aiken a text on the SL phone you gave him?"

Quanta answered. "No. *If* — and that's a big if — if he's going to play ball, you can't risk having Parks hear or see him receiving anything right now. It could upset everything. No, Swan will have to wait this one out." She looked back at me. "And you really think Parks is going to spill everything to this guy?"

"No. But I think this guy can get information out of Jayanti."

"Why?"

I looked down to break eye contact. "I don't know. I just have a feeling."

"Did you and Aiken discuss this arrangement beforehand?"

"Uh, no."

The frustrated sigh came through loud and clear from Washington D.C. "Let me make sure I understand your plan, Swan. You put yourself in a position where Aiken would be retaken by Parks. You then banked on the fact that you could defeat their hired killer. Next, you're counting on Aiken to obtain vital information from Pradesh *and* find you in order to save the day. Is that about right?"

I had to chuckle. "When you put it like that . . ." I looked back at the screen. "All right, so it sounds like a long shot. But in the heat of the moment it's what made sense to me. Jonas has a really odd relationship with Jay, and I think he's figuring out what a schmuck he's been. If he still has that SL phone, or if he can get his hands on it, he can contact me. I think he will."

"Lovely," Quanta said. "And if he doesn't?"

I chewed my lower lip for a second. "If he doesn't, I'll come up with Plan B."

PARKS HAD WHISPERED *West* to me, and I believed him. He thought I was about to be fish food — if there *are* fish in the San Antonio river. And regardless of what he said about not wanting to divulge information, let's get real: Bad guys always liked boasting about their plans, about their accomplishments, their victories, and their overall superiority over anyone who pursued them.

Sometimes it meant sending notes to the police. Others, like Son of Sam and the Zodiac killer, sent letters to journalists.

This guy was no different. Saying just that one word — *West* — probably got him aroused.

If we took the meager facts available to this point and plugged in that single vain utterance, it suggested one of the two towns where he and Jay had surfaced lately. Why exactly would Pradesh be at that conference in Scottsdale? She wasn't on a panel. She'd flat-out told me she wasn't attending any of the breakout sessions.

Networking, she'd said. Really? In the midst of a project to kill tens of thousands of people she's interested in padding her contacts?

So if we assumed that was a load of shit, why was she hanging out in the desert?

To work with Parks on details of their plan? Did that mean Scottsdale? Or Phoenix? Or some other city in Arizona?

The questions kept rolling through my head. What if the first place they'd struck was the ultimate target? What if those killings at Marquart Labs were just a preview of things to come in Santa Fe?

Of course, it could be neither Arizona nor New Mexico. Parks could be a big fat lying piece of shit.

I didn't think so. And that meant I'd placed an awful lot on hunches lately. Not generally a good practice when lives were on the line.

Christina would be at the restaurant in Washington for another hour, so I couldn't talk to her at the moment. And I needed a drink. Putting my shoes back on, I left the room and took the stairs down to the lobby bar.

The FBI agent, Kowalczyk, was perched on a stool.

"What's that?" I asked, sitting down and pointing at her cocktail.

"Old-fashioned."

The bartender ambled over and I indicated her drink. "The same, but with rye, please."

To Kowalczyk I said, "I hope your first name is easier to say."

She smiled. "Katarina."

"Oh, shit. Worlds collide."

"Yeah," she said. "Mother from Sweden, father from Latvia. So Kat works. Or my high school friends thought Trina was cute."

"Kat it is. How's the big Texan?"

"Brockington? They took him to Brooke, a hospital at Fort Sam Houston. Might have a skull fracture, definitely a bad concussion. But he'll pull through."

My drink arrived and we clinked glasses.

"By the way," she said. "That corpse you dumped into the water drifted downstream and scared the shit out of a bunch of people enjoying nachos."

I almost spit out my drink. "I didn't think the current would work that fast. Look at it this way. They'll have a great story to tell for the rest of their lives."

"The restaurant comped their nachos, at least. Couldn't you have left him on the pavement for us to collect?"

"Nope." I took another sip. "What else have you heard? Anything on Parks and Pradesh?"

"Yeah, we got a possible break," she said. "A couple of our agents canvassed tech offices here in the downtown area and showed them pictures of Parks. A woman who runs one of those coffee carts in the lobby of a building said she definitely saw him. Said he bought tea and a scone."

"Definitely? Why definitely?"

"Said he reminded her of her creepy uncle."

"We've all got one," I said. "Anybody else in the building confirm?"

"Not officially. But the agents said one of the companies on the 8th floor was very strange about it when shown his picture. They said they'd never seen or heard of him, but it came across as a lie. Like they were trying to protect someone."

I nodded. "Very good. Thank you. Text me the info and I'll call on them tomorrow."

"Want me to join you?"

"Thanks, but no. One federal agent is intimidating enough for people."

I realized I'd sucked down my drink already. I considered

ordering a second, then decided on iced tea instead. I can be such a lightweight sometimes.

We chatted for another twenty minutes, mostly comparing work notes, at least as much as I could share. Only one person at the FBI, an agent I'd worked with in the Caribbean, knew what Q2 was really about. And it sucked having to be vague with fellow agents who risked their necks, too. I always felt like an ass, happy to soak up their stories and hear them bitch about internal politics while I couldn't offer much in return. I found myself sometimes making shit up, just to placate their curiosity.

Kat Kowalczyk wasn't nosey, which made this particular banter much easier. As I was getting ready to leave she nodded to the other side of the bar.

"You have an admirer," she said.

I followed her gaze toward a pure Texas beauty, complete with large hair and a dazzling smile, which she aimed directly at me.

"With my scars she must think I'm a rodeo star," I said, standing.

"Not gonna saddle up?" Kat asked, amused.

"Nah. I'm just gonna mosey on back to my room."

For some reason this made her laugh. We said good night.

GETTING OFF THE ELEVATOR, I tried Christina and got her after four rings.

"You sound tired," she said. "Long day at the office?"

"Oh, same ol'," I said. "What was the special tonight?"

"Braised ribs and orzo. Sold out. What was the most exciting part of your day?"

"Um . . . probably when a guy threatened to cut off my ear."

"The one that's jacked up? Because he'd be doing all of us a favor."

"Funny. No, the other one."

"I assume you didn't let him do that."

"No. I talked him out of it."

"San Antonio, right? When are you coming home?"

I sighed, a completely genuine sigh. "Oh, babe. Wish I could right now. I've got some business tomorrow, then I think I'm headed back to Arizona."

"I'm jealous. We got an ice storm today."

That's the way our conversations usually went. Pretty rapid-fire, jumping from subject to subject.

Sometimes I wondered what a marriage counselor would say about our relationship. Hardly seeing each other, then brief snippets of phone conversation or a video call, and the kind of snappy talk you'd find in an old Cary Grant movie.

But the truth was, neither Christina nor I gave a rat's ass what a counselor might say about it, which we both knew would be negative. It worked for us. It hurt, and yet worked, if that made sense.

All of this was exacerbated by the wicked cocktail of emotions tumbling around my head. I'd taken a gamble by letting two murderers and an accomplice walk, I'd lost the confidence of my boss, I'd fought with — and killed — a brute who could've starred in the WWE, and now I was lonely. I sat in a hotel room in Texas and wished I was in an ice storm back in D.C.

There were times I wondered about the mind that kept getting uploaded and downloaded. I could never be sure if it was the exact same mind I'd started with at Q2. It was, after all, a product of evolution and wasn't built to be transferred back and forth in a stream of ones and zeroes. Could it become degraded through all the exchanges? We hadn't had the technology long enough to find out.

Or maybe we had, and the powers at the top, including Dr. Nayar — my Dr. Frankenstein — *knew* I was getting damaged, but did a cost-benefit analysis and determined the gradual erosion of my essence was a small price to pay for saving America's collective ass.

It was late, I was tired, and these thoughts weren't productive. Finding the technology geeks that Parks met with would be productive.

I said a few sappy things to Christina and told her good night.

Five minutes later I got a text from Jonas Aiken.

CHAPTER EIGHTEEN

The message was short, vague, and thoroughly frustrating.

Leaving town tomorrow. It's not what you think.

I almost threw my phone across the room. Leaving town for *where*, asshole? And *what's* not what I think? The poison plan? His relationship with Jayanti? His return to the dark side?

Goddamned rookies.

Then other thoughts rushed in. Like the possibility that Aiken was screwing with me; or worse, that Parks and Pradesh had his phone and were about to send me on the mother of all wild goose chases.

I couldn't text him back. Not yet, anyway. I still had to wait and hope. Not generally my tactic of choice.

But there was nothing else to be done except try to catch some sleep and see what developed in the morning. I turned on the ringer and set my phone next to the bed in case Aiken made a stealth call in the middle of the night.

He didn't.

In the morning the sun snuck through a tiny opening in the curtains and that sliver of light happened to line up perfectly on my face, rousing me at around 7:30. I'd managed a full night of rest, which was overdue.

After ordering room service and taking care of morning rituals, I opened the curtains and took in the wintery view. Standing there with a towel around my waist and my hair still wet from the shower, I visualized the work that lay before me. The most important task was a visit to the tech company that had acted screwy when asked to identify Steffan Parks. It was suspicious, but I'd be able to confirm or rule out their association with him in just a few minutes.

A knock on the door signaled the arrival of eggs, bacon, and coffee. While I fueled up I called Poole and put it on speaker.

"There's something odd about the murders in Santa Fe," she said.

"Tell me."

"We've been able to track down both Parks and Pradesh on the two days those happened."

"Okay. And?"

"And they weren't in New Mexico."

I was in the process of lifting a strip of extra-crispy bacon off the plate. I stopped and held it in the air. "How reliable is the information?"

"Pretty solid," she said. "Data shows that Parks was in the Washington area and Pradesh was already in Arizona, although not checked in at the Scottsdale resort. Of course, it's possible we've got it wrong, and either one or both of them *could've* been there to pull it off. Or—"

"Or there's another person involved," I said. Finally taking a bite of the bacon, I thought about this possible development.

Poole waited patiently while I took a drink of coffee and wiped my hands.

"Okay," I said. "Aiken told me this association of disgruntled scientists had several members. But he was confident that few, if any, would go to the extremes that Parks advocated. In fact he led me to believe *nobody* would help him."

"All it takes is one," Poole said.

She was right. So now, on top of everything else, we had to factor in the possibility that Parks had indeed recruited another mad scientist to his cause. If that was the case, this person was just as dangerous and deadly as any of them. They had confirmed kills on their resume.

This case was aggravating. At the moment it seemed like the only thing that had gone right was this morning's bacon.

I said to Poole, "I know he said he'd contact me if he found anything new, but would you please check in with that sheriff in Santa Fe. What was his name?"

"Tonkin."

"Yeah, him. He wasn't crazy about working with damned Feds, so he might've conveniently forgotten to call."

"Will do."

We hung up and I finished breakfast. Pouring my third coffee — hotel cups are small enough for children's tea parties — I got dressed and packed my things. If all went well I'd go straight from my tech meeting to the airport.

THE COMPANY on the 8th floor was called AppaDabba, which must've sounded breezy and playful to the founders. The logo was a finger on a phone screen with glitzy graphics to make it seem futuristic. Seemed corny to me.

But their offices were furnished in a way that conveyed

success and money, so what did I know? Maybe AppaDabba was the coolest name ever.

At the desk I displayed my fake government badge and asked for the most important person in the place. The bored receptionist made a call and a minute later I was shaking hands with a guy named Guy. He looked about 30, as casually dressed as you'd expect for a young tech guru, with a shaved head but full beard. Some people can pull that off. Guy couldn't.

He took me back to his corner office and indicated the chair across from his desk. We settled in and he gave me his best concerned look.

"I met yesterday with some of your people," he said. "Or were they not with you?"

"We work in tandem," I said. "But we're after the same thing." I turned my phone around and showed him the photo. "This is what we're after. Steffan Parks, one of your clients. I want to know what you built for him."

Guy frowned and did a slight shake of his head. "I think you have the wrong company. I'm not familiar with a Steven Parks."

I chuckled at the intentional mistake. "My friend, there are three things I'm going to share with you, and I want you to really listen closely.

"One, Steffan has already told us he did an app project with you, so you're lying. Two, lying to a government official, especially my department, will get your ass shut down before lunch and your doors will be locked. You can bet on that."

I put my phone back in my pocket. "And three, multiple departments in Washington will make sure you personally never get over this. You might be working in a call center by this summer."

He did what I expected, which was to put on his best outraged look. But before he could stammer a sentence I kept going.

"And here's the real heavy stuff, Guy. Steffan Parks has obviously bullshitted you on what his toy will do. So let me set you straight. What you've created for him will lead to the deaths of not dozens, not hundreds, but thousands of people. And guess what the government's next move against you will be? A murder charge. Not accessory to murder, but the big M itself, because you built it. So now you can even forget the call center, my little Texas buckaroo. Your skinny ass will be in a prison yard getting sized up for a little nighttime company, if you know what I mean."

I leaned forward. "So now, let me ask you again, asshole, and don't piss me off. What did your company build for Steffan Parks, and what will it do for him?"

His face had gone pale. I learned a long time ago to press these advantages before the subject could fully recover.

"Let's start with some simple questions first," I said. "Why the deception? Why tell us you weren't working for Parks?"

He leaned across his desk, his palms spread apart. "Listen, I am fully cooperating with you, okay? There was nothing to suggest any crime would be committed, let alone murder. So I had nothing to do with those plans. I'm—"

"Guy," I said, holding up a hand in the stop position. "I don't want to send you to prison, okay? That's not what I'm after. If Parks conned you, like he's conned a lot of other people, then you might come across as a victim instead of an accomplice. So answer my question: What did he do to make you lie about this?"

"Um, he, uh, he said this was proprietary information that could someday be used in a lot of other applications. So he demanded a complete NDA, and to never let anyone know we were working with him."

"Okay, a non-disclosure agreement I get. But didn't you get even a little suspicious that you couldn't utter his name?"

Guy took a breath. "I mean, you've heard of Steffan Parks before, right? The dude's an award-winning scientist. So of course I believed that people would want to pirate something he'd commissioned. He's not the first person to ask us for complete confidentiality. It's one of the reasons we're successful."

I nodded. "All right, fair enough. Now that we've wasted valuable time getting all that out of the way, why don't you tell me exactly what he hired you to do."

"It's a triggering device, but in the form of an app."

"Triggering device," I said. "So, almost like a remote detonator?"

He frowned. "No. It's similar to what you might use on a phone to connect with your home security system while you're out of town. Or some smart thermostats in houses can be controlled with a phone app. You turn down the air conditioning or turn up the heat when you leave the office and the house will be at the right temperature when you get home."

"How was his different from those applications?"

He thought about this for a moment, then turned around and got something off the credenza behind his desk. Facing me again he set a mechanical device between us.

"This," he said, "is a valve used by a natural gas company in Louisiana. They use it when they're processing the raw natural gas taken from the ground. Something to do with separating impurities." He shrugged. "Anyway, the important thing is they have to be able to open and close these valves quickly.

Yes, there's someone on site and they use actual levers and buttons and whatnot.

"But their chief engineer talked with us about creating an app that worked on both ends. So we built the app that goes onto a phone or tablet, and also created the receiving end that's built into these valves."

It was my turn to frown. "I don't understand what makes this so difficult. You mentioned all the home security systems and thermostats. I know people who use apps to open and close their garage. What makes this special?"

This produced a smile in young Guy, and I realized I'd tapped into his passion. Now that he was no longer fearful of becoming a cell-block date for someone, he was only too happy to explain.

"Those are mass produced. The software controls tens of thousands of them, and the only thing separating one from the other is the personal ID and the password. *These*," he said, pointing to the valve, "are custom built. We engineer both sides for specific tasks."

I sat back and digested what he was saying. "All right. So Parks wanted a custom app that worked on both ends of the signal. What do they do?"

"They release salt water into a container of fresh water."

"That's it?"

"Basically. Steffan Parks has done a lot of work with desalination systems, and a lot of that research involves controlling the ratio of fresh to salt water. So he wanted a device that would work for a large water treatment system. He would mix salt water with the fresh, and then use his methods to purify the whole thing. But he needed to remotely control the saturation level of salt."

I rubbed my hand against my chin and jaw, looking down

at the fancy tiled floor between my feet. Salt water to fresh water. Controlling the amount of salt that entered the treatment tanks. And . . .

Of course. This made complete sense. All those years of publishing papers on desalination work, all those projects the government paid for; it all created a perfect backdrop for what Parks was planning now. Certainly no one would question his order for a control valve into a water treatment plant. And his demand that it stay hush-hush wouldn't raise an eyebrow, either. Big science was big money, and intellectual property thieves abounded.

"You worked on both sides, correct?" I asked.

He nodded.

"So the command portion would simply be an app on his phone or tablet. What about the other side?"

"Yeah,that was the tricky part," Guy said. "We had to develop software that would work with a specially-built valve. See, most of the stuff we've talked about is all digital. Simple electrical signals tell your thermostat to kick on, and the thermostat does the real work along with the air conditioning system. For *this* project we had to work with a set of physical valves that Mr. Parks supplied so that it would produce the mechanical work, not just an electrical signal."

"And I assume you've made delivery of all this to Parks?"

He looked sheepish. "Yesterday."

"Do you have any of those valves still around?"

Guy hesitated, and I raised a threatening eyebrow.

"I'm sure we do," he said. "We took a handful of them to mess around with."

"Get me one," I said.

While he picked up a phone and placed a call to someone in his office, I stood and walked to the window. But I paid no attention to the view. My mind was on a valve system that Steffan Parks could now use to exploit a water treatment center. It wouldn't be salt water he released into a community's fresh water. It would be a derivative of tabun, the Nazi nerve agent. The same chemical used to murder three people in Santa Fe and one Q2 agent in Scottsdale.

Me.

CHAPTER NINETEEN

I t didn't look like much, but how many valves do? I went
from the AppaDabba offices to a pack-and-ship store, carefully swaddled the device in way too much bubble wrap, and
overnighted it to the geniuses working on the second floor of
the Q2 building in Washington. Inside the package was also
every scrap of information about the phone app that would
trigger the release.

Every few minutes I found myself checking my phone,
holding on to the belief I'd see a message from Jonas.

By one o'clock I was inside San Antonio's quaint but efficient airport, boarding a plane back to Phoenix. I had no proof
that's where the dirty deed was going down, but I stood a
better chance of digging up something there than I did
in Texas.

At least the conversation with Guy, the preppy techie, had
delivered some good intel. Parks was bent on introducing
poison into a city's water supply, and now we at least knew the
equipment he'd be working with. After buckling my seat belt
and lowering the window shade, I put on the noise cancelling

headphones I'd picked up in the concourse and settled in to think.

One thing that kept nagging me was the notion that additional players were involved. The fact that a third person may have poisoned the Marquart Labs employees in Santa Fe was a jolt. We'd assumed that Parks and Pradesh worked alone, two deranged scientists and lovers intent on murder and mayhem. If there was at least one more involved, who could say there weren't more?

Which brought me back to a sickening thought: How could we be sure we were dealing with only *one* target? Maybe it would be one to start, and then another, then another. The app developer had provided Steffan Parks with all the technical know-how he needed to employ his deadly chemical expertise. Would one major blow be enough to satisfy his lust for revenge, his insane demand for professional respect?

I didn't ponder the question for long.

The answer was no. Once would not be enough. Santa Fe had been an experiment, one with the secondary benefit of striking down an academic foe. The next event would be larger, deadlier, and worthy of every news source in the world.

Would a third, decisive blow cement his legacy? Just one brief meeting with him convinced me he wouldn't stop anytime soon.

Then I began mulling over my odd-couple pairing with Jonas Aiken. I'd taken him by gunpoint on a 900-mile joy ride and spent the majority of that time trying to understand his association with Parks. And then to finally crack the shell and discover his motivation was an obsession with Jayanti, an almost embarrassing puppy love? Strange. Even when faced with the harsh truth that she'd used him the entire time, he'd doggedly remained smitten.

He'd tipped off his crush that I — posing as Department of Defense rep Ed Phillips — might be on her trail, and we all know how that ended for me. So why the hell I was sitting here, on a Boeing 737, worried about *him*? I'd grown attached to him like you would to a pet, and I feared he was about to be put down. And yet when the time had come beneath that dark underpass, letting him go with Parks and Pradesh seemed like the right call. It was a supreme hunch, one I shouldn't second-guess. But I was anyway.

I still had confidence Jonas would come through. Maybe I *had* to have confidence because I'd placed so much faith in him.

The plane barreled down the runway and lifted off. Before a quick layover in Dallas I had an hour in the air to puzzle out other components of this case.

Assuming I was right, and the target city — at least the first one — was in Arizona, then what would it take for Parks to pull off his plan? He had his valves and he had the app to remotely operate them, and he had a homemade batch of poison. What he needed was access to a water supply.

But how would one go about gaining access to a facility like that? Security would be tight enough that they wouldn't let just anyone wander in and poke around.

At least I didn't think so. Who knew how those places operated?

I made a mental note for my first visit in the morning: A water treatment plant. No sense just guessing. And I'd have Poole arrange for every plant in Arizona to quietly step up their security measures for the time being.

The quiet aspect was important. If I'd learned anything in my years with Q2 it was the need to keep our investigations on the down-low. All it took was one copycat to hear an idea like this and they'd wanna see if they could get their names on the 24-hour news channels, too. It happens more than you think.

What if Parks had already figured out his access point? What if he had gallons of his poison already positioned, just awaiting the technology pack to make it all go?

And where would one store that much killer potion? It would take an awfully large supply to contaminate that much water.

Or would it?

Even through my headphones I heard the frustrated sigh escaping my lips. So many questions.

And there was still this potential third person on the opposing team. I doubted if Steffan Parks could actually recruit someone off the street into his plan; it would be another person who felt wronged. It might not even be a scientist, but just some other soul who had a beef with America and wanted to make a statement. A sick, repulsive statement, but a statement nonetheless.

After I'd joined Q2 one of my first official meetings with Quanta consisted of a long discussion about this very subject. She prepared me for the never-ending, relentless onslaught of people with grudges. *Everyone has a grudge, a slight they can't forgive or forget,* she said. *Most people live with it, bury it, or simply ignore it.*

But then, she told me, there are a few who are pathologically wired to seek their own warped form of justice. And when that justice involves the killing of large numbers of innocent people, Q2 must step in. Some might say we defend the defenseless, but that's not it exactly. It's more like we defend the unsuspecting.

We're not infallible, but the general public would freak out if they knew how many times a Q2 agent had prevented a catastrophe. Let's just say it happens several times a year. Sometimes with help from our buddies at another agency, like the FBI or NSA, sometimes through sheer, dogged determination to not let the bastards win.

Quanta once revealed that the psychological profile of an agent candidate must include one critical component: A maniacal competitive streak. The other law enforcement groups may or may not appreciate that quality, but at Q2 it's a requirement. You can be the at the top of your class in every other category, but if you don't have an innate desire to crush your competition at all times, then go peddle your resume to the CIA or your local state patrol.

And that's no knock on those guys; they're probably badasses in their own way. But there's competitive and there's *competitive*. You've probably known a few people in the latter category. Never enjoyed playing ping pong with them, did you?

It helps that in our case we're basically replaceable parts. Being hell-bent on winning is easier when you know you can always come back later to complete the job. That doesn't mean we're irresponsible with our host bodies, but knowing you have a spare sure takes some of the pressure off. Maybe juices that competitive spirit a touch more.

Apparently it was in my file somewhere that after not getting any scholarship offers to play football, I'd walked on at my university and tried out. With a hairline fracture in my leg. Taped it up, went out, and impressed the coaches enough to get an invitation to play.

Until my first practice two days later, when I creamed our star quarterback with a vicious — but legal — hit after he talked shit to me across the line of scrimmage. Hitting your own quarterback is frowned upon. I was kicked off the team.

It was just as well. I used the extra time to learn martial arts and take some advanced science classes, both of which later helped when I joined the military. And *that* specialized training, combined with an impressive combat record, led to my interview with Quanta.

So smearing that asshole QB with the big mouth ultimately got me this job.

Of course, he was drafted in the 2nd round and played seven years in the NFL, so he came out all right, too. He probably forgot that hit an hour after practice.

I never will.

That, my friend, is competitive.

I KNEW the next steps as soon as the plane touched down at DFW airport. With a quick plane change I'd be back in the air in 45 minutes. That left enough time to call Quanta.

"I'm sure there's at least one more person involved," I said, walking down the concourse to my new gate. "Maybe two. I doubt there's more than that, or Parks wouldn't be able to keep a lid on everything."

"Santa Fe?" she asked.

"Yes. That person probably didn't stick around town, though. Finding them might be too difficult right now. But the other one . . . we might have a shot there."

"What are you thinking?"

"If Parks is going to pull this off, he's going to need more help than Jayanti. He's going to need someone on the inside."

Quanta mused over this. "There are several water districts in Arizona, assuming you still think that's the target. And each district must have dozens of employees."

I'd spotted my gate, where people were just lining up to

begin boarding. "Yeah, I know, it's a lot of people. But maybe Poole and some helpers can cross-check all of them against anyone who's had a beef with a funding organization, or someone who's written anything combative about the government, or maybe been fired from a university lab."

"That's a tall order."

"Stopping this nut job is an even taller order. Any little break could make the difference."

There was a pause, and then she said, "And what about your friend, Aiken? I don't suppose you've heard from him, have you?"

I resisted the urge to respond with all-out snark. So far Quanta was right, and I had nothing substantial to show for my gambit with the skinny scientist. He was still on the loose, still embedded with the enemy, and, for all I knew, was toying with me.

"One vague text," I finally said. "But he'll come through."

"Hmm," was all she said in response. Once again, the disappointed parent.

"All right, I have to board in a minute. Tomorrow morning I'm going to start going door-to-door with water treatment plants in the Phoenix area. The sooner we can get on that cross-check of names the sooner I'll be able to narrow down the search on my end."

"Be sure to upload when you get in tonight."

"God, you're starting to sound like Poole."

We hung up. I walked over to the large floor-to-ceiling window and studied the plane parked at the gate, watching the frenetic activity going on around it. A squadron of workers, all with a specific task, each one critical to the success of the overall mission of the airline, moved in a choreographed dance of duty. Each individual unit had to be executed precisely or the plane would never even take off.

That was what Steffan Parks faced in his mission, too. His team of worker bees might be smaller, but their jobs had to be done to perfection for him to succeed.

I got the impression he was ready to taxi.

CHAPTER TWENTY

A mix-up at the car rental counter in Phoenix had me in a minivan. That was a first. The attendant said the mistake could be fixed in a few minutes, but I was tired and instead just went on my merry minivan way. It was okay as long as none of my spy friends saw me.

On the way to the hotel I checked my phone several times. No message from Jonas. That bastard. If he let me down I might shoot *him* before I took out Parks.

Exhaustion came on quickly. After sleepwalking through the hotel check-in, I pushed through the door of room 512 and barely got out of my clothes before collapsing onto the bed.

Quanta would have to wait until the morning to get her upload.

I was just falling asleep when my phone rang, startling me wide awake.

It was Jonas.

"You son of a bitch," I said, rubbing my eyes. "Where the hell are you?"

"I'm in Phoenix. Where are you?"

"I'm at a cemetery ordering your plot. What the hell took you so long to call?"

"What are you talking about? You think I can just excuse myself and say I have to call the Feds? Don't be stupid. I'm glad you got away from the beast, though. I wasn't really sure you would."

"He wasn't either, which is why he ended up in the river. If you're here, then—"

"Here?" he said. "You're in Phoenix, too?"

"Yeah. And that means we can meet. Tomorrow."

"I don't know . . ."

"I do. Tomorrow. Figure something out. If they went to the trouble of hauling your carcass back to Arizona they're not gonna kill you right away. At least for a while. You have news, right? Something?"

"I think so. All right. I'll get away. I'll say I have to go try to make things good with my wife."

I chortled. "That's actually pretty good. They won't wanna be anywhere near that mess. I have things to do, too, so let's say 11."

"Yeah, okay. But I need to get a new phone first, so my text will be coming from a different number."

"Why?"

He let out a long breath. "Because, secret agent, a couple of times I've thought they wanted to use my phone for something. Probably just to check things out. And if it's some third-grader's phone without Internet or anything—"

"Yeah, yeah," I said. "Fine. Text me by 10:30. And don't be late."

I lay back on the bed but now I was wired. He *thought* he had something. Of course, that was more than what *we* had.

After a few minutes I realized I'd now be up for a while. I

got out all my digital paraphernalia, curled up with the latest *People*, and uploaded.

THE CALL from Poole came at 6:15, right in the middle of a dream where I was being poisoned again, this time by Quanta. I'll let professional psychotherapists work that one out.

"Did I wake you?" she asked.

"Of course you woke me. Jesus, do you live at the office, Poole?"

"What? No, I have an apartment."

I had to laugh. Struggling to my feet I made my way to the bathroom, turning on the light and grimacing at the horrid sight in the mirror. This particular face would never really become comfortable to me. And that ear was disgusting.

"Okay, I'm gonna put you on speaker while I splash my face and try to return to the living. What do you have?"

She was obviously settling in before a computer screen. I distinctly heard clicks.

"We spent the night running down all of the science professionals working at various water treatment facilities in Arizona. There are many, as you might expect."

I began brushing my teeth.

"We still have a lot to run down, but so far six of them have conflicts in their background. Nothing extreme, but there. We've basically eliminated half of those because their work is pretty hands-off within minor water systems. The other three are more interesting."

"Okay," I mumbled through a mouth of paste.

"There's a man named Hart. He filed suit against his former university for loss of lab privileges. That was settled. He also sued his former employers for wrongful termination, and they also settled. He currently has a lawsuit pending against one of his professional organizations."

I spit into the sink. "What a pain in the ass. But probably not our guy."

"Why not?" Poole asked.

"His M.O. isn't violence. He uses lawyers as a weapon instead of poison to strike back at people. He *may* be a candidate here, but probably not a strong one. Who's next?"

"A woman named Oosterhaus. Censured by her university for what they called "injudicious conduct," and later fired from a government lab in Virginia."

"Oh, you know how much injudicious conduct turns me on," I said. "What'd she do? Pants the Dean?"

"The documents are sealed. So it'll take some digging." She paused. "What's 'pants the dean'?"

You had to love Poole. "Let's just say it's injudicious. Google Pantsing after we hang up. I'm interested in Ms. Oosterhaus. And the third?"

Poole clicked on something. "Name is Franks. Led a movement to abolish government involvement in his university's laboratories. Lots of protests and lectures, very anti-government. He's also written multiple pieces on the 'fraud of the grant system.' His words."

I left the bathroom and started the room's coffee maker. "How in the hell did these people land jobs at secure facilities like water treatment plants?"

"Traditional background checks wouldn't show any criminal activity," Poole said. "Their credentials are all fine, in terms of the work they've accomplished. They must've done well at their interviews."

I mumbled an agreement. But underneath all of this I felt a new concern, one I'd definitely address at my upcoming meetings with water officials. Just how tight was security at such vulnerable sites?

Poole and her helpers had more work to do. She'd text me links to files and information on the three prime candidates. It would be helpful to run their names past Aiken and see if any of them sounded familiar.

After ending the call I went back to bed and managed to sleep another hour. This time when I awoke I passed on room service and decided to go in search of an old-fashioned diner for breakfast. Some seriously bad food sounded seriously good.

Four blocks from the hotel I found just what I needed. They even had an old-fashioned, low-slung bar, with a saucy woman working behind it. She was as quick with a quip as she was with the coffee. While I devoured an omelet with a side pancake, I used a tablet to study up on water treatment facilities.

In the United States there were more than 16,000 publicly-owned plants, which pretty much took care of three-quarters of the population. The remainder were covered by either private firms or their own septic system. On an average day the country's wastewater systems treated more than 30 billion gallons of water. Which is great when everything is humming along.

But when a madman decides it's the most efficient way to make a point, you suddenly realize how susceptible we might be. We all just take for granted that what comes out of the tap will always be pristine. Nobody wants to think a simple glass of water could kill them. And policing 16,000 different sources had to be a nightmare.

Now I was anxious to continue my schooling with an actual engineer. By 9:30 I was being escorted back to the office of the administrator of one of Maricopa County's many plants.

He was a large, jovial fellow with a name to match. "Tiny Gonzales," he said, sticking out his hand.

The guy had to weigh 300 pounds. I shook his hand and smiled. "Hello Tiny. Eric."

He looked at the card I'd handed him — this one had an NSA logo on it — and was duly impressed. We sat down.

"What can I help you with?" he asked.

"We're looking into a possible threat against a water supply."

"*A* water supply? Which one?"

"That's the problem. We don't know. And it could all be a false alarm. But, as you know, Tiny, if we don't follow up it's all of our asses, am I right?"

He gave a deep, hearty chuckle. "What kind of threat are we looking at?"

"We don't know that for sure, either. I'm here to simply find out how your system works, and see where any vulnerable spots may exist. You could probably reel off a few of those without even thinking about it, couldn't you?"

His smile faded and he nodded. "Eric, there's not a plant in America that doesn't worry about this." He studied my face. "Want a quick tour?"

"I'd love one."

He pushed his large frame out of the chair and signaled for me to follow him down the hall. For the next 30 minutes I was treated to a behind-the-scenes look at everything that goes into cleansing, purifying, and delivering your tap water. It was almost beautiful how all of the components worked together.

There were various stages of filtration, the first to extract larger particles and debris, then finer levels that removed the smaller, nasty agents. There was actual water treatment, using algaecides and disinfectants, and several other stages, each designed to take wastewater and turn it back into drinking water. And it happened 24 hours a day, 365 days a year, constantly sifting, scrubbing, and sanitizing.

Toward the end of the tour I asked Tiny Gonzales a point-blank question.

"If someone wanted to contaminate a city's water supply, where would they be most likely to do it within the confines of a plant like this?"

He gave me a look that bordered on suspicion. I got the feeling he wanted another peek at my credentials. But after a moment of thought he gazed around and nodded.

"If someone could get inside, which would be damned difficult to do, I'd say they'd have to do it at the back end. After the filtration and sedimentation layers." He pointed toward the large room we'd just left. "Those containers? The water has to sit with the chlorine in order to permeate the supply. During times of normal usage it might be two hours, but during times of heavy volume it might only be half an hour."

He gave it some more thought. "Yeah. Probably either right before or right after the final doses of chlorine and fluoride are added. Those are the last stops before the water is pumped out."

I followed his gaze. "And there's nothing after that to check the safety of the water?"

"No." Then, glancing back at me, he added, "But I don't know how someone would sneak in here to do that. We have pretty tight security. Especially since 9-11."

I didn't want to ask him, but I had to. "All right. But suppose it was introduced into the water supply by an employee. How tight is *that* security?"

The look on his face told me all I needed to know.

THE TEXT CAME from an unfamiliar number. It was Jonas, who'd made good on his demand for a new phone. He wanted to meet at a bakery in Glendale, another of the Phoenix suburbs. Of course it was a food establishment; I imagined I'd be out a few bucks in order to stuff croissants and muffins into his bottomless pit of a stomach.

I texted back: *Make sure you're not followed.*

I got there at 11:15 and found him waiting. He stood up and steered me toward the counter. He'd already picked out what he wanted.

When we sat down with his large slice of carrot cake and my tea he started in.

"Here's what I know. The target is definitely somewhere in Arizona, and I think right here in the Phoenix area."

"And how do you know this?"

"I overheard Steffan talking to Jay. He said *'everything's here.'*"

I considered this. "Hell, Jonas, they could've intentionally let you snoop on their conversation, just to give you bullshit information."

"I don't think so."

"Where are they now? Are you staying with them?"

"No," he said. "They dropped me off at my place. I have no idea where they are. But they said to be available 24/7."

Not what I wanted to hear. "So *'everything's here.'* Does that mean it's already set up? Are the containers of poison already installed? What's the timeline?"

He took a large bite of his cake and talked through a full mouth. "The poison is definitely not in place yet. They're going to wait until just a few hours before they throw the switch. That way it can't be spotted and removed. In the meantime they've got their new timer system, and I guess they're wiring everything so it's ready to go at the same time. That's what the trip to San Antonio was all about."

"Listen, I need to know the exact plant. I'd just swoop in and pick up Parks and beat it out of him, but I'm afraid he's got a backup plan in place and will just rot in a cell before he reveals anything. And I don't want to see his goddamned smug face grinning through the bars while thousands of people die a miserable death."

Aiken looked thoughtful. "What if I can get Jayanti to open up?"

I sighed. "Jonas. Look, you're a big, romantic puppy dog. I get it. I'm the same way with my wife. But you don't understand what you're dealing with here."

"Yes, I—"

"No, you don't. You're a scientist and a hard worker and a husband — well, a shitty husband, as it turns out. But I'm the professional when it comes to this stuff. I've got a lot of experience with bad people. Your sweet Jayanti is not going to go soft. No amount of wooing by you is going to turn her. All right? Get that bullshit out of your head. You're an amateur."

"Which is what's gonna help me get the job done," he said. "The minute I turned you over at the Riverwalk they believed they could trust me." He pushed his empty plate toward the middle of the table. "And you're wrong," he said. "I can get her to turn. It's not too late."

"It *is* too late. She's already killed someone, dude. That's the epitome of too late."

This brought a glare but no argument.

I softened my tone. "And it's not just that, Jonas. You're going to get *yourself* killed. I can't fathom why they haven't yet, but if you keep screwing around, trying to play The Fixer, you're going to wind up with a few cc's of tabun in your bloodstream."

He shook his head. "All I've done is talk shit about you. I don't think they're suspicious of anything."

With a grunt I said, "Aren't they the ones who perfected Damnation Deniability? They probably see right through your shit-talk and realize what you're doing."

It was obvious from his expression he hadn't considered this. The same thoughts that bounced around my head were probably pinballing around his. Were they just toying with him? Did they really believe he was still an ally? There was no way of knowing.

"All right," I said. "Before you leave, have you heard of any scientists they might be working with? Any names they may have dropped?"

"Like who?"

I gave him the names Hart, Oosterhaus, and Franks. Aiken shook his head.

"No. But that doesn't mean they aren't working with them. I just don't get to hear very much about the actual plans. They keep me segregated from that."

Dammit.

"Okay. Any names at all? Anyone they might be communicating with?"

"Yeah. Their backup bodyguard is a guy named Troy something."

"That's very helpful. Troy something."

"Hey, I'll find out his last name. Stop giving me shit. Oh, and there's some other person I think they worked with in Santa Fe."

I sat forward, suddenly alert. "Yeah? Who's that?"

He concentrated. "I've only heard the name once, and it was before I met you. Something like . . ." His voice faded away.

I waited him out.

After a moment he said, "Maybe Bailey? I think some guy named Bailey. Or something like that."

"Definitely a guy?"

He thought about that. "Oh. No. I just assumed it was."

"Okay." What else could I say. "Keep your ears open. If you can get me the name of one person who may be on the inside, we'll know the treatment plant."

We stood up and faced each other awkwardly for a moment. Then, for the first time, we shook hands. This was one of the strangest partnerships I'd ever had. Truly an odd couple.

Before he left Aiken had me buy another piece of cake to go.

CHAPTER TWENTY-ONE

One thing about my job that sucks is how out of touch I get with current events. Once, while in-between bodies, my consciousness just lying in limbo within a computer hard drive, I missed a presidential election.

Sometimes I'd go weeks without hearing anything about my favorite sports teams. Then I'd spend an hour or two on a plane catching up and discovering our star player had injured his shoulder *again* and hadn't even played in the past month.

When your focus is preventing mass murder, your pop-culture peripheral vision takes a hit. Christina told me I'm probably lucky. But it's one of the reasons my uploading appointment with trash magazines was so exciting: *everything* was news to me.

After Aiken left I sat back down at the table in the bakery and noticed that the Super Bowl was only two weeks away. The last time I'd paid attention the season itself was barely halfway over.

I needed some time off.

Originally I'd planned on visiting another water treatment

plant in the early afternoon, but Tiny had taught me enough that I felt I had a good grasp on what we were dealing with. I trusted his detailed analysis, that contamination could best be accomplished in that final step of adding chlorine/fluoride. What better place to insert a killer concoction?

It also confirmed, at least in my mind, that an inside person was paramount to an operation this size. No way Parks, nor his murdering mistress, could get inside one of those facilities, especially toting the ingredients and tools necessary. If something didn't pop up soon on the names Poole had unearthed, we'd have to either keep digging for more or try another course altogether.

The two primary knaves in this case, after ditching Jonas, had once again gone underground, a development that had become as customary as it was aggravating. These two were able to live under the radar for short spurts of time, using false identities and untraceable forms of currency. Probably enormous amounts of cash. I'd seen it done before, often by foreign terrorists who'd snuck into the country. But amateur villains usually don't give enough thought or preparation to such tactics.

Parks and Pradesh had mastered it. If he'd seemed cocky during our quick exchange on the San Antonio Riverwalk, it's probably because he'd earned the right. We were chasing our tails as much as we were chasing him.

I finished my coffee and left. One block away a park was mostly deserted, and I settled onto the bench of a picnic table to place a call to Washington.

"You met with Aiken?" Quanta asked without small talk.

"Yeah. They brought him to town, dropped him off, and vanished. His gut tells him the target is definitely around here, though."

"And the names that Poole uncovered?"

"They mean nothing to him. Oh, he did have two other names. One is additional muscle. Troy. What can you do with that?"

She made a discouraged sound. "I'll pass it along."

"More importantly, he said there could be another team member who either helped in Santa Fe or was intricately involved. Bailey."

"Only one name again?"

I laughed. "And he wasn't even sure about *that*. All right, so he's the worst goddamned informant in history. But he's the only one we've got at the moment. The reluctant informant who's in love with one of the perps. Could be the most screwed-up case ever. Thanks for giving this one to me."

Quanta sighed, her other discouraged sound. I knew she was disappointed in my lack of progress, but at least she kept that low appraisal to herself. For now.

"Listen," I said. "There's another angle to all this that I think we should place more attention on. That's motive."

She hesitated, then said, "You think there's a motive other than the ones we've discussed?"

"No, I don't mean his ultimate motive for revenge. I'm talking about how and why he chose his target city."

This was greeted with silence, so I kept going.

"It just crossed my mind as I was talking with Aiken, the way he said he was pretty sure about the Phoenix area. I started wondering: *Why here*?"

Quanta offered an answer. "Could it just be the most convenient in terms of the inside help you described? If he has someone already working at a water treatment plant, it simply makes it easier."

I tapped a finger on the picnic table and watched a woman

walking two massive dogs through the park, almost being pulled along by them. Quanta could be right, but . . .

"Yeah, maybe," I said. "But think about Parks for a minute. Everything he's done has been calculated. He chose to work in desalination because it offered a way to become a hero world-wide and gain funding. He didn't choose that field for humanitarian reasons; he chose it because he thought it provided the quickest route to fame and wealth.

"When those efforts didn't pan out the way he expected, he hatched a plan to get back into the good graces of the government. How? By creating a toxin for the military. Again, something he was sure would be a priority for a country fighting ongoing battles around the globe. It was another shortcut back into the money. But it was vehemently rejected, as it should've been.

"And then, when he was outright humiliated by a fellow scientist for the work that had brought him the only real success he'd managed in his career, he took out his accuser. Murdered him and the people around him."

I smiled at the woman with the dogs as she walked by and gave me a small wave. I lowered my voice until she was out of range.

"Now he wants to show the country we were wrong in not working with him. So why here? Knowing Parks, he chose his target with a specific reason in mind. I don't think he's someone who just throws a dart at a map and attacks the first city that comes up."

Quanta said, "Granted, all of that makes sense. The problem is we have nothing to go on regarding that particular motive."

"Right. But I'm saying it's probably there. Somewhere. Something that makes Steffan Parks want to lash out at a sprawling city in the desert. It can't be a random choice. That's not his style."

Her sound of silence carried the kind of weight that told me I'd redeemed myself, at least in part. The idea of this particular motive hadn't even registered with me until today, but I quickly latched on to it as a way of solving the case. Why the hell would this deranged scientist want to poison a city in Arizona? We'd been chasing after him, trying to prevent a calamity, without slowing down to investigate the *why*?

Yes, revenge is a motivating factor in many heinous crimes. But even revenge can be broken down into constituent parts.

"Very good, Swan," was all Quanta said. But that was enough. She'd be on it.

BACK AT MY hotel I invested another 90 minutes into uploading. The chats with both Aiken and Quanta were too precious to be lost. Afterward I grabbed a quick nap, then at four o'clock changed into shorts and a long-sleeved running shirt and went out to work up a sweat.

For most of the run I tried to keep my mind off the case. Sometimes you can just overthink something to the point where it becomes a blur of coalesced color. I needed to flush out everything in order to see it all with fresh eyes. That's easier said than done, especially when deadlines loom. But I knew, if successful, it would help.

I spent the first mile thinking about Christina and a vacation long overdue. We'd mentioned the UK several times, and even plotted the non-touristy spots we longed to see. But those thoughts tended to be more depressing than uplifting, so I shook them away and shifted into a faster gear. I needed at least 7-minute miles in order to feel in adequate shape. Not every body I occupied had the proper conditioning to maintain that pace, but this one did. I silently offered appreciation to the convict I'd never know, the man who'd sacrificed his body for me.

That thought spun me down a different path entirely. For several years I'd essentially leased bodies, using them up before a new shell became necessary. There was always a period of acclimation, and no guarantee that my host would take to my physical requirements without a revolt.

I'd had knees go out, various aches and pains within joints for unknown reasons, and breathing difficulties that could be merely irritating or downright dangerous.

Then there were the quirks you tried hard to just accept. One might have a strange twitch in the face or hands, while another might get caught up in embarrassing sneezing fits. Recently I'd been in a body with the worst freakin' tastebuds of all time; all my favorite foods tasted like shit in that mouth. I couldn't bitch about these issues to anyone — well, except my wife, and even she barely tolerated my whining. Her classic reply was, "Yeah, when you start having cramps, I'll weep for you."

That was the last time I complained to her.

It had become a problem, too, in a way none of the Q2 scientists ever considered, and something I'd never made the mistake of bringing up. Because so many of the bodies had problems or idiosyncrasies, whenever I found myself in a pretty good one I worried that it affected my decision-making.

Think about it: If the temporary body you're occupying is a pain in the ass, you're less likely to worry about losing it. Conversely, get yourself a fairly nice one and you might be tempted to be less aggressive. You know, throttle back and play it a bit more carefully.

Just like someone driving a 15-year-old beater car will be more carefree than someone driving an Aston Martin. When I got a good body I sometimes worried about behaving like the person who parks clear across the parking lot to keep from getting a door ding.

This one was pretty good. It even tolerated my sprints. So far the only problem I'd had was occasional heartburn, but I didn't need spicy queso *all* the time.

I'D JUST BEGUN the return trip to the hotel, running through a neighborhood of pricey homes and daydreaming about retiring into one of them, when my phone vibrated in my front pocket.

It was Jonas.

"Yeah," I said, pulling up and breathing heavily.

His voice was panicked. "That Troy guy came for me. You've gotta get me outta here."

"Whoa, slow down. What do you mean he *came for you*? Where are you?"

I heard a door pushed open with a bang, then Aiken was obviously running.

"He's . . . he's at my building. I just happened to be standing near a window and saw him park across the street."

For a moment phone noise overrode anything he was saying. I yelled his name twice, but there was only the sound of furious activity for a while. Then, out of breath, he came back on the line.

"Shit. He's chasing me. Wait. I think . . . I think I may have lost him." He coughed twice. "Jesus, Eric, you have to help me."

"I will help you," I said. I began running back toward my hotel, then stopped and realized that would take too long. I'd call for a ride share.

"Jonas, stay hidden. Tell me exactly where you are and then hunker down, be quiet, and hold on while I get a ride."

He rattled off cross streets in the Glendale area. It sounded like he was crying.

"Okay, hang on," I said. Opening one of my ride-share apps, I requested a car.

"Jonas, you still there?" I asked. "Where's this Troy guy?"

His answer was in the form of a whisper. "I think he's half a block away. He's looking behind every wall and bush. Shit. Shit, Eric, he's getting closer. I have to go."

"Wait wait wait!" I yelled. "I have to know which way you're going."

He'd hung up.

Pop culture portrays spies and secret agents as purveyors of miracles. Jason Bourne or Ethan Hunt, in my situation, would've absconded with some innocent bystander's motorcycle and zipped across crowded city squares and down pedestrian tunnels to reach their destination in the nick of time.

Real life? I was standing there, cursing, sweating, and waiting for my ride. Sexy, right?

Screw Ethan Hunt and his fictional magic tricks.

Four minutes later the ride pulled up, a woman driving a Subaru. I jumped in and gave her the cross streets. She said it'd be about 20 minutes.

"There's an extra 50 bucks in it for you if you make it 15," I said.

She gave me a sideways glance. "Sir, I don't break the law for anyone. Please buckle your seatbelt. There's water in the door cup holder, if you like."

Great. I'd rustled up a solid citizen.

She came to complete stops, she stopped at yellow lights, and her music playlist must've been titled, "*I Have The Saddest Life in History.*"

About halfway there my phone rang again. It was Jonas.

"Where are you?" I asked.

"Shit, Eric, he's right there. And he has a gun."

"He has a gun *out*? Jesus, where are you, Jonas?"

The Subaru driver's head snapped around toward me. She actually hit the brakes and acted like she was going to stop. I pointed a finger at her and yelled, "I'm with the FBI. Do *not* stop this car, do you hear me? Floor it. Let's go. This is a matter of life and death."

She began shaking, but hit the accelerator again.

I couldn't believe I'd actually said *a matter of life and death*. Christ.

Into the phone I said, "Jonas, I have to know where you are. Tell me."

He stammered for a moment, and I could tell he was still crying. "It's . . . it's called Dust Devil Park."

I looked at the driver. "Do you know a Dust Devil Park?"

"No," she said, almost in tears herself.

"Shit," I muttered. I pulled it up on my phone and gave her basic directions. "Just get me as close as you can. Hurry."

She actually sped up.

"Jonas, I'm 7 minutes away. Are you hiding?"

"I'm trying. It's not easy."

"Just stay on the line with me." After a pause, I said, "Listen, have you learned anything else?"

His reply was the loudest he could manage while trying to remain hidden. "You bastard! I'm on the verge of being killed and you still want information? Save my ass and I might help you. Otherwise piss off."

I took a breath. "Hey. I'm almost there. Tell me this: Why is Steffan targeting Phoenix? He has to have told you something."

"No, asshole. He hasn't. I gotta go."

Before I could argue with him the line was dead again.

The Subaru driver actually rolled through a stop sign and pulled up next to the park. I threw a couple of $20 bills at her as a tip and jumped out.

That was the moment I realized something very important.

I didn't have *my* gun.

I mean, I'd been on a run. It's not often you need to be armed for that, unless you're in Baltimore.

Dust Devil wasn't that big. There was a skate park, currently empty because of the chill, a typical modern playground built for bubble-wrapped kids, and a covered pavilion-type area with a few teenagers, probably vaping. The only trees to speak of were sparse and widely scattered. Certainly no place to hide a terrified scientist, no matter how skinny he was.

Then I saw the restrooms on the far side. The same kind you saw at every city-run park.

I ran toward them, just as a man in jeans and a hoodie edged up to them. It had to be Troy. Even from a distance I could tell he had one hand in a pocket of the hoodie. I slowed to a jog, trying to seem as innocuous as possible. Just a harmless citizen, out for a run in the park.

Aiken, amateur that he was, had opted to hide in the most obvious place possible. Instead of staying in plain view, blending in with the crowd, he'd sequestered himself in a small, enclosed space. The sound of a gun might not even escape the concrete walls.

I grabbed my phone and called him. He didn't answer.

Still a hundred yards away I saw the killer push open the door of the men's room and slip inside. I picked up speed. But a moment later he was back outside and I slowed again. He wasn't leaving. He seemed perplexed.

Then he and I came to the same conclusion at the same time and I began sprinting again.

He moved over a few feet and shoved his way into the ladies room.

Seconds later I was proved wrong; you *could* hear shots through the concrete. There were three of them total, two quick ones, then a third to be sure.

I got to the door just as Troy emerged. In that instant I recognized him from the hotel surveillance video, where my body had been evacuated in a wheelchair. Troy had been the guy helping Cox.

Without breaking stride I threw myself into him like a middle linebacker and crushed him against the concrete wall. He let out a grunt as his head and shoulders made impact. The gun he'd held fell to the ground.

But he was good. Recovering immediately, he adopted a martial arts stance and, shaking off the initial blow, he created a little bit of space between us. It would be hand to hand.

I thought. Until he pulled out the knife.

Shit, nothing could ever just be easy. These guys loved their knives.

That first contact and resulting grunts had attracted the attention of a couple walking nearby. Now they were riveted, seeing two grown-ass men squaring off in combat. The woman had pulled out a phone and was undoubtedly calling 9-1-1.

"C'mon, asshole," Troy said, circling, the knife held like a pro.

"You're better than Cox," I said, squinting at him. "Why weren't you the first team?"

"I *am* the first team," he said, and slashed. It caught me along the chest, barely. I felt a slight trickle of blood.

"If you're this good with a knife," I said, "why shoot Jonas?"

He seemed amused by my conversation. "Because someone requested I put a bullet in his big pie hole."

"Steffan actually said *pie hole*? That doesn't sound like him."

He shifted position and brought the knife up again, this time just missing my right arm. The son of a bitch knew what he was doing. And he was obviously done talking.

I backed up and found myself against the concrete wall, cut off. I may have actually muttered, "Oh, shit."

This brought a wicked smile to Troy's face, and he prepared to finish me.

About that time one of the bystanders yelled, "Hey!" It didn't exactly distract my opponent, but it registered with him and gave me the split second I needed.

Feinting to my right, then dipping to my left, I sent a roundhouse kick against his wrist. The knife clattered to the pavement. Without waiting, I lunged and hit him in the jaw with a forearm. He was strong, and retaliated. His powerful right would've caught me square on the chin if I hadn't deflected it.

That's when I bent down and delivered another kick, connecting with his throat. His eyes popped and he staggered back a step. I threw a hard right into his face, breaking his nose. But as he fell backward onto the ground, he landed right next to the knife. My only defense was to pounce on him and we were soon engaged in a wrestling match with the blade. The bystanders were now both screaming.

I felt a streak of panic when it seemed like he was about to wrest control of the knife and drive it into me. At the last moment I twisted, gained a grip on his hand holding the knife, and plunged it into his chest. He let out a gasp, and blood squirted from his mouth.

Unsatisfied, I retrieved the blade and shoved it in again, this time into his heart. A death sigh escaped his lips and he went limp.

I rolled over and lay back on the ground, bleeding and breathing hard.

One of the witnesses yelled, "Hey, man! What the hell?"

CHAPTER TWENTY-TWO

It took all of one minute before I heard the sirens. Still on the ground, and with the witnesses careful to not get too close — who could blame them? — I called Poole and requested Sanitation. There had to be at least one nearby in a city this size.

That department had an official name, which wasn't important. Internally we called them Sanitation because their speciality was cleaning up messy incidents, like the one lying next to me with a knife sticking out of his chest. They would swoop in and deal with law enforcement and, if necessary, politicians who got uppity when it came to violence in their district.

I had no idea how they did it, but their repair skills were off the charts. They'd scrubbed more than a few sticky situations for me.

The police car now squealing to a stop would disgorge one or two officers who'd start by pulling their guns on me, and then would want to haul my ass in. I couldn't have that, and would need to stall them until my help arrived.

The call with Poole lasted less than 20 seconds. I told her I needed Sanitation at a place called Dust Devil Park in Glendale, Arizona, and time was of the essence. She didn't even say goodbye before disconnecting and going to work.

Sometimes Q2 operated like the best well-oiled machine in the world. I certainly needed that at the moment.

As expected, the lone police officer, who looked to be about 25 years old, went on alert when he saw the body and me next to it. I'd raised myself to a sitting position and had my hands held high, saving him the instruction.

"Before you say anything," I told him, "I'm with the FBI." Nobody would, or could, know what the hell Q2 was. We usurped the FBI's name all the time. "I have no identification, so I don't blame you for being skeptical. But one of my fellow agents is on the way and should be here within half an hour. Understood?"

He responded by pointing his gun at me and calling for backup.

A small crowd had now gathered and the officer had his hands full keeping me covered and the crowd back. At least he was cool enough to converse with me.

"Is he dead?" he asked.

"God, I hope so," I said, "because I went to a lot of trouble and contributed my own blood." I nodded to my left. "I believe you'll also find a body in the women's toilet. I haven't confirmed that, but this gentlemen shot him in the head. At least he said he did, and I heard the shots. Three of them. The gun is over there."

There was a little more back and forth, but the young officer was stuck. He couldn't go into the restroom to confirm my claim without risking me running away, so we waited. When the backup arrived — not one, not two, but three police cars, a fire truck, and an ambulance — relief washed over the first cop's face.

What happened in the next few minutes was standard protocol. I was yanked to my feet, and after it was determined that my wound wasn't fatal or even remarkably serious, I was pushed face-first against the wall, frisked, and cuffed behind my back. Someone read me my rights. Another cop came out of the bathroom and announced that, indeed, there was a second victim in a stall, missing most of his head.

Shit. As strange as our relationship was, I'd really grown fond of Jonas. What a pisser to die in a filthy restroom in a crappy little park.

Another car pulled up, of the unmarked variety. A police lieutenant strode up to the scene, and after a quick conversation with the first cop, walked over to me.

"You say you're FBI? But no ID?"

"I was out for a run and trouble found me. My ID is back at the hotel. But I have someone on the way. Should be any minute. Can we wait for them? And while we're waiting can someone please put some ointment on this cut? It stings like a mother."

He studied my face and must've felt it couldn't hurt to wait a few minutes. He looked down at the body.

"Who's this guy?"

"His first name is Troy and I don't care anymore what his last name is. We're working a case in this area and he's some hired muscle for a very bad person. I'd rather not say more at the moment."

"You might have to say a *lot* more, my friend."

Another car pulled up and a man and woman, dressed impeccably, flashed identification to get past the perimeter the cops had set up. These two new arrivals ignored me and walked directly up to the lieutenant. Again the badges came out, and, after a conversation I couldn't hear, the police lieutenant ordered my cuffs removed.

Bless Poole's heart.

An EMT was summoned. She removed my shirt and went to work cleaning up and disinfecting my wound. It wasn't as bad as it could've been, but it one place it required a few stitches. She sat me down on a bench, deadened it, then sewed me up, all the while stealing glances at my head.

Finally curiosity won out and she asked, "What happened to your ear?"

"I have no idea," I said.

She laughed. "So you just woke up one day and it was like that?"

"Pretty much."

There was no more chit-chat, but I liked these people; none of this *you've got to get to a hospital*. See it, sew it, shoo me away.

The crew from Q2 Sanitation had spoken in hushed tones with the police lieutenant the entire time I was being treated. Now the woman nodded for me to follow her while the man stayed behind and continued the conversation.

Back at their car she looked from me to the crime scene and back again.

"Do you need any further medical attention?" When I assured her I didn't she asked, "What about transportation? Can you get back to where you need to go, or will I need to drive you?"

"I can get back. Thanks for the help." I explained who Aiken was, *where* he was, and his importance to the case. She took no notes and I knew she didn't need to. Sanitation people were complete badasses in every way.

And that was it. With just a nod and not another word, she left me and rejoined her partner. A pretty standard interaction with that secretive department.

I pulled out my phone and called for a ride.

BACK IN MY room I took a long shower, carefully cleaning around the new red racing stripe running across my chest. Under the pounding hot water I allowed myself a few minutes to grieve for poor, love-struck Aiken. He'd gone from naive accomplice to wanna-be helper before settling into some vague middle ground.

Now he was dead. And I had no more concrete information than when I'd returned to Phoenix. Just another name which might not even be right, and a connection that was completely unknown.

I didn't know where Steffan Parks and Jayanti Pradesh were hiding, and I didn't know which water treatment plant could soon release deadly poison to an unsuspecting public.

I'd now eliminated two of Steffan's goons, so he'd need replacements. The next encounter would undoubtedly involve someone with more advanced skills in the thuggery department, and Troy had been pretty good. Parks had to know he was no longer playing in the minor leagues.

Once out of the shower I ordered food and propped myself up on the bed. I called Christina and left a voicemail with a gooey goodnight and assurances that I missed her. I really did. Surviving a death match usually brought out my drippy tendencies, regardless of the fact that being on the losing side was a temporary setback for me. It still triggered some evolutionary need to reflect and appreciate.

I hoped I'd never evolve out of that. Holding on to my little sliver of humanity through all of these various embodiments had recently become an obsession. Christina represented an anchor point. The day I stopped thinking of her when I was close to being killed would signal my transformation into a monster.

Of course, a cynic might deduce that Q2's insistence that field agents never enter into a long-term relationship — especially marriage — suggested they *wanted* us to make that transformation. Monsters may be scary, but they're less likely to suffer from emotional baggage. I was designed as a killing machine; machines aren't supposed to have a heart.

And wasn't that the issue with Data, the android on one of those Star Trek shows? He wanted to be more than, as he put it, a collection of circuits and sub-processors.

Was Q2 pushing me in the opposite direction? Would I make a better employee if I didn't rush to call my wife after almost getting killed?

Okay, I probably would. I could damn them for their intent — if it truly *was* their intent — but even my emotional, sappy mind recognized the superior position such a shift would bring about. In fact, the truth was that I was probably just one step along the way to fully autonomous artificial intelligence in human form.

Robot killers. Something akin to the *Terminator* and *Westworld*, to name some pop culture examples. Throw in HAL, the killer computer from *2001: A Space Odyssey*, and you see that we have a long history of imagining artificial intelligence that does dirty work.

And we often end up creating what we first imagine.

When the food arrived I was almost too tired to eat. I managed a few bites of my club sandwich before shutting off the light and navigating a tortured, restless sleep.

IN THE MORNING I got a call from Quanta.

"So you got yourself cut," she said without inquiring as to how I felt. "And lost another asset."

"He was a good guy," I said with a little more mustard than I'd intended. "I'm sorry he's gone."

"We can assume he was followed to his meeting with you yesterday. That's when they confirmed he was an impediment to their plan."

I let out a resigned breath. "Yeah. Probably. I specifically told him to be careful about that, but Jonas was too naive when it came to Parks and way too trusting of Pradesh. I don't think he ever believed she'd hurt him."

"So we can now write off your decision in San Antonio as flawed. You should've grabbed Parks when you had the chance."

I tamped down my temper. It wouldn't do to piss off the boss right now, no matter how much I disagreed with her. Instead of erupting I said, "I don't think so. We never would've found out about this Bailey person, or whatever their name is."

"You think Aiken's life was a good trade for a murky name?"

"Depends on if we're able to catch Bailey or whoever he or she is. If that saves hundreds of lives, then yeah, I guess it was a good trade." My voice was getting chippy again. I changed the subject. "Where are we with that motivation we talked about? Have we isolated a reason why Steffan Parks might choose an Arizona target?"

"That's why I called. Your thought process in this area, at least, may have paid off."

"So I'm not a total screw-up, is that what you're saying?"

"Not totally." Most people would have a twinkle in their voice when they said this. Quanta stated it as fact.

"You mentioned Parks and his galvanizing moments," she said. "He does have a history of lashing out directly at people he feels have harmed him. His murder of Leon Haas is but one example."

"Right," I said. "So something associated with Arizona, or specifically the Phoenix area, had to inspire him to bring his poison here. What was it?"

Quanta said, "We went back over his history with the United States government. Since winning his awards he'd been very well compensated through grants and other programs. Most of it quite lucrative, actually.

"But when things began to fall apart, those programs were gradually cut back and then completely eliminated. The killing blow, so to speak, was when he lost a substantial, multi-year grant for research and development of one of his desalination devices."

I'd been staring out my hotel room window, listening to this. Now I sat down. "And?"

"And the woman who led the committee that eventually revoked his grant was a representative by the name of Suzanne Thresh. Congresswoman Thresh also delivered the censure of Steffan Parks when he submitted his plan for a military application of his tabun-laced poison."

"Uh-huh," I said, now riveted. "Let me guess: Congresswoman Thresh is from Arizona."

"That's correct," Quanta said. "And she's scheduled to speak at a fundraising dinner in Mesa tomorrow night."

CHAPTER TWENTY-THREE

I sat back in my chair, absorbing this news.

We had no proof this was *the* connection we were looking for. But it was all we had and, at least in my mind, it was everything. And it might shrink our search area from an entire state to a suburb of Arizona's most populous city.

Mesa itself was not tiny by any measure. With more than half a million people it was not only the largest suburb in the country, it was one of the largest cities, period.

And now it might be ground zero for a madman.

Quanta and I discussed this briefly. She stressed that nothing was confirmed yet, and that it was still possible another city would be the target. But I could tell she was equally confident that we'd found our motivating factor.

We had to be *sure*. There were too many lives at risk to ignore other possibilities.

"What about the three suspected accomplices you told me about? Hart, Oosterhaus, and Franks. One of them must work for Mesa Water."

She let out a frustrated breath. "No. Hart is in Tucson,

Oosterhaus is in Chandler, and Franks is in Phoenix. All three of them have been checked in terms of criminal record, and, other than speeding tickets and other minor infractions, they're all clean."

"Shit," I muttered. "They could've made this a lot easier."

We hung up. I looked at the remains of my barely-touched dinner from the night before and realized how hungry I was. Waiting around for room service was out of the question. I got dressed and went downstairs to the hotel restaurant for some overpriced French toast and copious amounts of coffee.

Just as I was sopping up a puddle of syrup with the last piece of toast, I sensed a presence next to my table. Looking up it took me a moment before the name came back to me.

"Agent Kowalczyk. This has to be the most remarkable coincidence in history. You're staying at this hotel, too?"

She smirked at my dripping sarcasm.

"Because," I said, setting down my fork and wiping the corner of my mouth with a napkin, "there's no way you'd be assigned to help me here in Arizona without someone telling me. Right?"

She pulled up a chair and sat down.

"Don't be mad at me, Eric. I have to follow orders just like you. You *do* follow orders, don't you? Or are you the wild mustang we always read about, the maverick who goes his own way?"

I answered by sipping my coffee in silence.

"For what it's worth," she said, "I'm not trying to horn in on your assignment. I was just told the agent I worked with in San Antonio might need another set of eyes and ears."

"Good thing you have a full set of each. What else were you told?"

"That the suspects we dealt with in Texas are now in

Phoenix and perhaps attempting to poison a large number of people. They said you'd fill me in on the rest."

I grunted. "Oh. So I'm supposed to finish the briefing, too."

"Might make it easier for me to help if I'm not guessing." She paused, then added softly, "Look, I'm sorry if you're angry. But I didn't ask to be sent here."

She was right, and I was being an ass for no reason. I just hated it when Quanta sprang things on me. She tended to do that when she felt I'd dropped the ball. Which, if I looked at things from *her* perspective, I could grudgingly understand.

I tossed my napkin on the table. "All right. It's just a surprise, that's all. I'll pull up my big boy britches and get over it. Things have just been . . . challenging in the last 24 hours."

This produced an empathetic look from Kowalczyk. Professional operatives, regardless of the agency, all dealt with the same challenges I'd hinted at. When someone had a bad day, everyone knew what that usually meant.

"Unless you're in a hurry, I'll get some coffee, too, and you can give me the highlights," she said. "I just flew in and I'm pretty exhausted."

"Of course." I caught the attention of the server and had him bring a fresh pot to the table.

Over the next 20 minutes I explained as much of the case as I could, leaving out certain elements that Kowalczyk — Kat, if I remembered correctly — wasn't privy to. My murder in Scottsdale was one example. Anything about my agency, for that matter.

Much of the background on Parks she'd been told; the killings in Santa Fe, however, were news to her. When I got to the part about Jonas's death in the public restroom she cringed.

"That's a shame," she said. "I only had to babysit him for a while, but he was a likable guy, in a dorky kind of way."

I nodded. "Got a bit too attached myself. And I'm supposed to know better than that." Taking a deep breath I plunged forward. "So now we're dealing with Congresswoman Thresh coming to town. All the signs point to Parks planning something spectacular with her appearance."

"What do *you* think?"

"I think it makes more sense than assuming he just picked a city out of a hat. But really, I don't see that we have much choice. We can't cover dozens of water plants. We're going to reinforce security at every treatment plant in and around Mesa.

"And when did you say Thresh is here?" she asked.

"Tomorrow night. That gives us less than 36 hours to save the day."

I fell silent after that, deep in thought. Kowalczyk picked up on my mood.

"You seem perplexed," she said. "Something else bothering you?"

"Yeah. It's too easy."

"What do you mean?"

It took me a moment to put my thoughts into words. "Think about it. Parks has known we were on his trail for a few days now. He has to know we've figured out his beef with the congresswoman. And with all that, he has to know we'll have security teams three deep around every place he could try his poison trick."

Kat ran a finger around the top of her coffee cup, considering this. Then she said, "Maybe we're thinking too big. What if Parks isn't staging some bombastic act of terrorism, but instead just wants to take out Thresh. Maybe find a way to poison her at the banquet."

"Maybe."

"But you don't think so."

I shrugged. "Look, we don't really know shit, and we haven't from the get-go. Everything we've learned has been stitched together from tiny pieces here and there. It's one of the most frustrating cases I've handled. It would be one thing if we knew for sure what Parks had planned. But we don't know what or where."

I sat back and ran a hand through my hair. "No, it has to be something big. Otherwise he wouldn't have had that special device developed in Texas. That means he's up to more than just poisoning one water glass."

With that I picked up my own glass of water on the table and examined it. "I don't like having to react every time. It would be nice to be proactive just once on this case."

Kowalczyk nodded. She mixed some half-and-half into her fresh cup of coffee and stirred it thoughtfully for a moment. "So what the hell do we do next?" she asked.

I sat back. "Kat, that's the best question yet. Part of me believes the next move isn't ours."

"What do you mean?"

"There's something about Parks and Pradesh that makes me think I'm going to hear from one of them. The more they live this lifestyle, the more I think they want to flaunt it."

"The downfall of most idiotic criminals," Kat said.

"He knows we're scrambling for anything right now. And since he's lost another team member — this Troy guy — Parks will probably want to put on an act that it doesn't trouble him."

My new partner laced her fingers together on the table and asked, "What do you need me to do?"

I gave it some thought before answering. "I'll tell you what; you know those potential allies of Parks who work in the water treatment industry?"

"You want me to check them out?"

"Yeah. In fact, would you go and actually talk with a couple of them? Hart strikes me as just a loudmouth crybaby, plus he's down in Tucson. I think we can back-burner him for the moment. But the other two, Oosterhaus and Franks, could be candidates."

"And where are they?"

"Chandler and Phoenix. Maybe they have nothing to do with Parks, but an eyeball-to-eyeball meeting can stir things up. Remember, none of the people involved in this were professional criminals before all this started. They're supposedly just nerdy scientists. A visit from an FBI agent could shake one of them up to the point where you get something useful."

"Okay, I'll get right on it."

I thanked her and said I'd forward their names and departments.

We got up to leave, and she put a hand on my forearm.

"Oh, someone said to tell you hello. He would've been the one flying here to help you but he's tied up with another case. Said he worked with you recently, though."

"Who's that?"

"Agent Fife."

I had to laugh. "That son of a bitch. Ask him if he's getting better at being on time."

ANOTHER RUN SOUNDED GOOD, especially since the one the day before had ended in such a nasty way. But it also felt like time had become too precious. A workout would have to wait until everything played out.

Instead I sat down at the desk in my room and began

making notes the old-fashioned way. On a piece of hotel stationery I scribbled out a few columns. At the top of the first I put *Santa Fe*; next to that *Arcetri*; and finally *Mesa/Thresh*.

For the next hour I listed what we knew — even if it was scant information — below each heading. Regardless of its perceived importance, it went on the page. It was mostly a depressing exercise, but one that had served me well in the past. Many times a clue or vital tidbit hid within notes like these, and it took actually looking at them to make something click.

This was the real work of an agent, anyway. Talking with Christina I once compared it to a football game, where the vast majority of the clock was spent in the huddle, walking back to the huddle, or just standing around. If you condensed all the plays, I told her, a 60-minute NFL game — which takes about three hours in real time — had less than 11 minutes of action.

You invest three hours of your life to savor those 11 minutes.

An agent for Q2 was expected to think his/her way through the bulk of a case just to get into a position where the action counted. We didn't spend all day fighting criminals; most of our time was spent figuring out where the hell they were.

The Santa Fe column intrigued me. We'd assumed that was just a layover for Parks and Pradesh, a quick revenge killing before focusing on the main event. Now I wondered if there was more that could be attached to those deaths. Specifically, the importance of the person or persons who'd done the deeds. Was the same person responsible for the Marquart Labs murders and the killing of David Torres? Was it a small team?

And would Stacey Haas be the next to go? Did we need to warn her, maybe even hide her for the time being?

All of these thoughts shifted my attention to the next

column. I thought about this group of pissed off scientists, calling themselves by a name that, to them, represented the ultimate in repression and humiliation of the sciences. When Aiken first told me about the Arcetri I hadn't assigned much concern to them or their 'cause.' Now there were four more bodies added to the count, more than doubling the Santa Fe tally, and suddenly I couldn't take these angry lab coats lightly any more.

If they were successful with their poison plan in Arizona, it could embolden them to expand their retaliation against grievances worldwide. And, even more troubling, it could open the door for copycat groups to do the same.

I was desperate to know much more about the Arcetri.

The third column was light on detail. We were working under a lot of assumptions and few hard facts. By now Quanta would've been in touch with Congresswoman Thresh to share our concerns. I didn't expect a career politician to cancel an event organized to make her fat stacks of campaign cash.

I sat back at my desk and let out a long, slow breath. Parks would be counting on that political greed. He was probably rubbing his hands together in glee.

Just as I was about to send a text to Poole, another came in. I stared at the screen in disbelief.

It was from the SL phone I'd given to Jonas. The one he'd supposedly ditched in order to get his own. The one that should've been discarded.

My finger hovered over the notification for a moment before opening it.

It said: *I assume you're our friend from the river in San Antonio. We should probably talk before I release hell.*

It was simply signed: *SP.*

CHAPTER TWENTY-FOUR

I don't have a psychic bone in my body — regardless of which body I inhabit. But I felt pretty full of myself after predicting such a message from Parks or Pradesh when I'd spoken over coffee with Kowalczyk.

The reply to Steffan's simple request would have to be well thought out. I'd had only one opportunity to speak with this knave, and I couldn't let him wriggle off the hook now. There were multiple ways he might be spooked; the key would be to use a bit of mystique to hold his attention.

First things first. I messaged Poole, alerting her to the contact. Then I tied in Q2 so both Poole and Quanta could observe my thread with Parks without his knowledge, like a blind cc in an email.

Then I composed the reply.

If you'll quit trying to kill me I'd love to chat. When and where?

It took almost an hour for him to respond, and I'd started to think he'd merely wanted to see if there *would* be a response.

Then came this text from a different number: *I'll call you at 12:15.*

I didn't bother to confirm. Saying nothing was better than saying the wrong thing.

Quanta rang through a few minutes later.

"We accessed the tracking device in the SL phone," she said. "It hasn't moved since the original text. It's about 40 miles north of Phoenix, off Interstate 17."

"He ditched it as soon as he got my number and confirmed who I was. He's not stupid. He knew we'd track it once he used it. So now he can just call me with a series of burner phones."

I paused, then added, "Of course, I could send Agent Kowalczyk to pick up the SL, if you'd like. She's very dependable."

"Oh," she said. "I recognize that. It's your hurt voice."

"I understand why you sent for her. I just think a heads-up would've been nice."

"That would've just given you more time to pout. What task did you give her?"

"Checking out Oosterhaus and Franks. Have you spoken with Thresh yet about cancelling her trip?"

"Her people say absolutely not. In their words, '*we don't cower from terrorists.*'"

I grunted. "It's okay to die a gruesome, agonizing death, but cowering is strictly forbidden."

"Apparently. At least they're doubling her normal security force."

"Which Parks will simply treat as a challenge. I guarantee you if this was just a standard visit to her district she'd cancel. The fact that it's a major fundraiser makes that out of the question." I paused, then asked: "What about the stuff I sent you? The valve and the app data?"

"Exactly what you predicted," she said. "Our friends on the 2nd floor confirmed that Parks will use the app on his phone to dial up this particular valve. He can not only open and close it, he can set a timer with it."

"So he could set that today and then just wait for the poison to be in place."

"Potentially," Quanta said. "Listen, I know you wanted Parks to somehow tip his hand about the date and the location. But things are spiraling out of control. It's time to grab him and bring him in. We'll have to take our chances that we can stop everything with him in custody."

"All right. I'll work on that. But he and Pradesh have impressed me with their ghost act. If anything he'll get even more elusive since I keep killing his goon squad. Which makes me wonder if he's got a spare in place yet."

Quanta said, "He has the money to equip himself with people and supplies. I'm sure there will be someone else assigned specifically to handle you."

Which was a polite way of saying *kill you.*

"Assuming he's punctual, I have an hour until he calls," I said. "We can talk after that."

We ended the call. Quanta and Poole would be listening to the conversation, and I'm sure every effort would be made to pinpoint his location. But if Parks was as bright as I thought he was, he'd be on the move during the call, probably the passenger in a speeding car driven by Jayanti.

I needed to get some fresh air and to think, so I left the hotel and walked a few blocks. The sun did its best to warm the city, but at 63 degrees it was just an average January day for the Phoenix area. I exchanged polite greetings with several people who were also soaking up the meager sunshine. I wondered if any of those faces belonged to people who lived in the fallout zone we anticipated in Mesa.

There was no way to alert them. You couldn't just broadcast a warning to stop drinking water when you had no concrete proof of when or where a threat existed. The panic could potentially create its own lethal consequences. And yet was it fair to everyone in that potential kill zone to sit on our suspicions?

It wasn't the first time this dilemma had come up in my work. In fact, it was fairly common. Walking down this peaceful city street I was tempted to stop each person and tell them to leave town for a few days, to just get away. They'd think I was a madman, but at least it would help to vanquish the guilt I felt, staring into their faces.

Instead I smiled and nodded. It made me feel like a murderer myself, a grinning executioner who knew the blade was about to fall.

And that wasn't my only quandary. Quanta now expected an arrest, while I thought our chances of actually coming face to face with Steffan Parks, prior to the Thresh banquet, were remote. If we could thwart his plan, he might stick his head out. At the very least I wanted to personally handle Jayanti. I still had a score to settle with her.

I got back to my room just after 12. I sat down and waited.

Parks was indeed punctual. At 12:15 the phone rang, from yet another number.

"If memory serves," he said, "your name is Eric. Is that correct?"

"At your service."

He chuckled. "You have quite a way of wiggling out of trouble. How many times do you think you can manage that?"

"Oh, I have more lives than a cat. You'd shit your pants if I told you how many."

"Oh, that's right. You're one of the clever ones. Maybe one of the most clever ones with a badge I've ever met. Would that be an FBI badge?"

"Close enough. Listen, why don't we set up a place to meet so we don't have to do this over the phone?"

Another short laugh. "Eric, not only will that not happen, but this call will only last a short time."

"Tracing you would be nearly impossible, Steffan."

"And totally impossible when I hang up. Let's practice that, shall we?"

And he was gone.

A minute later it rang again. Yet another number.

"I see. You're going to use a different phone each time and keep them short. Congratulations. You're officially the most paranoid psychopath I've ever chased. And I've chased a few."

"Do you want to spend our limited time being cute, or would you like to really talk?" he asked.

"All right, so you won't meet in person. Tell me this: Since you know we're going to be all over the fundraising dinner for Congresswoman Thresh, why bother trying anything?"

He was quiet for a spell, and I could tell I'd surprised him. Then he said, "I was right; you are a clever one. I won't deny that I have a special interest in hurting Ms. Thresh."

"You're going to an awful lot of trouble just to avenge a little public embarrassment."

Parks scoffed. "Embarrassment? That's what you call it? When an entire career, an entire professional life has been reduced to ashes, and then for the ashes to be ground under heel? No, this isn't about something as banal as simple embarrassment. And it isn't even just about me, which you and your friends seem to believe."

I decided to play the next card. "You're talking about the Arcetri?"

Again he paused. When he spoke his voice took on a calm, respectful tone. "Well, well. You have moved to the head of the class, Eric. First rate. It takes a lot to impress me, and I never expect that from a government stooge."

"Yeah, I do my homework, Professor. But let's talk about your little organization."

"*My* organization? Oh, that's not accurate at all. They don't belong to me, nor do they follow my commands. It's a true democracy, you might say."

"All right. But it's an organization built around vindictiveness. It's powered by anger and feelings of victimization. How long can an agency survive when it's supported by that platform?"

"You've guessed right on so many things," he said. "But now you've reached a pathetically wrong conclusion. Wrong and dangerous. You and those you work for have already made mistakes by misjudging us in the first place. Misjudgment now will have disastrous consequences. Is that clear?"

Before I could answer he disconnected again. I forced myself to relax, taking deep breaths. Time dragged by, so I retrieved a diet soda from the mini bar. It was nearly ten minutes before he called back.

"I don't feel like discussing the Arcetri," he said. "But I will offer a warning. You and others have taken advantage of people of science for centuries. You've held them back because of your ritualistic and supernatural fears. You've contaminated their research efforts with your seedy, personal biases. And you've controlled them with your purses. Those days have reached an end. Men and women of science have delivered miracles to an ungrateful public. Now *we* will decide what to study and how to implement our findings."

"While murdering a few people along the way," I said.

"Don't disappoint me now, Eric. You've been doing so well."

I didn't want him to hang up for good. It was time to proceed with caution.

"Listen, Steffan, don't lump me in with the ungrateful public you referenced. There are a lot more of us who are appreciative of science and its wonders than you think. All I'm asking is that you not take it out on innocent people because of a few asshole politicians."

"The people elect their asshole politicians," Parks said. "They give them a mandate to control and humiliate. There aren't as many innocent people as you suggest."

I sighed. "If you go through with what I think you're planning, there *will* be a lot of innocent people hurt or killed. Including children."

He scoffed again. "Don't talk to me about children. When good people in almost every field of science are punished and denied a good living, their children aren't considered for a moment, are they? And it'll keep happening for centuries to come, assuming our idiotic race manages to keep from killing itself off entirely."

"Here's the thing, Steffan. I don't disagree with you about your treatment, or the treatment of others throughout the years. It's true; we've taken advantage of — and mistreated — the people who have made our lives easier and more fulfilled. But please, let's find a way of talking about it, rather than killing out of spite and revenge."

This was greeted with silence and I thought he might've

hung up again. But then he spoke in a voice that was hushed and pained.

"Eric, it's been a pleasure talking to someone who, at least on the surface, seems to have a grasp of the injustices my people have endured for centuries. Or more like millennia. But—"

"Don't hang up," I said. "Let's talk about this."

He gave a low, sad laugh. "Talk? No more talk, Eric. I've said I'm going to hurt Ms. Thresh, and I mean to carry it out. Nothing you can do will stop that. And once it's done we'll have the attention of more than just a few miserable senators and congresspeople. We'll have the attention of the world.

"And," he added, "we've only just begun."

CHAPTER TWENTY-FIVE

Quanta was calling, but I didn't feel like answering. Not yet. It had only been five minutes since Steffan Parks had ended our call for good, and I hadn't moved. The soda sat neglected on the table before me. Somewhere in the hall outside my room a child was crying and a parent was yelling. I ignored all of it.

My mind sifted through everything I'd heard, and the frightening part was that I found I couldn't fault Parks for his indignation. What he said made sense — right up to the part where he seized revenge by murdering thousands of people.

Why couldn't someone with that particular grievance find a way to get people and politicians to listen without resorting to slaughter?

It dawned on me that the same argument could be made for many groups who felt slighted. We feel our own pain down to the core, but are usually oblivious to the pain of others. It has to affect us personally before we'll sit up and take notice. And sometimes not even then.

I had to square my instinct to agree with Parks with my disappointment and fear of his ultimate plan.

When Quanta called back a second time I finally answered.

"Well?" she asked.

"You heard every word he said. There's no chance of talking him down from this scheme. I don't think he has a shred of regret for the damage he'll do. All he's concerned with is avenging every scientist who's ever been victimized, going back centuries. And the thing is, he has a valid point."

"Swan—" she started to say.

"Relax," I said, cutting her off. "I'm not saying I agree with his methods of retribution. I'm saying I at least understand his charge. We *are* guilty, you know. It's just that his response is . . . insane." I paused, then added, "It's too bad."

I had to hand it to Quanta. She was good at reading me when I fell into these moods. She knew that a Q2 agent was not just a killing machine for the government, at least not yet. We were human beings, too. Freaks, perhaps, because of our strange tendency to inhabit multiple bodies. But still human, nonetheless.

She waited until I reached my own conclusion, the mark of a superior manager of people.

"We'll take him down," I said, resigned to the fact that Parks could not be swayed. "Now it's just a matter of reaching him before he can kill Thresh and half the population of Mesa."

AGENT KOWALCZYK SHOWED up around 4 o'clock. I met her downstairs at the hotel bar where I allowed myself one cocktail.

I briefed her on my conversation with Parks. She listened,

asking a question here and there, drinking a club soda and lime.

"It's not all negative," she said when I'd finished. "At least he confirmed a couple things. He's after Thresh, and he's not troubled about taking down thousands of people to get his cause recognized by the masses."

It sounded so casual. Thousands dead in order to get noticed.

But she was right.

"He can't get away with it, though," Kat said. "We have people installed in all of the water treatment plants that serve Mesa, and we've added people to the Phoenix plants, too. The staffs there are on full alert. No one could possibly do anything without getting noticed immediately. I mean, it's impossible for him to pull this off."

"If that's really what he has in mind," I said.

"If it's not, I can't imagine what he *does* have planned. There's also a full complement of agents set up to surround the congresswoman. Hell, they're even supplying every single thing she'll eat or drink. It's like the official tasters the pharaohs used to employ. I'm telling you, Parks can't get to Thresh and he can't poison the Mesa water supply. Unless he's some sort of goddamned magician."

"That's the thing, Kat. I think the son of a bitch could very well be the kind of magician we're not expecting. He's too smooth, even in the face of so many agents descending upon the city. It's like he doesn't care." I stared at her. "Why is that? Why doesn't he care?"

She didn't answer, just sipped her club soda.

I waved a hand in frustration. "Time is running short. Tell me what you got out of your meetings today."

"It was pretty obvious to me. Franks is a major asshole, but he's not involved in any way."

"What do you mean?"

"He took offense to being questioned at all. Said he didn't always agree with Steffan Parks, but could understand why he was angry."

I smiled. "Yeah, that rules him out, all right. If there's no Damnation Denial, there's no collaboration. What about Oosterhaus?"

She pulled out a small notebook. "Classic response from a nervous accomplice. As soon as I brought up Steffan Parks she started fidgeting. At first said she didn't know him well. Then, when I pressed her, she started in with your . . . what did you call it? Damn something?"

"Yeah, Damnation Deniability. Something I learned from poor Jonas Aiken. Their technique is to throw their companions under the bus. That somehow proves their innocence. So Oosterhaus ripped on him?"

"Said he was someone she not only didn't like, but that needed to be put away."

"Good one. What else?"

"Said she hadn't talked to him in years. Which we know is a lie. But there's still a problem with her."

"She doesn't work in Mesa," I said. "Does she ever go there?"

"I called the manager of operations in Mesa. He's never heard of her."

I rubbed my forehead. "That's strange. She *behaves* like she's involved, but she doesn't appear to be. At least not in this particular operation."

"So you think she might be working on some other operation? Something down the road?"

"God, I don't know." I wanted another drink, but couldn't chance that. Too much at stake right now.

We sat in silence for a few minutes, watching the other hotel guests at the bar, some of them loud, some of them shy and reserved. Maybe some of them dead within a few hours. The thought was sobering.

Kowalczyk finished her club soda and pushed the glass toward the bartender. "We're watching Oosterhaus until Thresh leaves town. There's an agent following her wherever she goes. If she heads toward Mesa we'll know right away."

All I could do was nod. It still seemed fruitless. Parks wasn't doing what we expected of him. He couldn't be. And that meant Allison Oosterhaus wouldn't be going to Mesa to poison anyone.

But maybe it was as simple as just striking down Thresh. Parks had made it clear to me that his goal was to hurt her. Those were his words: *I have a special interest in hurting Ms. Thresh.*

So what if our security measures were misguided? What if his plan wasn't to knock off the congresswoman at her fundraiser? What if he planned on doing it somewhere else while she was in town? Or maybe even on her flight to Arizona? Or . . .

It pissed me off. I wanted a simple answer to a complex question; and revenge, while often a basic human reaction, could also become remarkably complex.

I shared my thoughts about Thresh with Kat. She pondered it for a moment, then shook her head.

"I don't know, Eric. She's being guarded around the clock, and no one is serving her who isn't on her staff. And those people have been vetted beyond question. The only way Parks could possibly get to her is maybe with a sniper's bullet. I don't think that's his plan, do you?"

No. I didn't. Parks wanted his punishment to fit the perceived crime. He was obstinate, if nothing else. To him, I was sure, the crime was meant to be poetic in its sick, demented application.

I changed the subject and brought up the Arcetri. Kowalczyk was fascinated by the concept while also terrified of the implications. She asked me how many scientists might be involved.

"Around the world? It's probably like any other organization; it'll start small and pick up followers. My fear is that some big score, at least a score in their eyes, will encourage hundreds who otherwise would never imagine themselves participating in something like that."

I tapped a finger on the bar and relived my phone call with Parks. He'd said, *We've only just begun.*

It may cost me my man license, but I liked that song.

WE WERE 24 hours away from the fundraising dinner. Something was going down, one way or another. I sat in my hotel room, pondering everything that had happened, all of the conversations, the chases, the charades, the killings. More people would die in the next day. Would it be one, two, three, or death on a massive scale?

I hoped that Christina would be available to talk, and I got lucky. She was still at the restaurant, but picked up after three rings.

"What's the special tonight?" I asked.

"Um . . . chicken with Asian beans and a plum relish."

"Is that one a challenge or easy?"

"So easy. What did you have?"

"Not hungry."

She clucked her tongue. "I know what that means. It's not going well. I'm sorry, babe. Everything gonna be okay?"

I had a tendency to do this: to call Christina when things sucked. I'd often find myself alone like this, usually in a hotel room, staring at the walls and wondering why things so often went through the shit stage before rounding the home stretch and — sometimes — working out just fine. Or not.

Christina was my best friend, my confidant, and my therapist, all rolled into one. She was sweet and supportive, but at the same time tolerated only a limited amount of whining. When my quota was up, she shut off the sympathy tap and applied a solid kick to the ass. Through the years I'd learned to gauge for myself when that time was approaching and dialed it back.

"It's a bitch at the moment," I said. "But there's always hope."

"Sure. And meditation," she said. "Supplication to the universe for divine intervention. Don't forget that one."

"I'll try anything. Never been too good at supplication, though. Is there an app for that?"

"Wouldn't be surprised."

I chuckled. "All right, pity party over. Tell me something to take my mind off things. It might clear my neural pathways by listening to you talk about your day."

She had to pull the phone away and direct someone to remove something from the flame. Perhaps the Asian beans. This was part of her job: being a food conductor, holding the baton and leading an orchestra of cooks, sous chefs, and servers. And she was damned good at it.

Then she was back with me. "What? Oh, my day. Uh, I almost got a cat."

"Almost? What stopped you?"

"Litter boxes disgust me. I still might do it. Just tabling the idea for now."

I said, "We could put a kitty door between our units and the little guy could wander back and forth. Get a diverse upbringing. When he was tired of your neat and tidy world he could come over and piss on my carpet."

She laughed, a generous laugh if I'd ever heard one. I decided to return to one of our previous topics.

"Any more talk with Antonio about being a surrogate?"

"Yes. They're excited that I'm even open to the idea."

"Which way are you leaning?" I asked.

"Still 50-50. But I did meet with them at their doctor's office, to find out more about it. Swan, it's such a remarkable process, and couldn't be more beautiful. If you could've seen the look on Antonio's face, and the way Marissa just hung on every word. They would make wonderful parents. God, I was practically balling at one point."

In normal circumstances this is where I might throw in a snarky comment — and she'd fire back with one. But I was getting a little misty-eyed myself, just listening to her talk about it.

"Is there a timetable?" I asked.

"The doctor says it could be done at any time, and I agreed to meet with him again tomorrow. So they're just waiting on my answer. The fact that *you're* supportive might nudge me into doing it. They're really the sweetest couple you've ever seen."

I shifted the phone to my other ear. "I know I could say *Wait and let's talk about it*, but it's not a permanent change for us. I mean, if I lived an ordinary life and was home every day things might be different. But I think this is a personal decision for you. Thank you for bringing me into the discussion, but yeah, I'll support you whichever way you go, babe."

She was quiet, so I let that drape over us a minute. Then there was a commotion in the background and she told me she had to go. She was at work, after all. I gave a mushy goodbye and lay back on my bed.

The thought of Christina pregnant was interesting. She wouldn't walk away from the experience as a traditional parent in the family sense. She'd relinquish the child right away.

But she'd be a parent in some respects, nonetheless. I found that to be a beautiful thing, and I couldn't imagine a better person to bring a new life into the world for another couple. She hadn't even agreed to do it yet, and I still felt a rush of pride and admiration for her. I was a lucky guy, and I knew it.

She deserved better than what I could do for her. For some reason she'd hitched her wagon to me and my ridiculous life. Lives, actually.

A moment later my brain connected the concept of her ushering in a new life while I was 2,300 miles away, dealing with the *extinction* of life. My calling. My lot in life. My area of expertise.

As I'd done so many times, I tried to convince myself that somebody had to do it.

At this particular moment in time it disgusted me.

I shut off the light and watched the advance of twilight through my window, wondering how many people would be dead by the time the sun set again.

CHAPTER TWENTY-SIX

A garbage truck, making the rounds early, awoke me before sunrise. I checked the time on my phone. 6:55.

I'd managed a solid nine hours of sleep, and that was unusual for me. Well, unless I inhabited a body that agreed with a normal sleep cycle, and then I had the pleasure a little more often. This body most certainly did.

I was also famished, and that might've contributed to the wake signal. I'd skipped dinner, opting for my one cocktail and then a bottled water. It was bound to be a helluva day, and I needed protein.

Without bothering to shower I put on a baseball cap and went down to the hotel restaurant, where I destroyed six eggs, bacon, an English muffin, and lots of coffee. I was back in my room by eight, rejuvenated and in a much better head space. The mindset was triggered by a feeling of resignation, the knowledge that shit was going down today whether I was ready for it or not. I chose to be ready. Steffan Parks didn't deserve a hall pass.

I used the next two hours to upload, making sure everything was saved for posterity and any future Eric Swan. I was so dialed in to the case and the impending climax that I couldn't even get into my *Us Weekly*. This time, though, I just couldn't muster any interest in the reality stars and pop singers. The Bachelorette would have to get along without me.

That was followed by a long run, then a shower, and before noon I was ready to take on the day and any calamity it might deliver.

In a succession of calls I spoke with Quanta, Poole, and Kowalczyk. We all agreed to the following schedule for the day:

I'd head over to the conference center where Thresh would be speaking. Her plane was scheduled to touch down at 4:15. That gave me a few hours to meet with the staff, the security personnel, and two of the congresswoman's advance staff.

Although Thresh had refused to postpone the dinner — no politician ever turns down tens of thousands of dollars — she'd at least agreed to the heightened security and a meeting with me, which would take place around 5 o'clock. My cover was that of a special consultant to the FBI.

Kowalczyk would monitor the comings and goings of Oosterhaus. At the moment, the agent parked outside her house reported all quiet. Oosterhaus had not gone to work. That concerned me, but could also be completely innocent. She was, after all, stationed far from the action.

Just for safety's sake, another agent was tailing Franks. He'd been at his Phoenix office since 8:30.

More than three dozen people, including Phoenix and Mesa police, conference center security, and eight additional FBI agents had pictures of Steffan Parks and Jayanti Pradesh. Unless they were not only scientists but masters of disguise, too, they weren't getting into the building.

And yet, with all of that, I was still bothered by the utter lack of concern shown by Parks. Something was wrong.

For the moment there was nothing I could do about it.

I PULLED up in my stylish minivan and eyed the conference center, which was not what I expected. Although clean and functional, it lacked the pizazz one would normally associate with a big-shot dinner. I was introduced to one of Representative Thresh's aides, and she politely explained that the congresswoman rotated her attention throughout the state. Scottsdale gleamed with celebrities and big money, Phoenix and Tucson sported big business, and the rural communities injected the necessary dose of pure middle America. A politician's job required that they connect with all of their donors at some point. Tonight, the aide said, it was Mesa's turn.

Kowalczyk introduced me to another FBI agent, a man named Tahoma who'd been raised on Navajo land in the state. A local. His firm handshake and piercing eyes were almost intimidating. It was good to have him on the team.

Together the three of us made two loops around the banquet room and adjoining corridors. Everything seemed to be secure, but I didn't know exactly what we were looking for. Kowalczyk said the water in the building was being checked every 30 minutes. Special care was being paid to the catering service. Not counting the over-the-top precautions, everything was normal.

Next we went over the guest list. Tahoma said every name had been background-checked, and security at the door would be intense but not overbearing. The idea was to make sure of the identity of each person entering, but not to alarm anyone. Security checks would be done with a smile.

Kowalczyk was notified that the plane carrying Thresh had landed and she was in a limo convoy headed straight to the center. I nodded and went off to a quiet office to check in one more time with Quanta and Poole.

"Are you happy with the level of security?" Quanta asked.

"It's impressive. No one's getting in here with a rocket launcher, that's for sure. I don't think anyone could even sneak a tennis racquet past the door. But is that what we're guarding against?"

"Mesa Water is on full alert," Poole said. "Phoenix and Scottsdale report the same. All the others in the area have added extra security to make sure only employees can enter and exit."

"All right. I meet with Ms. Thresh in—" I looked at my phone's screen. "—in about 25 minutes. I'm told she's appreciative of the extra security and grateful for the concern. She just doesn't want to spook her constituents."

Quanta acknowledged this, then said, "As a last minute precaution we're sending a helicopter to park outside the conference center. Just in case we need to evacuate someone quickly."

I grunted. "*Someone*, meaning Thresh."

She ignored this. "There's also a full medical team coming. In fact, they should be there any minute. After that, I can't think of any other precaution. You?"

"No. Let's hope we don't need it."

IT ONLY TOOK a few minutes to brief the emergency medical people. They'd been hand-picked because of their background training in poison control and treatment. I spent a few minutes letting them know the specifics of this tabun-based threat.

What I didn't say was that, once it was in a person's system, there wasn't much that could be done. I still felt better about having them on premises.

Minutes later the bustle of activity at the back entrance told me that Representative Thresh had arrived, later than planned. It was 5:15 and the hoopla was scheduled to begin when she took the stage at six. In the meantime, according to her aides, she'd meet with the VIPs who'd ponied up mega-dollars. It was like Taylor Swift meeting radio and record executives backstage before a concert. Those people got special treatment before the ordinary fans because they'd helped make success possible.

What irked me was the fact that I was not at the front of that line. In fact, I hadn't even seen the congresswoman yet.

"She's going to talk with you in just a few minutes," her main handler said to me.

"What's *a few minutes*?" I asked with a tone that displayed my irritation. "This is very important."

In reply I got one of the most condescending smiles of all time. "I'm sure within 10 minutes," the assistant said. "She needs to have a quick chat with the people who paid to have her in Washington. That, too, is very important, as I'm sure you understand."

I opened my mouth to pull real rank, but instead simply nodded. I made eye contact with Kowalczyk, who shook her head as if to say *Idiots*.

It wasn't 10 minutes. It was 25. When I was taken back to her posh private reception room at 5:45, Thresh turned on the professional smile that had helped her defeat a popular incumbent. She used the politician's two-handed hand shake and gave me a look that said she was here to solve all of my problems.

Eleanor Thresh was in her late-40s, medium height, and in remarkably good shape. Her hair was short and professional, her clothing perfect, the jewelry just this side of ostentatious. Working in Washington, D.C. I understood that the best officials learned how to dress and accessorize based on the audience. This would be a room full of muckety-mucks, and Thresh made sure that her clothes and jewelry — the necklace, diamond earrings, and sparkly bracelets — were in just the right price range: not the most expensive in the room, which could offend, but enough to let her sit at the table.

She spoke first. "I want you to know how much I appreciate all that you and your team have done to make sure everything is safe and secure for our guests tonight."

"We're doing our best," I said, then nodded to the small group of helpers gathered around her. "If it's okay with you, Congresswoman, I'd like a moment to visit with you privately."

Her first reaction was to look at her aide, who shook her head. I put on my most severe face.

"It's of vital importance, and could mean the safety of not just the people here tonight, but across your entire constituency."

Those were the magic words. She led the way to a far corner of the room. Kowalczyk joined us.

"By now you've heard about the potential threats from a scientist you've had interaction with," I said. "Have you, or anyone on your staff, had any contact from Steffan Parks in the last few days or weeks?"

She shook her head slowly. "No. Nothing. I recall how upset he was at the loss of his funding, but that wasn't entirely my doing."

"I understand that. But he does hold you personally responsible. In fact, Mr. Parks holds several people responsible for the unfortunate turns that his career has taken. Which is why Agent Kowalczyk and I are here tonight, along with a few dozen others. What you saw as a matter of duty to the taxpayers, he saw as a personal attack. And, unfortunately, he's on a mission to right what he feels are wrongs."

For the first time her face showed real concern. She glanced at the group of people on the far side of the room, then to Kat, then back to me.

"Let me tell you about the only direct, one-on-one conversation I've had with Mr. Parks," she said, her voice low. "Our committee hadn't yet decided on any action at the time; it was a possibility that we'd have to cut funding, but the vote hadn't taken place yet.

"He came to my office and, although he didn't have an official appointment, I felt he deserved a few minutes to pitch for continued support. After all, the man won a Nobel Prize, that should be worth something, right?"

I nodded and let her continue.

"For the first minute I thought he was one of the most charming people I've ever met, and I've met a few, as you can imagine. His manner was calm and respectful. But the moment I even mentioned how the budget might require us to make some changes, he . . . he came unhinged, as my mother would've said. He didn't exactly shout, but his voice took on a rather ominous, threatening tone. Two of my assistants were there, including Benjamin, who's a former wrestler, thank goodness. Benjamin stood ready in case Mr. Parks tried something physical."

"And did he?" I asked.

"No. But he did lean toward me and say a budget wasn't the only thing that could get cut. I believe I actually took a step backward. He was so . . . *menacing*. Not just his voice, but his entire demeanor. All I did at that point was give a look to Benjamin, and he ushered Mr. Parks out. That was the last time I saw him, or even heard from him."

"But you've been aware of his actions since?"

"Oh, yes. I was briefed on his reaction to the fact that his proposal to the Pentagon was denied. As it should've been. No humane individual would ever think our country should operate in that manner. And I've been told that he may have been involved in the killing of a fellow scientist. Is that correct?"

"He's the prime suspect, along with some colleagues."

The congresswoman shuddered. "I'm sorry to hear about that. But really, I have a hard time believing he'd try to get revenge here tonight. Again, I'm very grateful for all the work you and Agent Kowalczyk have put into the security."

She looked over to where her aide motioned. "I'm so sorry, but I have to speak with some other people before the dinner begins. Is there anything else I can answer for you?"

I thought about it. "I'm told you don't have any other plans while you're back in Arizona. Is that right?"

She nodded. "I won't even be spending the night. I'm on a plane as of 10:10 tonight and back in Washington three hours later." She chuckled. "Much to the chagrin of my parents. They're always furious if I don't stop by to see them."

Through instinct I almost reached out and grabbed her arm. "Your parents? I was told your parents lived in Idaho."

"They do, most of the year. But they're senior citizens, you know, and have suddenly decided to be true snow birds. This year they're spending October through April here."

Kat and I exchanged a stunned look.

"Where?" I said, a little more loudly than I intended.

Another look of alarm crossed Eleanor Thresh's face. "In Sun City. It's about an hour—"

I didn't let her finish the sentence. I bolted toward the door, and felt Kat right behind me.

Sun City. Just to the northwest of Phoenix. A popular destination for the snow birds the congresswoman had mentioned. Including her parents.

As I raced toward the building exit, a replay of my phone conversation with Steffan Parks rolled through my mind. The part where he made his intentions clear.

I have a special interest in hurting Ms. Thresh.

Dammit! He never said he was going to *kill* her. He said he would hurt her.

Parks wasn't going to poison the people of Phoenix or Mesa.

He was going to murder the people of Sun City.

CHAPTER TWENTY-SEVEN

I was halfway to my van in the parking lot when I got the idea. I stopped so fast that Kat nearly ran into me from behind.

"What is it?" she asked.

I pointed across the parking lot in the other direction. "Traffic will be miserable right now. Unless we take that."

She followed my gaze. "The helicopter? But that's in case of an emergency with the congresswoman."

"*This* is the emergency. Your agent Tahoma can keep an eye on things, but nothing's going to happen here."

"You don't know that."

I didn't wait to argue. As I began running toward the chopper I called back over my shoulder, "Sure I do." Then I added, "Coming?"

She gave a large groan of frustration but started after me.

The pilot was named Grogan, small and wiry, and also former military. He listened intently as both Kat and I showed our badges and told him we needed a lift. He got out a phone to make a call of confirmation and I gently put a hand on his forearm.

"Mr. Grogan, we're going to have to make that call in the air. Things are that serious."

He squinted as he looked into my face, trying to decide on the spot if he could violate his orders.

I added, "We need you to deviate from protocol. You've done it before, I'm sure. It's how shit gets done and lives get saved. Am I right?"

He glanced at Kowalczyk, who said, "It's not just a few lives; it's maybe tens of thousands."

Looking back at me he hesitated, then gave a quick nod. "Climb in."

It took a minute to get everything up to speed and the rotors spinning. I used that time to patch my phone into the radio headset Grogan handed to me.

"Poole," I said as she came on. "Emergency alert. We're on our way to Sun City." To Grogan I asked: "ETA?"

He'd just started the process of lifting off. "Call it 14 minutes. Maybe 12 if I can get in touch with local air traffic control for emergency clearance."

"Poole," I said. "We'll be on the ground in 12 to 14 minutes. I need to know which location. Can you send that to both me and Agent Kowalczyk?"

I turned in my seat to Kat.

"What about your agent in Chandler? Can they confirm that Oosterhaus is still immobile?"

Her face was grim. "She's not answering. I have someone on the way now."

I sat back and rubbed my forehead. In a matter of minutes things had turned into one big jolly shit show. If the poison was already in place in Sun City, then Parks was merely a phone swipe away from sending a lethal solution through 24-inch ductile iron pipes to an unsuspecting public.

If Oosterhaus was hooking it up now, we might have a small window of opportunity to stop it.

Poole called me back. There was one primary plant that would most likely be the target — and she couldn't raise anyone there. Police had been notified and were en route. They'd arrive about the same time we did. I gave the coordinates to the pilot. He nodded and gave a thumbs up.

I gazed out the side window and took in the gridlock of traffic below. Without this last-minute addition of the helicopter at the conference center it would've taken us maybe an hour to get to Sun City. But even with this quick airlift we might be too late.

Grogan's voice piped through my headset. "Halfway. Say six minutes."

Kat leaned forward and touched my arm to get my attention. I turned to look at her phone's screen.

The FBI agent assigned to watch Oosterhaus had just been found in her car, outside the house.

She was dead. No external sign of foul play.

I looked at Kat. "She was poisoned."

I turned back to the window, silently cursing. All along, from the time I'd first heard his name while sitting in Quanta's kitchen, I'd made the worst mistake of the entire mission. I'd automatically assumed that Steffan Parks was an amateur when it came to crime. He was a scientist — granted, an award-winner, but that wouldn't necessarily make someone gifted in the art of villainy.

Parks, though, was different. And I'd underestimated him at every step.

He'd masterminded the murders in Santa Fe without being caught.

He'd commissioned and retrieved the tech devices he needed in San Antonio and danced out of town.

He'd assembled a team of fellow dissidents from an association known as the Arcetri to help construct his scheme, and employed various thugs to do the dirty work. His thugs had been offed, but Parks had scampered free.

He'd taken the one potential inside connection I had — Jonas Aiken — and pretty much toyed with me, letting me believe I'd get the data I needed. He'd brought the lovesick fool all the way back to Arizona to bolster my confidence and to kill some more time before Thresh arrived. Then, in a snap, he'd pulled the rug out and left my mole dead in a public restroom.

And now he'd fooled all of us with a classic case of misdirection. The world's greatest magicians kept you watching one hand while they did whatever they wished with the other. In the end you felt like a fool for not picking up on it.

That was me: Steffan's fool. And he was no amateur.

There were many of us who would not only feel foolish if this ended tragically, but would be held accountable by the highest powers. And where would Parks be while we were crucified for failing to save an entire community from a madman?

He'd be off with Jayanti, no doubt, laughing. Then he'd offer his wicked services to an enemy of the state who'd certainly leap at the chance to do business with a killer who could so easily baffle the United States and its supposedly-well-trained agents.

It would be a catastrophe on multiple levels.

My brooding was interrupted by a shift in the helicopter's flight path. We veered to the right and Grogan began to bring it down a touch. The cars below us still crawled, but up ahead I saw what had to be the water treatment plant. They never gleamed like the Emerald City; rather, they were built to be as inconspicuous as possible. From the air I counted an assortment of five buildings, covering a large city block like a compound. This plant, like most, was a drab tan, unmarked, and completely unlovable from the outside.

I guess when you thought about the process going on *inside* it made sense they would be kept so nondescript.

There were two police cars in the parking lot, and two more that were stationed in the street. A few passersby on foot were gathered, taking in the spectacle. It had to be the first time in their lives they'd seen drama at Sewage City, or whatever the locals called it.

Since it was after six o'clock there was room at the far edge of the parking lot, and Grogan set down the chopper amidst a whirlwind of dirt and dust. I shook his hand and thanked him for fudging on his orders. He responded with a standard "Roger that," and wished us luck.

Kowalczyk and I ducked beneath the rotors and hurried to the main door. Four police officers, looking wide-eyed and tense, dutifully examined our badges then nodded. The one in charge, Sgt. Oakes, was beefy but sharp. He quickly filled us in.

They'd arrived six minutes before us. The doors to the facility were locked and there was no answer. One of the officers had made a quick run around the perimeter, and discovered no other unlocked entrance before reaching chain link fences with razor wire along the top. They were awaiting instructions and the arrival of a lieutenant.

"We're not waiting," I said, and while this prompted more concerned looks, no one spoke up.

With a solid kick I broke open the door and the six of us carefully edged inside. The main room was vacant.

I pointed toward a door on the right and two of the patrol officers, with guns now drawn, worked toward it. Kowalczyk joined them. Sgt. Oakes, the other officer, and I made for a hallway to the left. It, too, was deserted.

Shoving in an earpiece, I connected with Poole.

"We're inside," I said. "Help me with directions."

"Stand by," she said. A moment later she came back. "You want to head toward the back, and that will take you out a door into a large lot. The building you want will be about 30 yards to the southwest."

I acknowledged this and led our small team down the dimly-lit hallway. Normally I'd tread lightly through a potentially hazardous zone, but my gut told me all the action was taking place in that posterior building. Still, we moved at a pace where we wouldn't be caught off-guard by someone jumping out from one of the dark offices.

"Eric," Kat said from behind me. I stopped and let her catch up.

"Four people in that room off the lobby. One dead, the other three terrified out of their minds. The one who was killed was assigned here as part of the extra security we ordered. They were all told if they came anywhere near the door they'd be shot. And to make the point they bashed another one of the men across his forehead. An ambulance is almost here."

"Shit," I muttered. "Did they say how long ago this began?"

"About fifteen minutes."

I didn't know if that was good for us or disastrous. Oosterhaus might only need minutes.

Poole spoke up in my ear. "One mystery is solved. Oosterhaus does work for Chandler water, but she also serves as a consultant for two other districts."

"Including Sun City," I said.

"Correct. She's helped them for the past two months."

Another victory for Parks. A private consultation like that wouldn't show up in most checks, and it allowed Oosterhaus entry to the plant anytime without suspicion. Apparently once he learned of Thresh's parents' snow bird plans, he put everything into motion. My guess was that he'd been ready for a while, and just waiting for a location and a visit from Thresh. The Arizona connection was perfect.

We reached the back door of the main building. I checked in with Poole.

"There's a courtyard and two buildings," she reported. "Remember, you want the one to the southwest. There's no cover between the buildings, however. You'll be exposed to fire if they're waiting."

I gave a short grunt of a laugh. "We arrived in a helicopter. They know we're here."

The Sun City police sergeant moved next to me, gun drawn. "How many people are we talking about?" he asked.

"I don't know. But I guarantee at least one who's armed."

I reached for the door handle, then turned back to Oakes. "Oh, and something else you should know. These people specialize in poisoning their enemies. So if you see anything that resembles a syringe or a spear or who knows what, be alert. The shit they use will kill you within a minute."

He gave me a look like I was crazy, and maybe I was. I'd lived with the insanity of Parks and Pradesh for so long that it all seemed routine to me. It had to sound like action-movie nonsense to anyone else.

Time was wasting away. I positioned our group so that I'd go first, followed by Oakes, the other officer, and then Kowalczyk at the rear, providing cover.

I pushed open the door, stuck my head out quickly then brought it back. When that didn't prompt gunfire I did it again, taking a moment to get the lay of the land.

It was just as Poole had described, an open space of ground between our main building and two other structures. Security lights bathed the area. It was just what an offensive team like ours hated to see, while someone defending the other side loved the clear shooting lanes.

There was nothing to be done about it at the moment. I took a deep breath, then bent down and hustled outside. Oakes knew about proper spacing and followed that protocol. The second police officer did the same. We all ran.

When I was within a few feet of the other building a spate of shots rang out. I heard Oakes grunt behind me, and a louder cry from his partner. Immediately there was return fire from Kat.

I was so close to the building that I dove to the ground near its base, out of the glare of the lights. A moment later Oakes hit the ground beside me. He was breathing hard and holding on to a spot near his hip.

"Bad?" I asked.

He removed a blood-stained hand. "Hurts like a bitch," he said with a grimace. "I'll need to do something about it soon."

We both looked back. The other police officer was down, unmoving, and it didn't look good.

Kowalczyk was nowhere to be seen.

Then I heard her whistle. Looking across to the other

building I could just make out her shape in the faint shadows. When the shots began she'd detoured to the closest cover.

We were separated.

I gave her a quick hand signal to hold tight for a moment, then turned back to Oakes.

"Did you get a glimpse of where those shots came from?"

He was in serious pain, but nodded. "Yeah. This building, the window on the far right."

We were out of that line of fire, but Kat would be cut down if she ventured out again.

Things had gotten bad very quickly. The other two police officers were back with the people they'd discovered in the front office. There were two more patrol cars out front, in the street, but I wasn't exactly sure what they could do, even if they followed our path. The gunman — or gunmen — now were ready for battle. Anyone else who came out that back door would be torn apart.

With the Sun City sergeant busy bleeding next to me, and with Kat pinned down across the way, that meant one thing.

I'd have to go in alone.

CHAPTER TWENTY-EIGHT

Under normal circumstances I could've stayed put, helped the sergeant, and waited for the cavalry in the form of a SWAT team and a regiment of patrol officers. That would've been nice.

Instead, with every passing minute the chances of Steffan Parks swiping right — or whatever he'd do to unleash the stream of tabun into the water supply — increased. He was camped out somewhere, comfortably waiting for the thumbs-up from Oosterhaus that the deadly potion was in place.

All of that was bad. But I realized it wasn't ideal for Parks, either. He'd gone through the trouble of having the phone app built so he could commit the crime at his leisure, with his chemicals in place well in advance. Thresh's visit, however, was a last minute affair, put together in days. But it was an opportunity Parks couldn't pass up. Sure, he could've killed the congresswoman's parents at any time, but he was definitely the kind who loved the high drama of actually having her in town, just miles from the kill zone. Somehow, to his warped way of thinking, that increased the hurt exponentially.

He also knew we were on his tail and he couldn't wait for the next chance. This was it.

So with his accomplice Oosterhaus under surveillance and with me as a wildcard, he'd been forced to make additional arrangements. It might've slowed down the execution of his plan, but it hadn't stopped it. It was an inconvenience.

I turned to Oakes. "I have to get in there. You gonna be all right?"

His eyes were red-rimmed from fighting the pain. Hey, I've been shot before; movie tough guys shrug it off and barely break their stride, but that's utter bullshit. It's agonizing.

"Just do me a favor," he said, breathing hard. "Take them down. Hard. Not for me . . ."

I followed his gaze that had moved to the center of the courtyard. One of his partners, a young police officer, was crumpled in a puddle of blood.

"Count on it," I said. "Hang tight. Help is coming."

He replied with just a curt nod.

I looked back to where Kat was positioned. She had a clear view of the door I'd need to enter, and her angle was good. I dialed her up.

"This sucks," she said. "What's your plan?"

"I'm going to lean out and put a couple of shots toward the window where they're set up," I said. "I won't hit them, but it might cause them to duck for a moment. I need you to reach out and put a full clip into the door handle for me."

She understood what I was thinking. With that door bolted, I'd linger too long trying to kick it open. She could do most of the preliminary work with her SIG Sauer. I doubted these doors were built to withstand a military assault.

With one more glance at Oakes and a pat on his shoulder, I took a breath, rolled out from the cover of the building and fired four shots at the window. Within two seconds Kowalczyk cut loose.

Her shooting skills were magnificent. After the first two shots went a touch high, she pretty much obliterated the hardware around the door handle. I bolted from my position, threw my shoulder into the door, and felt the satisfactory crunch as it spilled open.

I was on the ground inside, rolling to my left, and saw two men kneeling below the window. They were ready for me, but that didn't matter. I had a round into the first one's head before he could do much, and was about to place another into the second man's chest.

But he was much quicker than his friend. As I trained the Glock on him and squeezed off a round, he dove backwards, through an open office door and out of sight. I saw a streak of blood.

"Shit," I said through my mouthpiece to Kat. "One down, another is hit but has taken cover. It'll be the room to the right of that window. I can't stay to battle with him."

"Go," was all she said, but I was already on the move.

This building was smaller than the main offices but still had a long series of rooms. Once again I'd have to move as quickly as possible while staying alert for an ambush. There was very little lighting, and a rhythmic, pulsing sound grew louder as I made my way along. It would help to cover my approach, but also mask anyone waiting ahead.

I knelt down as I entered the room where most of the sound originated.

"Poole," I said, trying to remain as quiet as possible. "I'm in a second, larger room. It's noisy. Am I still moving ahead?"

She was right there. "Yes. Building plans say the chlorination facilities are farther along. You'll pass through one more room before getting there."

I muttered below my breath, then crept forward.

The machinery kicking out the obnoxious sound was smaller than I'd expected, but was apparently hard at work cleansing the water supply for its customers. Reaching the end of the room, I looked back to make sure my wounded adversary wasn't following. The path was clear.

The next room was oddly quiet, with just a hypnotizing hum to announce that anything was going on. It was a low-frequency note, and I felt it in my stomach more than I heard it. It was strangely soothing.

But the good feeling didn't last long. I discovered my way ahead into the chlorination room was blocked by a large, metal door. It was the kind that was kick-proof, and looked to be bullet-proof, as well. If it was locked, I was screwed. I'd have to wait for reinforcements.

I held my breath and pushed against it.

It slowly swung open with a metallic groan.

The average person might thank the gods for easy access; I'd been around enough to know that when a bad guy leaves a door open, they have other plans for you. It was pure Parks and his desire for showmanship.

This room was also dimly lit. I understood that was done strictly for my arrival. I paused as long as I could to let my eyes acclimate, and just as I was ready to take a step I heard movement behind me.

I whirled around, Glock raised, and saw Kat entering the humming room. When she saw me she hurried over and crouched by my side.

"Well, that was quick," I said.

"Hey, I took note of your one critique of Agent Fife. I wasn't about to be late."

"And the bully back there with the gun?"

She gave me a quick glance. "You did better than you thought. When I got into the room he had one hand up and the other cupped across a wound in his chest. He's now cuffed to a railing."

"Still bleeding?"

"Of course. I don't have time to play nurse. Someone will be along in a few minutes."

I nodded and looked back into the chlorination room. "This is ground zero," I told her. "Ready?"

She held up her weapon in response. "I'll go to the right."

With a quiet count to three, we jumped ahead, separating. But the moment we entered the room there were more shots. I heard Kat cry out, followed by the sound of her hitting the ground.

I'd made it to a large metal bin and was crouched behind it. Into the mouthpiece I said, "Kat."

There was no answer, so I repeated it. A moment later her voice came through my earpiece. It was low and sounded terrible.

"Son of a bitch," she said. "Hit."

"Where?"

I could hear her breathing in gasps. "Left side." She let out a groan.

This was ridiculous. All of my partners were getting nailed, and yet I was the one with the extra lives.

As I contemplated my next move, Kat spoke up. "Don't wait for me. Go ahead."

It was the only play. Even if Kowalczyk bled out, I

couldn't afford to move over to her. Somewhere in the darkness ahead many more murders were about to take place.

I snuck toward a faint light ahead, ducking behind another bin as a shot skipped across the ground beside me. I peeked back around the corner and saw someone kneeling beside a large barrel, the kind that held 40 or so gallons, and what looked like one of those large tanks you find at an aquarium.

It was Oosterhaus. She was working on the vat of poison, hooking up the barrel to the chlorination tank. The dolly they'd used to roll the tabun vat into the room was parked to the side.

One shot from me could save thousands of people. Although by now Poole and Q2 had probably alerted the local media to warn people against drinking the water — who knew what story they'd invented? — there was no way they could reach everyone. Thousands of people would still be exposed to the poison. I didn't want to just shoot Oosterhaus, but would she stop otherwise?

I opened my mouth to shout a single warning to her and felt a crunch against my back.

Spilling onto the concrete floor and losing my Glock, I managed to roll to the side just as a metal pipe smacked into the ground. I felt blood seeping through the back of my shirt, a sign the pipe either had a ragged end or maybe a screw sticking out of it. I peered through the low light and studied the man wielding the weapon.

Parks obviously had recruited an entire Shit Squad, and this latest specimen had a wolfish grin on his face. There was a gun tucked into his waistband, and I wondered why he hadn't just offed me with it.

That's when I saw a shape walking up from the gloom. As soon as it took the form of a woman I didn't need two guesses to figure out who it was.

"Put the pipe down, Glen, and cover him with a real weapon," Jayanti said. "No games with this one."

The pipe clattered to the floor and he pointed a gun at my face.

Jayanti moved closer and nodded.

"Of course it's you," she said. "You're the asshole from San Antonio. The one who killed Cox."

"And Troy in the park," I said. "Plus another couple back that-a-way." I nodded toward the one she'd called Glen. "I'm adding him to my collection in just a minute. By the way, where's your nutty boyfriend? Why isn't he here helping? Or does he always refuse to get his own hands dirty?"

With a condescending smile she walked up to me and ripped my headset away, severing the contact with Poole and Kowalczyk.

"He's busy in the land of enchantment," she said. "You, on the other hand? You're done."

But instead of ordering her goon to shoot me, she raised a hand from her side. Even in the low light I saw the glisten of a syringe.

"Oh, c'mon, Jay," I said. "Not again. How many times can you poison me? Frankly, it's getting old."

She took a step toward me. "You say the strangest things. You did at the Riverwalk, too. Are you just trying to be odd for show? If anything is getting old, it's your wit."

"You sound just like my wife." I held out my left arm. "If you're going to do it, I'd prefer this arm."

It had just the effect I wanted. She got within two feet of me and paused, wondering what the trick was. Glen was also confused, and took his eyes off me to see what his employer was going to do.

In a rush I flew to Jayanti, grabbed her by the wrists, and

watched the lethal syringe fly harmlessly to the ground. I spun her around and positioned her between me and Glen. It had happened in less than three seconds.

"Don't shoot your boss," I said to the hired beef.

Jayanti hissed at him. "Shoot him! He won't do anything. Shoot him now."

I'd counted on his hesitation and got it. As he looked between me and Jayanti's savagely-contorted face, I used the opening to shove her into him as hard as I could. I followed with a kick into his face that shattered teeth. Pradesh fell to the ground and I completed the lesson by striking her gunman as hard as I could in his larynx. With a gasp he dropped to one knee, then collapsed onto his side, holding his crushed wind pipe. He'd be dead soon.

I picked up Glen's gun, then grabbed Jayanti by the arm and pulled her to her feet.

"C'mon," I said. "Let's go stop some mayhem."

She didn't cooperate well, and I ended up mostly dragging her toward the spot where Oosterhaus was working. The scientist had obviously been aware of the scuffle going on, but to her credit hadn't stopped working. Now I pointed the gun at her as we approached.

"That's enough, Allison," I said. "There are about a hundred cops and SWAT members ready to descend. You won't get out of here, and if you finish your work I can't vouch for how well you'll be treated. It's their family members you're poisoning, you know."

She looked at Pradesh, who, even with one arm pinned behind her, surprisingly chuckled and said, "Finish the job."

I waved the gun. "Allison, make no mistake. I *will* shoot you."

After a few seconds her smile matched that of Jayanti, and it was clear I was dealing with two complete lunatics.

"Listen, Mr. Government Man," Jayanti said, and I realized that was her stock name for agents. "Allison only has about a minute left. Isn't that right?"

The scientist nodded, still with a deranged smile on her face.

I stretched out my hand holding the gun, and squared it with Oosterhaus's eyes. "She has less than that. Besides, just how do you think you two could escape, anyway? Every exit will be covered by a dozen police officers by now."

Jayanti laughed again. "You think we're going to walk out a door?"

I hate being stumped, and I especially dislike feeling stupid in front of people I'm supposed to triumph over. My mind churned through the possibilities. If they didn't plan on exiting through the door . . .

Of course. The pipes carrying the treated water out of the storage tanks went down a tunnel, which undoubtedly had a service walkway alongside. Pradesh and her evil scientist friend would be able to get several blocks away before taking a service entrance up to the street. From there they would scatter into the wind.

They'd planned it all perfectly. The only obstacle had been the late notice from Thresh regarding her visit. If not for that, everything would've been done with no complications.

"Well," I said. "You'll be going out the front door this time, right into the backseat of a car."

At that moment — because nothing in my job could ever be easy — I caught something in my peripheral vision. It was Jayanti's free hand.

All I could do in that split-second was drop the gun and

intercept her wrist with my gun hand. Once again I saw the gleam of a hypodermic needle.

"Jesus Christ," I said. "How many of these things do you carry around?"

She kicked at me, and tried pulling her wrist from my grip. She was small, but strong in a stubborn, wiry way. For a moment we wrestled, and in the faint light I saw the golden liquid inside the syringe. It carried death.

Oosterhaus used the altercation to turn back to her work. She was moments away from finishing.

I twisted Pradesh's hand backward. After chasing her for so long, after visualizing revenge, and after lamenting that someone I admired could be such a snake, it had come down to this: A battle inside a sewage plant.

"Let it go, Jay," I said. "No need to —"

Her face turned toward mine and she spit at me, then uttered an animalistic roar and actually tried to lean forward and *bite* me.

That did it. Grudging respect or not, I'd had enough of her act. Summoning the necessary strength, I spun her around so her back was to me. I forced up the arm pinned behind her, which caused her to cry out.

Then, with one savage rip, I pulled her other arm down quickly, plunging the syringe into the center of her throat. With a determined stroke, I emptied the contents into her.

She let out a gasp and her body went rigid. I held on tight. Then, as she began to shake, I leaned down to her ear.

"Silly girl," I whispered. "You didn't think of *everything*, did you?"

Childish or not, I wanted those words, the final words she'd uttered to me in her hotel room, to be the last thing she ever heard.

She struggled for a moment, trying to fight the inevitable, then gave a piercing scream. From listening to the recording of my own murder in a Scottsdale hotel room I knew what the poison was doing to her body. But while my own exposure had been small and gradual, Pradesh had just received a substantial dose. The agony she now experienced would be indescribable.

I let go of her arm and she collapsed to the concrete floor, convulsing and crying out.

Without waiting for her to expire, I stepped over Pradesh on my way to Oosterhaus, who'd stopped again and was watching, wide-eyed, as her boss contorted in a grisly death spasm, screams reverberating from every wall. They were similar to the sounds I'd made after my own taste of tabun.

I grabbed Oosterhaus by the upper arm and pulled her face to within inches of mine. In the gruffest, angriest voice I could conjure, I said, "And now, Ms. Oosterhaus. If you don't want to be next, rip this shit out."

CHAPTER TWENTY-NINE

It was almost nine o'clock. The wind had picked up, and dust swirled outside the grounds of the Sun City water treatment plant. I sat on one of the bench seats in the back of an ambulance, talking with Kat Kowalczyk. She lay there, two different IVs feeding her veins.

"How close did they come?" she asked, slightly dopy from the medication.

"Oh, God, we had ages to spare. Wasn't even dramatic."

She managed a laugh. "Liar."

I rested a hand on her shoulder. "Hey, thank you for running in to help me. You're officially much more prompt than Fife."

"A lot of good I did."

"Are you kidding? You filled them with overconfidence."

"Shut up."

With a soft pat I told her, "The EMT says you're going to be fine. Then you'll have a scar to prove to the Bureau's top dogs how tough you are. So quit griping and get some rest. I'll check in with you later."

I stepped out of the ambulance into the chilly night air and the blinding glare of emergency lights from a squadron of police cars. Sergeant Oakes was also going to be all right, but would be out of service for a few months. Unfortunately the young officer who'd been cut down in the yard didn't make it. The cost of this mission had been high, but the risk to the population had been eliminated. Barely.

I could've felt happy about the outcome, but I didn't. I couldn't.

Steffan Parks was still at large. And still just as dangerous.

My phone vibrated and I took the call from Quanta.

"Well done," she said. "Are you okay?"

"I am. Agent Kowalczyk is going to the hospital. She'll be out of action for a while." I paused. "She's good. We should make a note of her."

Quanta spoke with a twinge of humor to her voice. "You're not suggesting another new agent for Q2, are you? You can't keep doing that."

I thought of the woman I'd recommended after the escapade in the Caribbean. "Just keep it in mind. You know, in case I retire."

"I don't expect that anytime soon."

She was right. It wasn't unusual after a difficult case for me to make similar noises. But Quanta knew it would come to nothing. She was professional enough to let me vent.

I kicked at a discarded fast food cup along the side of the street. "You know we're not finished with this, right?"

"Parks," was all she said.

"Not just Parks. There's also his accomplice in Santa Fe. That's where I'm headed first thing in the morning."

"And you think he's there?"

"Jayanti told me he was."

"She *told* you?"

I'd reached the end of the street, and turned back toward the plant. "She said Parks was in the land of enchantment."

Quanta was quiet for a moment. "The New Mexico state motto."

"Uh-huh. He's gone back, either to collect his only surviving partner on this case or to kill them so they can't tell us anything. Then I expect him to disappear again. I can't have that."

"Do I need to tell you to upload tonight?" she asked.

"Nope."

THE PLANE QUANTA had arranged for me was waiting when I got to the airport at seven the next morning. It was a Gulfstream, a treat for sure. Over the years I'd grown to appreciate the rare chance to ride in style. It usually happened only after I'd delivered in a tough spot.

My boss, at times, could be very good to me.

It was a speedy flight, and I was in another BMW by nine. As I sped away from the Santa Fe airport I called Sheriff Tonkin.

"I don't have any news for you, if that's what you're after," he said in his usual unfriendly tone.

"I didn't expect any," I said. "But I might have some for you."

His pause was brief. "Okay. Go ahead."

"Not yet."

A long, frustrated sigh came across the car's speaker system. "Does that mean you don't know anything yet, or you're not going to tell me yet?"

"The latter."

"So you're obstructing, now," he said.

"Hard for me to obstruct when I'm working toward the same result you are: Bringing people to justice. Let's say I'm being cautious."

"To hell with caution. If you know something, you tell me now."

"Sheriff, I will explain everything to you soon. Probably by the end of the day. But for now I just wanted to give you a courtesy call to say I'm back in town and working on the case. You'll have to cut me some slack for a few more hours. Can you do that?"

He was silent for a minute, then uttered a low curse. "I've never liked you Feds. And you're about the worst yet."

With that he hung up.

I couldn't help but smile. Tonkin was an ornery son of a bitch, but I liked him. What I couldn't tell him was that, while ordinarily I'd be happy to share what I knew, the fact that his niece had been one of the murder victims made this different. His emotions might affect the way he approached things, and I couldn't have that. There were two people I had to bring in, and I couldn't worry about a sheriff with a personal grudge.

I was one to talk. I'd spent the bulk of my career with Q2 carrying around one hell of a grudge. And I would until I'd put that particular issue to rest.

A red light gave me a few extra moments to consider that personal vendetta, one that I knew was both unprofessional and possibly compromising. But I didn't care. In a bizarre way, it powered me. Kept me sharp, and moving forward. As long as Beadle prowled the Earth, I'd keep serving and protecting.

Until I choked the life out of him with my bare hands.

The light turned green. I left the intersection and those thoughts behind me.

THE NEIGHBORHOOD WAS QUIET, but I saw movement through a window of the house. I sat in the car for a few minutes, preparing myself for one of the hardest jobs I'd ever done.

I got out and, instead of going to the front door, walked around the side of the house into the back yard. It was equally quiet, and out of view of any of the neighbors. I saw movement again through another window, waited until it was clear, then let myself in through the unlocked sliding door.

I sat down at the round kitchen table and waited.

She came walking into the kitchen from the front room and froze, looking at me in fear.

I pulled out my phony FBI badge. "Relax, Ms. Haas. And have a seat."

Poor Jonas. He'd heard *Bailey*, when it actually was *Stacey*.

I could tell she was contemplating the advantage of running toward the front door. To make it easier for her to stay, I remained calm. Even crossed one leg over the other.

While she stood there thinking, I casually studied her. The last time I'd been in this house I'd occupied a different body. I'd also been *pre*occupied with reminiscing when I should've been investigating. The whole mushy wad of memories had overwhelmed me and I lost the ability to detach from my youthful fascination with Stacey Bromley, now Mrs. Stacey Haas, the widow of a well-respected scientist.

A lot had happened since my last visit. The haze from my old romantic history had burned away with the deaths of several people. My eyes were now wide open and clear.

She walked to the table and sat down.

"What are you doing here?" she asked. "Is this about Leon's murder?"

"It sure is."

She adopted an angry look. "Then why did you break into my house? Why not ring the doorbell?"

"Technically I didn't break in. I just walked in through an unlocked door. But let me ask the questions. Starting with: What time are you expecting Steffan to arrive?"

The start this gave her almost made me laugh. Stacey had done a bit of acting in college, but that skill was no longer honed.

"Steffan? Steffan Parks? He better *not* show his face around here. I'll—"

I cut her off with a wave. "So many things clued me in, although, granted, it took longer than it should have. I think I first got an inkling that something wasn't right when Jonas Aiken schooled me on Steffan's little trick called Damnation Deniability. Stupid name, I'll give you that. But in a way it makes sense."

Stacey Haas kept up the startled look. "I don't know what you're—"

"Yeah, you do know. And when I found out that he had a co-conspirator here in Santa Fe, I started putting some pieces together. One of the first was Damnation Deniability. Who'd damned Steffan Parks the most? Why, the grieving widow."

She gave a disgusted snort. "And you don't think a grieving widow would damn her husband's killer?"

"Of course she would. But you overplayed the part. You not only went after him for allegedly killing your husband, but for everything under the sun. His research, his methods, his results. You even scorched him personally. It was all designed to sell me on the fact that he was a horrible man you'd have nothing to do with. But, of course, you've been on Team Steffan for years, haven't you?"

"You're insane."

I waved a flippant hand. "Probably more of a prerequisite for this job than an impediment. The really nice touch, though, the part that impressed me the most when I looked back, was you going over the head of the coroner to hire that independent pathologist. No chance in hell you'd be suspected if you were so adamant on finding the real cause of death. If you'd been guilty, you'd happily let the world believe Leon had accidentally poisoned himself, right? That threw the sheriff off your trail for sure, and made you appear completely innocent.

"But you and I both know you're not innocent, and you're certainly not a poor, grieving widow. With just a little bit of digging we'll be able to prove a solid connection between you and the once-esteemed Mr. Parks that goes all the way back to your days at UC."

I let the casual look on my face dissolve into a mask of pure bad-assery. "So let's cut out the horseshit, okay? You're about to be booked on four counts of first-degree murder. Do you want to continue this charade of innocence and face life without parole, or do you want one shot to make things at least slightly easier for you?"

She stared at me for a long time. But her mask of purity and principles had fallen away.

I kept going. "You know, believe it or not, things can go way worse for you, Stacey. If I drop you off at the Sheriff's office, you'll be booked, but at least you'll be safe. On the other hand, I could quietly, off the record, ask the Sheriff to drop by here. I'll step outside and the Sheriff might be forced to defend himself against an armed suspect. He might have to gun you down, probably right here on this abominable-looking tile."

Her face had gone pale. "Why would he do that? I'm not armed."

"Not yet you're not. But what you didn't know when you poisoned your husband at Marquart Labs was the young, fresh-faced scientist helping your husband — the one who died alongside him — was the much-beloved niece of Sheriff Tonkin. And I've been around him enough to know he'd be more than happy to forego a trial and appeals process that could take years. I get the feeling the sheriff is a true relic of the old west and its simple forms of justice. No doubt he has a nice collection of firearms that could be found in the right hand of your bullet-riddled corpse. Get my drift?"

She didn't answer but instead looked down at her lap. Although Sheriff Tonkin was way too principled, despite his gruff tones, to ever kill a defenseless suspect, Stacey didn't know that.

"Of course you get it," I said. "You always were a very smart girl. In most respects. Not your decisions about men, obviously. You could've made much better choices years ago."

"What?" she mumbled.

I grinned. "Never mind. So, can we go back to my original question? What time will Steffan be here?"

She didn't answer for a full minute. Just sat there, staring down, in complete shock. When she finally spoke, it came out as a whisper.

"Noon."

I looked at the time on my phone.

"Oh, what a relief. I thought you were gonna say late this afternoon or tonight. Now tell me about the other lab worker. Why was David Torres killed?"

"He . . . he wasn't supposed to be killed. Things just . . . turned."

"Turned how? Are you saying *Torres* turned?" I paused, letting things work themselves out in my head. "He did, didn't he? He was in on the killings at the lab."

She nodded. "Then he found out that Amy was there. He had feelings for Amy, which I didn't know anything about. Anyway, he started talking crazy, like he was going to turn himself in and confess everything."

"And you certainly couldn't have that. So he became your third victim."

Stacey didn't answer.

"Anyway, that helps fill in some holes," I said. "We're actually making some progress here, Mrs. Haas. Good. I'm anxious to get this all wrapped up so I can go home to a woman who *does* appreciate me."

She looked up, a pained look on her face. "What are you going on about? What is this?"

This time I laughed out loud. "Don't worry about it. You just sit there like a good little murderer and when we corral Steffan we'll all take a ride downtown. Got anything to drink?"

At a quarter till noon I gently tied one of Stacey's wrists to the arm of her chair and went to unlock the front door. Then I moved back into the kitchen and stood by the fridge, out of sight of anyone who came in until it was too late for them.

At ten past twelve there was a double tap on the front door, then another a moment later. Per the instructions I'd given her, Stacey called out for Steffan to come in.

After a brief hesitation — probably an evolved animal

sense of danger — the door pushed open and I heard Steffan say, "Stacey?"

"In here," she said, although without much enthusiasm. I gave her a warning look. She added, "In the kitchen. Come on in."

The door closed and a moment later Steffan Parks walked into the room. He reached out to touch Stacey on the shoulder, then stopped when he spotted me against the counter. My Glock was pointed at his heart.

"I don't suppose they have Alamo T-shirts in Santa Fe, do they?" I asked.

After a moment he let his outstretched hand fall back to his side. "What a surprise," he said. "Should I assume this is why I haven't heard from Ms. Pradesh?"

"She would have a helluva time contacting you now, Steffan."

He raised an eyebrow. "My, you're a regular killing machine, aren't you, Eric? It is Eric, as I recall, isn't it?"

"That's right. Do me a favor, will ya? Sit down and place both hands face down on the table. That's good. Thank you."

I moved over and pulled out the seat directly across from him. I kept the gun centered on his chest.

"You know," I said, "after all this time and all the travel miles, I couldn't be happier that you just walked right in. And without muscle this time." I leaned to my left and tried to look toward the front door. "Or will another one of your inept meatheads be wandering in?"

He smiled. "Sadly, no." Then he turned his gaze to Stacey. "Has he hurt you?"

She shook her head without making eye contact with him.

"Mrs. Haas," I said, "this is where he pretends that he cares a great deal about what happens to you. But you'll notice he's not shedding any tears after finding out his girlfriend is dead."

Stacey slowly raised her head to look at me. Parks did the same. They both had a flat expression on their faces.

It took a few seconds, but finally clicked.

"Oh . . . my . . . God," I said. "You two are . . ."

I pointed a finger at Steffan and said to Stacey in a loud, whiny voice, "What's *he* got that I didn't have?"

They both just stared at me like I was a crazy man. To drive the point home, I dissolved into the hardest laugh I'd had in a long time.

CHAPTER THIRTY

The garden outside Quanta's house was much more impressive in the summer months. Now, as February began, it was mostly a frost-covered wonderland. I studied it through her kitchen's sliding glass door, rolling a hot mug of tea back and forth in my hands.

There was life hibernating beneath that cold layer outside, waiting for a chance to rebound from its slumber and bloom again. We only think it's dead, but it bides its time, knowing the right moment to come back and prove us wrong.

Not too unlike my experience with the Q2 investing program.

I was mentally exhausted but any down-time would have to wait until after finishing Quanta's version of a de-briefing. And for that I had to wait until she finished meditating inside the house's atrium, where it was summer year-round.

I'd left Christina a message that I was back in town and would be home late that afternoon. She didn't bother to ask for how long.

It had been one of the strangest cases of my career,

including a bizarre connection with my pre-Q2 past. Generally I don't remember many details about that original life. It's as if it never really existed. The memories could be confused with images from an old film watched long ago. Sometimes I wondered if the constant uploading and downloading had corrupted some of the older files.

Then Stacey Haas had shown up and shaken that reality back to life, and as a result had done me a huge favor. She'd reminded me that no matter how many convict bodies I inhabited across the years, there was an individual — just *one* person — steering the car. Someone who'd lived, loved, lost, and laughed through as many good and bad times as anyone.

And someone who would try harder to remember that in the years to come, no matter how difficult the circumstances.

I was still warming my hands with the tea mug when Quanta came in and filled a glass with water from the tap. She took the seat beside me and followed my gaze beyond the door. We sat like that for a long time, enjoying the mid-winter silence.

Then she spoke in a low voice. "I've always thought of you as a spy and covert operations manager, Swan. This time you surprised me with your detective act."

"You mean the part about Mrs. Haas? Mostly just a strong hunch until she confirmed it under duress. I can't believe I didn't see it earlier."

Quanta shrugged. "She was out of town when her husband and his associate were killed. And she was nowhere near David Torres when he was murdered, either."

"The beauty of planting poison," I said. "When she met Torres in the parking lot of the lab for their drive to Albuquerque she went inside for a minute and discreetly put a dose of poison in the coffee maker's water reservoir. It would never seem suspicious if she came to the office. And it explains why the sheriff couldn't find any prints from Parks or Pradesh. Fingerprints from Stacey Haas would be expected.

"I also should've realized she never really loved Leon Haas. He was a . . . a nice contact for her. And a convenient one for the only person she really *did* ever care about: Parks."

"How could you have realized that?" Quanta asked.

I looked at her and gave my own half shrug. "Let's just say I know some things about Stacey Haas and her history. Seeing her settled down, living the life of the supportive wife, just didn't jive with her past."

It was obvious Quanta was curious about what I claimed to know. At the same time she recognized that it didn't matter now. Both Stacey and Steffan were in custody and would stand trial for murder, attempted murder, and a shitload of other charges. I had no doubt the government would toss in counts of terrorism.

"But Leon Haas's crusade to discredit Parks," Quanta said. "Was that really his idea?"

"I doubt it," I said. "It was the first volley in the Damnation Deniability scheme. Stacey had known both Leon and Steffan back at the University of Chicago. It was easy for her to stir things up. Perhaps Leon even had a tinge of jealousy about Parks, going back years. He may have leapt at the chance to bring him down."

"Instead it got him killed."

I gave a quick nod. "Which was part of the ultimate plan. Their practice run, so to speak, and a chance for Stacey to inherit a vast sum of money to further fund their dark plans together."

"And Jayanti?" Quanta asked.

"Another sad pawn. Steffan exploited her ruthless side

while stringing her along with phony romance. Which, come to think of it, is exactly what *she* did with Aiken. So they all turned out to be one big lying, dysfunctional collection of cads.

"Anyway, Parks never cared one bit about Jayanti. It explains why he didn't mind using her to rope Aiken into helping. Or, for that matter, why he was fine letting her be the prime suspect for the murders in Santa Fe. She died never knowing that everything he did with her was one big act. Or hell, maybe she knew and didn't care. People put up walls. If she hadn't murdered me I might even feel sorry for her."

"Look, you prevented 42 gallons of tabun-based poison to filter through a city's water supply. Our guys say that was plenty in the short term to kill at least ten thousand."

We lapsed into silence again until I changed the subject. "There's a loose thread we're going to have to talk about eventually."

"The Arcetri."

"Yes. As much as we'd like to believe Steffan's arrest means the end of them, I wouldn't be surprised if they resurfaced."

"Because?"

"Because their skills are boundless and their grievances are legitimate."

She sat back and considered that while she took a long drink of water. Then she said, "We'll begin compiling a dossier on known and potential members. Just in case."

"Right," I said. "Just in case."

THE LAST STEPS up to the 7th floor of the Stadler Building were always hard. I still refused to take the elevator.

Inside my condo I didn't bother to hang up my coat,

throwing it across a bar stool in the kitchen. I'd just opened the bottle of Willamette Valley Pinot Noir and was filling two glasses when the panel in the living room slid open. A moment later Christina was by my side, an arm around my shoulder. She planted a loving kiss on my cheek.

"Welcome home," she said into my mangled ear. Then she stubbed it with a finger and frowned. "This is truly disgusting. I don't suppose you'd have some plastic surgery done on it."

"No chance. But think about it this way: I might be killed soon and you won't have to look at it after that."

"No," she said. "Just my luck you'll have this body for a year. I guess I'll just have to live with it for a while."

I started to hand her one of the glasses of wine, but she waved it away and held up the mug of tea she'd brought over. We touched glass to mug and each took a sip.

She pointed to a package I had on the counter. "What's that? A surprise for me?"

"One for you and one for Poole. I promised her a treat from New Mexico, but actually got it in Arizona. It's called Horno Bread."

She gave me a real kiss this time. "You're the sweetest spy I've ever known."

We walked into the living room where I opened the curtains, exposing the view I didn't appreciate often enough. We settled next to each other on the couch.

"I'm assuming your case ended well," she said.

"It did for me and the citizens of Arizona. But everyone around me seemed to get shot."

"By you?" she asked.

"Very funny. You'll be happy to know I didn't even go through an entire magazine's worth of ammunition on the entire case."

"Well, don't tell me what you *did* use."

"Not even the syringe? That was pretty cool."

"No. Let's just enjoy the pretty lights."

She rested her head on my shoulder. I kicked off my shoes and put my feet up on the coffee table, a move that was forbidden on Christina's side of the living quarters. I stroked her hair for a minute then said, "You wanna know the strangest part of this trip?"

She mumbled a contented yes.

"I captured an old girlfriend and turned her over to the police."

Christina laughed. "The one you told me about from college?"

"The same. For murder, even."

"Good thing you dumped her back then."

I couldn't bring myself to set her straight. Better to let her think she'd won the prize.

"I have some good news, too," I said. "Quanta is adamant that I'll get at least ten days off."

"And you believe her?"

"I want to."

"So I have you until you need to save the country again."

"Correct."

She squeezed my arm. "That's great, babe. I might need your help around here."

Laughing into her hair I said, "Don't be ridiculous. You know I don't have a single handyman gene in any of my bodies. Besides, I intend to spend all ten days either right here or in one of our beds."

"Oh, I'm not asking you to fix the sink or put in a dimmer switch."

I raised my wine glass to my lips and, just before taking a sip, said, "What kind of help do you need, then?"

She pulled away from me and looked right into my eyes. Her face was beaming and her eyes had never looked more beautiful.

"I don't know yet," she said. "I've never been pregnant before."